The Guide To
MİDDLE EARTH

THE GUIDE TO
MIDDLE EARTH

The unauthorised guide to
the world of JRR Tolkien

Iain Lowson, Peter Mackenzie
and Keith Marshall

Reynolds & Hearn Ltd
London

To all those high school pupils writing their dissertations
on LotR against their teacher's advice: good on you!

To Rona: blue, beautiful and best. With love.

To Sandi, Ashley and Michael for making me believe.
And to Dad, for memories of mutton.

First published in 2001 by
Reynolds & Hearn Ltd
61a Priory Road
Kew Gardens
Richmond
Surrey TW9 3DH

A CIP catalogue record for this book is available
from the British Library.

ISBN 1 903111 23 4

Cover illustration by Carl Lyons
Designed by Paul Chamberlain
Printed and bound in Great Britain by Biddles Ltd

Contents

CHAPTER ONE

THE LEARNING
OF THE WISE

ow did you first encounter the work of J R R Tolkien? Did a school friend read *The Lord of the Rings* and then insist you did, loaning you their dog-eared copy and then demanding daily updates on how far you had got? Had you read *The Hobbit* when you were little, or even had it read to you, and then decided to find out what happened next? Did you listen to the excellent BBC Radio dramatisations of *The Hobbit* or *The Lord of the Rings*? Or did you simply want to know what all the fuss was about, and how a story about Elves and Dwarves and the like could possibly be the most popular novel of all time?

However you first entered the fantastical world of Tolkien's Middle-earth, you discovered a living, breathing world filled with wonderful things and with terrible things, with great good, heroism and valour, and great evil, deception and cowardice. Tolkien's world has a depth of detail and a rich mythological and historical background that sings from every page and draws its readers in. Once you have visited Middle-earth once, you carry it with you wherever you go.

Of course, it could be that you have never read any of Tolkien's work. It could be you are hoping this book will allow you to bluff your way through a conversation with a Hobbit fan. Well, you may just be in luck.

This book sets out to introduce the Tolkien beginner to some of the hidden depths of the Professor's works. It will concentrate primarily on five main volumes: *The Silmarillion*, *The Hobbit*, and the three volumes of *The Lord of the Rings*; namely *The Fellowship of the Ring*, *The*

Two Towers, and *The Return of the King*. It will look at events, places, characters and races. This guide also discusses many of the themes that run through Tolkien's books and touches on the motivation behind them. However, it is not an in-depth philological discussion.[1]

No single book can hope to deal in any depth with all of the many themes, philosophies and viewpoints that commentators have unearthed through the years. The final chapter points out some further reading for the Professor's more diligent pupils, as well as looking briefly at Tolkien on the Internet and in other media, including film, radio, games and even plastic action figures!

As a first step on the road to a better understanding of Middle-earth, it is worth looking at the life of the remarkable man who created it: Professor John Ronald Reuel Tolkien. While there are many who would say that to study an author's life with a view to understanding their work is fruitless[2], there are certain events in Tolkien's life that did have a profound effect on his work and on his attitude to the world around him. Also, in a work as profoundly personal as Tolkien's mythology, the character of the author has an inevitable bearing on the work.

J R R Tolkien was born in Bloemfontein, South Africa, in 1892. It was a country he stayed in for only a very few years. His mother, Mabel, had taken Ronald and his brother Hilary on a visit to England (as much because of Ronald's health as her own desire to return to Britain), leaving his father, Arthur Reuel Tolkien, a moderately successful banker, at home. Arthur Tolkien contracted rheumatic fever in November 1895, which became pneumonia. He suffered a severe haemorrhage in February of the following year and died, leaving his wife and children with only the smallest of incomes.

With the help and support of the family, Tolkien's mother did her very best for her children, and John Ronald Reuel's childhood, while not idyllic, was very fondly remembered. At various times, the children's lives were split between the countryside and the city, specifically Birmingham. Ronald's memories of country life were ever associated with memories of his mother, on whom he doted. In the summer of 1896, the family moved to Sarehole, which Ronald and Hilary (then only two and a half) loved. The two had many 'adventures' – chased for trespassing near the Sarehole Mill by the 'White Ogre', and by the 'Black Ogre' farmer, who objected to the theft of his mushrooms.

Tolkien's mother was his teacher at this time, and she introduced him to Latin and to French. Tolkien preferred the former. Reading from the *Red Fairy Book* of Andrew Lang, Tolkien encountered his first dragon, in the tale of the hero Sigurd. In June 1900, Mabel Tolkien became a Catholic. In an age of strong and openly declared religious beliefs, Mabel incurred the wrath and stated enmity of the majority of her own and her late husband's family. Only the intervention of a kindly uncle from the Tolkien family made it possible for the fees to be paid that allowed Ronald entrance to King Edward's School in the nearby city of Birmingham.

The family moved back into the city in 1900 to be closer to the school. Ronald missed the country terribly. However, a new language presented itself to fascinate Tolkien. Coal trucks from a number of Welsh collieries passed by his window, and he struggled to comprehend the names they bore.

In 1902, the family moved to Edgbaston, and the boys to St Philips School. It was a Catholic school, but the boys spent only a short time there, as the standards were not appropriate. Eventually, Ronald won a scholarship back to King Edward's. There, Tolkien began learning Greek and, thanks to an inspirational teacher, Middle English. Tolkien was delighted by Middle English, and endeavoured to learn more of it.

Mabel Tolkien had befriended one Father Francis Morgan, who was to have a lasting influence on Ronald's life. In 1904, after Ronald and Hilary had been very ill with first measles and then whooping cough, Mabel Tolkien also fell ill, and was diagnosed as having diabetes. She convalesced, at the suggestion of Father Morgan, in a country cottage in Worcestershire. Father Francis visited regularly, and the boys thrived during a wonderful summer. They all stayed on, though the school term had begun again, but Mabel's condition took a turn for the worse. In November of 1904, she died. Ronald was devastated.

Father Morgan became guardian to Ronald and his brother. The boys went to live with an Aunt in Edgbaston, though King Edward's School and the Catholic Oratory became home-from-home to Ronald and Hilary. The loss of both his mother and the countryside surroundings caused Ronald's love of both to be immutably intertwined.

Tolkien's study of language intensified, and he began exploring Anglo-Saxon, also known as Old English. The story of Beowulf drew him in. When he went back to the study of Middle English, he read *Sir Gawain and the Green Knight* and *Pearl*. Tolkien would make new editions of both in later life. Finally, Tolkien began to acquaint himself with Old Norse, and to read Sigurd's story in its original form. At this young age, Tolkien began to create languages of his own. This began, at first, in partnership with his cousin Mary, and the two created languages and whole alphabets. Tolkien delighted in the sounds as much as the meanings. Even then, he saw a need to understand the history behind a language, and devised such a history for his own creations.

In 1908, Tolkien moved to new lodgings and met fellow tenant Edith Bratt. By 1909, the two had decided they were in love. Their innocent 'affair' was frowned upon. Father Morgan was furious. Despite warnings, the two were spotted together twice. As a consequence, Father Morgan demanded that Ronald should have no further contact or communication of any sort with Edith until he was 21. Tolkien very reluctantly obeyed.

In December of 1910, Tolkien succeeded at his second attempt to gain a scholarship to Oxford. He was immensely proud, though sad to be leaving King Edward's. There, his personality had become established. Though prone to private melancholy and pessimism he was, in the company of his exclusively male friends, the life and soul of the Tea Club (later the Barrovian Society, and finally the T.C.B.S.) which he formed with, amongst others, fellow library administrator Christopher Wiseman. Tolkien played rugby, wrote poetry, and read to the T.C.B.S. from his favourite Middle English and Old Norse poems and sagas. He joined the Debating Society, though he had a reputation as an indistinct speaker, except when reciting. As well as all of this, Tolkien also found time to discover Finnish mythology, which he enjoyed enormously.

Between school and Oxford, Tolkien took a trip to Switzerland, visiting Interlaken (which rests between two beautiful lakes and is surrounded by snow-capped mountains) and walking extensively. Ronald, before returning home, bought a postcard of *Der Berggeist* by J Madelener. The mountain spirit of the title was an old man, cloaked, and Tolkien later ascribed the origin of Gandalf to this painting.

Though still working on his invented languages, Tolkien threw himself into Oxford life, if not into his studies. His special subject was Comparative Philology (the study of languages) and, at long last and with great enthusiasm, Tolkien began to study the Welsh language. The discovery in around 1912 of a Finnish grammar led to Tolkien setting aside the Gothic influences on his private languages. He began a new language, one that would someday become the High Elvish Quenya.

Very early in 1913, Tolkien wrote to Edith Bratt professing undying love and a desire to wed. Ever the romantic, Tolkien could not perceive of any difficulties, despite the fact that so much time had passed. The fact that Edith was engaged to someone else, which Tolkien discovered when she replied, also proved no deterrent. In the end, Edith happily broke off her engagement to one George Field and became engaged to Ronald.

At the beginning of the Oxford summer term of 1913, Tolkien switched from Classics to English, specifically English Language. During his studies, he came across a number of Anglo-Saxon poems. He found the name 'Earendel' in one. Its definition, 'a shining light', could not encompass the feelings the name stirred in Tolkien. At the same time, Ronald's specialist subject, Old Norse, brought him further contact with the Icelandic sagas. The mythology struck a deep chord with Tolkien. A holiday in 1914 to Cornwall, and the countryside he saw there, provided further inspiration. Shortly after, Tolkien wrote a poem titled 'The Voyage of Earendel the Evening Star'. This marks the birth of his own mythology.

Tolkien was, for all his life (with perhaps a slight lapse in his early days at Oxford), a deeply religious man, and a staunch Catholic. His mother he saw as a persecuted martyr, and her plight further strengthened Tolkien's faith. Some might find it strange that a devout Christian should write of Elves, Dwarves and a mythology wherein a non-Christian pantheon is worshipped. It has been suggested, by those with a blinkered outlook and a dangerous agenda, that the writing (and even reading) of one denies true belief in the other. In fact, Tolkien's beliefs are strongly present in his mythology, clearly defining right and wrong, good and evil. Tolkien is simply more subtle in his presentation of his beliefs than was, for example, his friend and confidant C S Lewis in his Narnia books. Tolkien believed that man dwindled somehow as he moved further from God. Despite the fact that the peoples of Middle-earth lessen through the Ages (to which we devote a whole chapter of this book), it would be dangerous to suggest that the fate of Middle-earth's peoples is in any way a lesson for us, as Tolkien was strongly suspicious of the use of allegory in writing.

Through 1914 and 1915, perhaps spurred on by approving comments on his poetry from members of the T.C.B.S., Tolkien continued the development of his language and mythology. He decided that his created language was spoken by the Elves encountered by Earendel, and the story of his voyage contained much that would be familiar to a reader of *The Silmarillion*.

This was wartime, however. Having passed from Oxford with First Class honours in 1915, Tolkien became a Second Lieutenant with the Lancashire Fusiliers. He married Edith in March of 1916, and shipped to war-torn France in June. The alternating drudgery and horror of the War, in which Tolkien saw action at Bouzincourt in the Somme campaign, impressed upon him a respect and admiration for the ordinary soldier over the officer class, for whom Tolkien had little time. This respect carried over into his mythology, and Sam Gamgee owes much of his character to the English soldiers Tolkien encountered.

Tolkien was struck down by trench fever. Shipped home in November 1916, Tolkien saw out the rest of the War in England. Tolkien lost many friends to the War, including some T.C.B.S. friends.

In his last communication with Tolkien before his death, George Smith, a T.C.B.S. member, made indirect reference to Tolkien's planned mythology, saying in effect that he should make a start. Another T.C.B.S. member, from his posting with the Royal Navy, was more direct. So it was that, in 1917, John Ronald Reuel Tolkien began *The Book of Lost Tales*, starting with 'The Fall of Gondolin'. In his early draft, the nature of Tolkien's elves was well established. Late on in the year, 'The Children of Húrin' was composed. At this time, Tolkien was convalescing from yet another recurrence of the illness that had denied him any prospect of overseas service. Edith was pregnant and, in November of 1917, John Francis Reuel Tolkien was born. Tolkien had been posted to Yorkshire. He and Edith took frequent country walks, during which Edith was moved to dance and sing. From this romantic interlude was born the bitter-sweet story of Beren and Luthien.

The War ended in 1918, and Tolkien worked first in Oxford, then at the University of Leeds. In 1920, Michael Hilary Reuel Tolkien was born. Meanwhile, *The Book of Lost Tales* was continued, though other work often took precedence. *Sir Gawain and the Green Knight*, for example, on which Tolkien worked with Eric Gordon, was published in 1925.

By 1923, *The Book of Lost Tales* was nearing completion. However, Tolkien now began a complete revision of the work. In 1924 he became the Professor of English Language at Leeds University. His third son, Christopher Reuel Tolkien, was born the same year. In 1925, Tolkien returned to Oxford as Professor of Anglo-Saxon. Despite the encouragement of friends such as C S Lewis, whom Tolkien met in 1925, *The Silmarillion* (as *The Book of Lost Tales* was now called) remained unfinished but frequently revised. Other stories came and went, often told to entertain his children, including daughter Priscilla, who was born in 1929. Some of the characters in those tales made their way into Tolkien's ever developing mythology. Other works, such as the illustrated letters from Father Christmas, saw publication many years later. By the 1930s, the person who knew most about *The Silmarillion* was

Christopher Tolkien, who often heard stories from and relating to it. It would be a long time before anyone else knew as much. Tolkien's storytelling had suddenly taken a different turn. In an idle moment he had started writing *The Hobbit* , a tale which first sprouted from a single line jotted on an empty page of an exam paper.

Begun around 1930, *The Hobbit* was all but complete by the end of 1932, when C S Lewis saw it. Always a children's story, it was not originally intended to be part of *The Silmarillion*'s mythology. As with *The Silmarillion*, it was left unfinished. The friend of a former pupil, who worked for publishers Allen & Unwin, was sent to Tolkien with a recommendation that she borrow the manuscript of *The Hobbit*. She did so, and quickly asked Tolkien to complete the tale. In October of 1936, the complete book reached the publishers. This was not an end to *The Hobbit*, however. Tolkien undertook a revision of the book early in 1937. Despite irritation with the publishers over the matter of maps and illustrations, the book saw publication in September of 1937. It was enthusiastically received, and was awarded the *New York Herald Tribune* prize for the best juvenile book of the season. Soon the demands for more about Hobbits began to come from both publishers and public.

Initially, Tolkien sought instead publication for *The Silmarillion*. This was rejected by the publishers. The manuscript was not well presented, and the material represented too radical a departure from the style and content of *The Hobbit*. In mid-December 1937, Tolkien admitted that he had begun a new Hobbit story. It was to be a long, often frustrating creative process. It was not until the autumn of 1938 that the sequel to *The Hobbit* found strong direction. At the same time it found a title: *The Lord of the Rings*. No more was it a children's story: it had become firmly set in the older mythology of *The Silmarillion*.

Well into what we now know as Book 2 by the summer of 1939, the lead character moved from being called 'Bingo' to 'Frodo'. By 1940, Tolkien was half way through Book 2. There was a break at this point of about a year. By the end of 1942, Tolkien felt he was nearly done, and he communicated as much to his publishers. However, by the middle of the next year Tolkien stopped again, stuck in the complexity of his creation. In April of 1944, after encouragement from C S Lewis, Tolkien began Book 4, bringing the Ring-bearer to Mordor at last. Nothing much was done to *The Lord of the Rings* in 1945, the same year Tolkien became Merton Professor of English Language and Literature. In 1947, however, Rayner Unwin was shown a manuscript that amounted to the majority of *The Lord of the Rings*. In the autumn the book was finished but, true to form, Tolkien began a revision, then another, then more. Many months passed before C S Lewis saw the completed story, late on in 1949. Further troubles with publishers, largely Tolkien's own doing, delayed matters. It was not until September of 1952 that Allen & Unwin finally got hold of the manuscript. The publishers decided to divide the book into three. Tolkien completed some final checks to the first volume, and *The Fellowship of the Ring* was published in August 1954. *The Two Towers* followed in November. Tolkien, however, caused further delays. The appendices for *The Return of the King* were not completed until May 1955, with publication finally coming in October. Despite the cautious expectations of the publishers, the book became an immediate success, first as a hardback and then in paperback form. By the 1960s, *The Lord of the Rings* had become a cult book among students and young people all over Europe and, especially, in the USA. Tolkien became world-famous, and (rather reluctantly) found himself dealing with the intrusions into his private life which fame now caused.

Fans of *The Hobbit* and *The Lord of the Rings* were well aware of the existence of *The Silmarillion*, and there were many requests for it. Tolkien retired from university life in 1959 aiming, amongst other things, to concentrate on *The Silmarillion*. Moving house and the revisions of other works delayed matters, as did the decision to re-work the existing text. Other works saw publication, including *Smith of Wootton Major*, *Tree and Leaf*, and *The Adventures of Tom Bombadil*. But it was not until 1971 that any real progress on *The Silmarillion* was made. However Edith Tolkien, who had not been in good health, fell ill in November and died. Tolkien returned to

Oxford in March 1972. He and Christopher, frequently his father's confidant during the writing of *The Lord of the Rings*, talked often of *The Silmarillion*. It was always Tolkien's intention that, if anything were to happen to him, Christopher should finish the book. This was to be the case as, in September 1973, Tolkien fell ill suddenly and died of a chest infection, aged 81.

The mythology of *The Book of Lost Tales*, and subsequently *The Silmarillion*, was to Tolkien a living history that he had discovered rather than written. It was the history that underpinned the language he had created. As more than one friend understood, it was alive to Tolkien only so long as it continued to be 'discovered' and written down. It was, one supposes, both inevitable and perhaps necessary that Professor Tolkien did not complete *The Silmarillion* or publish it in his lifetime.

In his foreword to *The Silmarillion*, Christopher Tolkien describes the preparation of the book as being a 'difficult and doubtful task'. By the time it fell to him to begin work on *The Silmarillion*, as literary executor of his father's estate, the sheer volume of material Christopher Tolkien had to work through must have been, to say the least, daunting. In the summer of 1974, Christopher invited Canadian author Guy Gavriel Kay to join him in the UK and to assist with the editing of Tolkien's work. Kay worked with Christopher through to 1975. It is a credit to Christopher Tolkien that he did not try to present in one volume all of the – sometimes contradictory – information at his disposal. In the end, published four years or so after the death of J R R Tolkien, *The Silmarillion* is a compendium of five distinct works, all of which are stories from the same mythology.

It is to that mythology, and to *The Silmarillion*, that we now turn.

CHAPTER TWO
CREATION

A cts of creation have a profound significance throughout the history of Middle-earth. To understand better the nature of creation in Tolkien's world, it helps to examine in some detail the first act of creation in Middle-earth's history. Many readers of *The Silmarillion* skim quickly through 'Ainulindalë' – the great song of Ilúvatar, the rebellion of Melkor, and the descent of the Valar into Eä. This is a pity, because it is a complex chapter, dense with meaning. This opening chapter gives us a model of the creative process: what it *is* to create; and also what it *means* to create.

First Ilúvatar creates the Ainur (the gods subordinate to him). He does this by an act of pure thought. Then he instructs the Ainur in the art of music, and for a while the gods make music individually. Ilúvatar then reveals to the gods collectively a great musical theme to which they are all to contribute. He makes it clear that they may improvise around the theme, but not depart from it. Also, he states that they will have the capability to perform this task '...since I have kindled you with the Flame Imperishable'[3] This Flame must be the ultimate essence of creativity. We are told that prior to the song, Melkor, greatest and wisest of the Ainur,[4] desired the power to create for himself, and hunted for the Imperishable Flame in the Void. We are also told that '...he found not the Fire, for it is with Ilúvatar.'[5] Not even the most powerful of the Ainur possesses one spark of the Fire unless Ilúvatar grants it to them.

The gods begin the song. For a while all is well, but then Melkor attempts to introduce his own theme into the music. Ilúvatar begins a new theme, and once again Melkor disrupts it. The third theme of Ilúvatar cunningly subverts Melkor's subversion, weaving parts of his rebellious music back into the main theme, and producing a song

> deep and wide and beautiful, but slow and blended with an immeasurable sorrow, from which its beauty chiefly came.[6]

Battling against this song is the raucous, confident, yet repetitive music of Melkor. Ilúvatar then reveals to the Ainur the purpose of their music: the creation of the universe, and the world that will become Middle-earth.[7] However, they see things that are not part of their making: the Elves and Men of Middle-earth. It is reported that these living aspects of the universe are brought forth by the third theme of Ilúvatar alone, and are not part of the first theme into which the Ainur have some creative input. It is significant that the third theme is the one that makes use of the anarchy of Melkor's contribution.[8] Ilúvatar himself explains to Melkor that the secret and corrupt thoughts of his mind have been assimilated into the created universe, making the whole even greater. He goes on to demonstrate to the Ainur that the hostile elements Melkor sought to introduce into 'this little realm within the Deeps of Time'[9] have actually made the world more glorious: the bitter cold has created snow and frost, and the searing heat has made possible the clouds, the rain and the mists. With a rather beautiful image Ilúvatar explains that Ulmo, the god who will become associated with water, will be drawn by the clouds towards his friend Manwë, the god of the air. Ulmo realises something very important about the nature of creation at this point:

> 'Truly, Water is become now fairer than my heart imagined, neither had my secret thought conceived the snowflake, nor in all my music was contained the falling of the rain...'[10]

Ulmo realises that the imperfections Melkor thought to introduce to the universe have actually resulted in an even more glorious creation than a seemingly perfect one.[11]

'Let things be!'

Ilúvatar now does something that will seem familiar to those acquainted with the Judeo-Christian tradition. He makes the potential world the Ainur have seen actual, and he does so with a word, 'Eä!', 'Let things be!' And, fascinatingly, the world created takes the name of the command that created it. It becomes known as 'Eä', which as a noun means 'the World that Is.' The act of creation has become its own object.

Many of the greatest Ainur (including Melkor) descend into Eä, agreeing to surrender much of their power, and become bound to it irrevocably. They become the Valar, the gods of Middle-earth. Interestingly, they find that they have arrived at the very beginning of Eä's history and that they will have to labour to bring forth the world that they glimpsed *in potentia* in their song. Finally, Melkor attempts to claim Eä for his own, and the rest of the Valar have to fight to preserve the creation they are attempting to complete.

The creation of Eä is extended, complex, and non-linear. This close-bonded, complex relationship is representative of creation as a whole in Middle-earth. It is the breaking of this pact, normally by selfishness or covetousness, that causes strife. Rose A Zimbardo says something similar when she attempts to describe the chain of created beings in Middle-earth:

> The All in *The Lord of the Rings* is a chain of being, a scale
> of creatures, ... Good is the cooperation of all levels of being,
> a harmony but not an interpenetration of all kinds, for each
> kind of being has its particular excellence and consequently
> its peculiar contribution to make to the order of the whole.[12]

In other words, it is not a creation with no gaps and with everything in its place that Tolkien describes, but a creation where there is an unbroken chain of force leading back to Ilúvatar, the prime cause.

We need to draw a distinction between *creating* and *making*.

Pure creation in Middle-earth stems ultimately from Ilúvatar, a fact that Melkor discovers prior to the creation of Eä:

Yet he found not the Fire, for it is with Ilúvatar.[13]

Many characters throughout the history of Middle-earth make things. Few are involved in the transmission of the 'Flame Imperishable' that derives from Eä's first cause. The Valar's first inventions are the great Lamps they build to illuminate Middle-earth. Aulë makes them, Yavanna fills them with light, and Manwë 'hallows' them. Even though they are consecrated in this way, presumably to Ilúvatar, there is no sense of the Lamps as anything other than artefacts. Indeed, the very first era of the history of Middle-earth is defined by the struggle between Melkor busily corrupting the growth of the world, and the Valar attempting to maintain it. In this task the Valar fail, and this is Melkor's first making: the spoiling of the world's original beauty and the casting down of the Lamps:

And the shape of Arda and the symmetry of its waters
and lands was marred in that time, so that the first
designs of the Valar were never after restored. [14]

And yet, as promised by Ilúvatar, this original evil making is incorporated into the developing beauty and perfection of Middle-earth. To replace the fallen Lamps the Valar create the Two Trees of Valinor. This, quite apart from being one of the most beautiful moments in the history of Middle-earth, is a profound moment in the *development* of Middle-earth. The Two Trees bloom and fade at seven-hour intervals, each giving out light, and with a one-hour period of soft light when one is waxing and the other waning. The text is clear about the implication of this cycle:

Thus began the days of Bliss of Valinor, and thus began
also the Count of Time.[15]

The trees together make the first clock, and recorded time has begun in Middle-earth. This marks a *Felix Culpa*. An act of great destruction forces the Valar to attempt a task far beyond what they first attempted with the Lamps. The Trees are a true creation in ways that the Lamps were not. Most obviously, the Trees are alive whereas the Lamps were inanimate. Much more detail is revealed about the Trees than the Lamps. Each one is individual. Each has a different appearance, gives forth a different kind of light, and most tellingly, has an individual name and sex. Telperion, the eldest, is male and gives out a silver light; Laurelin is female and gives out a golden light.

Manwë hallows the Lamps *to* Ilúvatar. In order to bring forth the Trees, Yavanna draws power *from* Ilúvatar:

> ...she sat there long upon the green grass and sang a song
> of power, in which was set all her thought of things that
> grow in the earth.[16]

The use of song is no coincidence. Yavanna is drawing on her part in the Creation Song orchestrated by Ilúvatar himself. We notice also that Aulë has no part in the birth of the Trees. Embodying craft and artifice, he was a necessary part of the act of tribute to Ilúvatar that was the making of the Lamps. The Trees, however, derive not from an act of tribute, but from an act of prayer. Ilúvatar is *involved* in the creation of the Trees: there is a way for Yavanna to channel the creative force that only Ilúvatar possesses. When the Valar made the Lamps, Angels were talking to God. When the Valar bring forth the Trees, God is talking to Angels.

We should also notice that the power of song runs through the very essence of the world itself, maintained by Ulmo:

> In the deep places he gives thought to music great and ter-
> rible; and the echo of that music runs through all the
> veins of the world ...[17]

It is interesting to read of the world as a living organism with veins, and life-giving stuff that runs through them, even if this does sound more like metaphor than a modern Gaian theory of Earth as a vital whole. And yet, to label this description as a metaphor doesn't seem quite right either. It is a subtle point, but Ulmo is definitely doing *something* to maintain the vitality of the world. The following description is too concrete in detail to suggest otherwise:

> And thus it was by the power of Ulmo that even under
> the darkness of Melkor life coursed still through many
> secret lodes, and the Earth did not die...[18]

If the song Ulmo sings is a metaphor for some kind of sustaining force, it is no less powerful or actual for all that. By extension, the world is no less alive or organically whole either. It seems that a true act of creation requires a link back to the original song of creation *and* Ilúvatar's gift of the Flame Imperishable. When Melkor or Sauron attempt to create by corrupting, only the first element is present and the attempt is eventually re-subverted to good, as dictated by the Third Theme of the Song of Creation. As we shall see later, however, Sauron does manage to cheat this rule of creation once, but with dreadful consequences to himself. It is song that signals an unbroken chain from the original Creation to its antecedents. Yavanna sings to bring forth the trees, Ulmo sings to sustain the life of the world, and after Melkor has drained them Yavanna will sing again to bring forth a final fruit and a final flower from the dead husks of the Trees. Thus song is a fundamental part of the genesis of light in Middle-earth, and is a sustaining force at the heart of it. Tolkien makes it clear that Ulmo never ceases to propagate his sustaining force throughout the arteries of the world:

> ... nor has he ever forsaken Middle-earth, and whatsoever
> may since have befallen of ruin or change he has not ceased
> to take thought for it, and will not until the end of days.[19]

It is a pleasant thought that when the characters of Middle-earth pause for song, to celebrate, to stiffen their resolve, or simply to lift their spirits, they are channelling a part of the original creative force of the universe.

The history of the Dwarves is dealt with elsewhere. We need to glance at it here, because it reveals further aspects of creation in Middle-earth. The Valar Aulë *makes* the Dwarves (the verb is surely significant) because he desires 'to have learners to whom he could teach his lore and his crafts…'.[20] There is disobedience in his act. Tolkien says that he was 'unwilling to await the fulfilment of the designs of Ilúvatar.'[21] However, there is no malice in his actions. Unlike Melkor, who desired to create in order to have power and dominion over others, Aulë merely wishes to have students to teach. When Ilúvatar, perceiving what he has done, appears before him and demands an explanation for his disobedience, Aulë is instantly contrite. He offers to destroy his makings, but as he lifts his hammer to do so, the Dwarves shrink back in fear. Ilúvatar explains that he has already granted them proper life. Had he not, they should not have flinched from Aulë's blow.

Aulë *made* the Dwarves as automatons. Ilúvatar granted them real life. Thus the Dwarves come into existence before the Elves, who Ilúvatar had planned as his firstborn. The Dwarves derive their being from an act of loving disobedience (the desire of a son to imitate his father), and an act of loving forgiveness (the indulgence of a father for his son). Yet if Ilúvatar grants their true existence as free-thinking beings, their maker dictates their natures. Aulë keeps his project secret even from his wife Yavanna, who we remember singing to bring forth the trees. There is small love of growing things within the Dwarves. Their natures are as stony as that of their maker, and great grief is prophesied between the Dwarves and the Elves, and between the Dwarves and the growing things of Middle-earth. It is easy to pass over the creation that follows that of the Dwarves. Fearing for the living things of Middle-earth at the hands of Aulë's Dwarves, Yavanna petitions Manwë for help. Ilúvatar speaks through Manwë, promising that the forests shall have their own means of protection:

'But in the forests shall walk the Shepherds of the Trees.'[22]

These are the Ents, the children of Yavanna – as the Dwarves are the children of Aulë.[23]

The Dwarves are created before the Elves, but are not permitted to wake before them. In preparation for the coming of the Elves, Varda attempts one of the most beautiful acts of creation in the history of Middle-earth. She creates the stars – or rather she creates the major constellations, the stars and planets. She uses the silver dew of Telperion the Tree to do this. Again, the chain of creation runs unbroken back to Ilúvatar, through one of the Trees and through Yavanna's Song, to the first music of Middle-earth. For this deed Varda becomes revered by the Elves beyond all the other Valar, as the stars are the first things they see when they awake.[24] Even the name that the Elves give to Varda, 'Elbereth' or 'Star Queen', has great power to dismay the forces of evil. Frodo calls her name during the attack by the Nazgûl on Weathertop, and afterwards Aragorn states that the name of Elbereth was more deadly to the Witch-king than the sword Frodo stabbed him with.[25] It is with the Phial of Galadriel, full of captured starlight, that Frodo at first drives Shelob back;[26] and it is with the same phial that Sam breaks the malice of the Watchers at Cirith Ungol.[27]

THE SILMARILS

If the creation of the stars is one of the most beautiful in the history of Middle-earth, then surely only the creation of the Rings of Power can match the creation of the Silmarils for significance. Long after the first waking of the Elves, and the journeys of their various tribes to Valinor, Fëanor, the greatest smith of the Noldor, makes the three Silmarils. Fëanor shares many characteristics with figures from Western myth. As wrathful as Achilles, as proud and stubborn as Milton's Satan – well could he have used the words 'Better to reign in Hell than serve in Heaven' in his rebel-rousing speech to the Noldor after the destruction of the Trees.

Tolkien makes it very clear that only Fëanor understood of what substance the Silmarils were made.[28] This material was like diamond, only stronger – and there the resemblance between these gems and the most precious stones our world has to offer today ends. The fire that seems to live in the heart of a cut and polished diamond is a mere function of the refractive and reflective powers of its facets and its substance. The Silmarils were truly *alive* with the captured light of the Trees. Fëanor had not entirely created the Silmarils. But he had come close. Like Aulë, he can make substance. Unlike Aulë, he had actually *imprisoned* some of the light of the Trees in that substance. It is not too much to suggest that Fëanor actually managed to steal some of the light of the Trees for his own purposes, and thus by extension to steal some of the original Music of Creation itself. To be sure, Fëanor's motive in doing this is entirely benign. A premonition (and a true one) has come upon him, and he desires to find a way to preserve the light of the Trees for all time. Yet a time comes when Melkor destroys the Trees, and corrupted by lies and fear, Fëanor refuses to unmake the gems in order that the light of the Trees might be freed, and the Trees be made again.[29] Fëanor's developing paranoia as Melkor poisons his heart with lies prefigures the subsequent desire of the Noldor for the knowledge of Ring-making that Sauron offers them. Fëanor's original desire to preserve the light of the Trees is gradually corrupted, as he forgets that the light of the gems is the one thing he has not created:

> For Fëanor began to love the Silmarils with a greedy love, and grudged the sight of them to all save his father and his seven sons; he seldom remembered now that the light within them was not his own.[30]

What has begun as an act of almost pure creation must in the end be interpreted as an act of theft, just as Melkor steals the Silmarils for himself after his destruction of the Trees. The forces of darkness lack the ability truly to create anything. For creation to occur there must be an unselfish communication between the creator and

Ilúvatar. Corruption, however, is the preferred method of evil in Middle-earth, and the corruption of the magnificent soul of Fëanor[31] is described in the text as Melkor's most evil act.

And yet, as always, the destruction of the Trees is turned in the history of Middle-earth to ultimate good. Yavanna puts forth all her power and sings to the ruined husks of the Trees. Laurelin brings forth one last golden fruit, Telperion one last flower of silver. These become the Sun and the Moon, both great banes of Melkor, or Morgoth ('The Enemy') as he becomes known. Indeed, Morgoth never willingly ventures forth from his dungeons after the creation of the Sun. Once again, his malice is turned against itself. It is also worth noting that Morgoth gets small joy from his possession of the Silmarils. They burn to his touch, they weary him when he bears them on his crown, and finally they are taken from him.

The One Ring

The creation of the Sun and the Moon mark the last great acts of creation or making until the middle of the Second Age, and the making of the Rings of Power.

In the previous sections we dealt with the great acts of creation of the First Age of Middle-earth. These events were vast in scale, as in the creation of the Lamps; or God-like in scope, as in the creation of the Silmarils. The creation events of the First Age are marked by their vastness and philosophical complexity; yet they are also marked by the simplicity of the narrative that surrounds them. However, it is the fate of Middle-earth that it moves from a history of gods through that of myths, to that of legends. This concept is examined in more detail in chapter three, The Lessening of the Ages. Accompanying this movement there is a corresponding lessening in the size and profundity of events, coupled with an increasing complexity of narrative, or how these events *relate* to each other. Thus it is necessary to examine the creation of the Rings within the events they arise from, and which they affect.

Many treasures in history and literature have inspired greed in those that sought them. They have been the causes of great woe, but their inanimate natures have been essentially passive. In *The Lord of the Rings,* the One Ring is unique. It possesses an ethical dimension that is inherently evil, and is actively involved in the promotion of evil. It is also, as we shall see, the only true creation in Middle-earth that does not derive its being partially from an act of primary volition by Ilúvatar.

In the thirteenth century of the Second Age of Middle earth, Sauron, attempting to draw the Elves under his influence, adopts the name 'Annatar', the 'Lord of Gifts'[32] and goes among the Elves. He offers to teach them new knowledge and skills. The greatest and wisest of the Elves, Elrond and Gil-galad, reject him. But the Elves dwelling in Eregion, west of Moria, receive him eagerly.[33] Sauron's appearance at this time is still fair and his demeanour noble, and over the next few hundred years he guides the smiths of Ost-in-Edhil towards their greatest efforts. Early in the sixteenth century of the Second Age the Elves of Eregion begin forging the Rings of Power. They make many Rings, but the Three Great Elven Rings are completed around the year 1590.

Meanwhile Sauron takes himself secretly to Mordor. In the Sammath Naur, the Chambers of Fire in Mount Doom, Sauron forges the One Ring, designed to dominate all the other Rings that have been forged with his techniques and lore.[34] However, if the Noldor Elves of Eregion have a fault, it is their desire to create works of wonder and subtlety. They could never have been accused of stupidity, and the moment Sauron sets the One Ring on his finger they immediately perceive his designs upon them. They take off their Rings and, in the war against Sauron that follows, they hide from him the Three Great Elven Rings that have been forged with his lore, but without his ever touching them.

Sauron wages unceasing war on the Elves of Eregion. He slays Celebrimbor and lays Eregion waste, but he never recovers the Three Great Rings. The Rings he has recovered, he distributes amongst two other peoples of Middle Earth. With the Dwarves he has little more success than with the Elves. They accept seven Rings from him, but prove remarkably hardy and difficult to dominate. However their natural greed is greatly amplified and this has many unhappy consequences throughout the history of Middle-earth. The Battle of the Five Armies at the climax of *The Hobbit*, for instance, is a direct result of Thorin's greed and suspicion – when he refuses to treat fairly with Bard and the people of Dale, and to pay them the share of the dragon hoard that is rightfully theirs. In the history of the Dwarves related in the Appendices to *The Lord of the Rings*, it is the malice of one of the Dwarven Rings that preys on Thrain's mind after the fall of the Lonely Mountain, and finally causes him to attempt a return. Gandalf finds Thrain tormented and insane in the dungeons of Dol Guldur, years prior to the events described within *The Hobbit*. Lastly, it is worth noting that even a Dwarf as basically decent as Balin (and he is by far the most likeable of the Dwarves in *The Hobbit*) is driven by the desire to find the last Dwarven Ring to return to Moria, where only an untimely death awaits him.

Sauron gives the Nine Rings to mortal men, and here he enjoys his greatest success. The fate of the nine Ring-wearers is truly horrifying. They obtain power and wealth, and their lives are vastly extended. They can become invisible to the sight of others, and they can see things that mortals cannot. Yet through the Rings they wear they fall entirely under the domination of the One Ruling Ring, and pass from the realm of the living into a realm of non-life, existing within shadows, existing almost as shadows. They become Sauron's most terrible servants, the Nazgûl – the Nine Ringwraiths which Sauron sends after the Hobbits.

Sauron forges the One Ring for the specific purpose of the domination of a free people – the Elves. It is the One Ring that empowers the Nine and the Seven, and as we shall see, also the Three Elven Rings. Sauron can only make the Ring powerful enough to do this by committing to it a great part of his own strength. The creation of the Ring actually makes Sauron weaker, not stronger. As Paul Kocher points out,[35] the forging of the Ring is indicative of Sauron's overwhelming arrogance – he never considers that he might lose the Ring, and hence a huge part of his strength. The seeds of Sauron's destruction are sown from the moment when, in his vanity, he makes the Ring and divides his own essence.

In the year 3430 of the Second Age, the Last Alliance between Men and Elves is formed and in 3441, after a desperate battle, Sauron is defeated and overthrown by Gil-galad and Elendil (the ancestor of Aragorn) who both perish in the battle. Elendil's son Isildur cuts the One Ruling Ring from Sauron's finger. For Sauron, the unthinkable has happened. With his nature divided by the Ring, he no longer has the capacity to suffer mortal wounds with impunity. With the Ring taken from him, his final destruction hangs by a thread.

At this point the Ring's active malevolence manifests itself. Isildur, ignoring the advice of Elrond and Círdan, who both urge that the Ring should be destroyed in the fire in which it was made, takes the Ring for himself. Here are Isildur's words justifying his choice, found by Gandalf in a scroll in the library at Minas Tirith:

> But for my part I will risk no hurt to this thing: of all the works of Sauron the only fair. It is precious to me, though I buy it with great pain.[36]

The use of the word 'precious' here is vital. It is the word Gollum uses to describe the Ring, and it is the word Bilbo finds himself using when Gandalf presses him to leave the Ring to Frodo in the first chapter of *The Lord of the Rings*. It is a clear sign that the evil of the Ring is already at work.

Isildur is spared the horror of the ultimate fate of a mortal Ring-bearer. In the second year of the Third Age, as he is returning from Gondor to Eriador to take up his father's kingdom, he is ambushed by Orcs near the River Anduin. Wearing the Ring he is invisible to the Orcs, but when he attempts to swim the river the Ring betrays him and slips from his finger. He is sighted by the Orcs and shot with many arrows. The Ring then passes out of the history of Middle-earth for an extended period. During the 2461 years it languishes at the bottom of the Great River, Sauron, greatly weakened, returns to Middle-earth and slowly begins consolidating his power.

In the year 2463 of the Third Age, the Ring is found by Déagol (a member of a race related to the Hobbits) whilst fishing on the Great River. Déagol is immediately murdered by Sméagol (Gollum), his cousin, who takes the Ring and flees to the caves under the Misty Mountains with it. In 2941, the Ring slips from Gollum's finger and is found by Bilbo Baggins[37]. Gandalf has this to say about these events:

> '...There was more than one power at work, Frodo. The
> Ring was trying to get back to its master. ...So now, when
> its master was awake once more and sending out his dark
> thought from Mirkwood,[38] it abandoned Gollum. Only to
> be picked up by the most unlikely person imaginable:
> Bilbo from the Shire!'[39]

The true nature of the Ring is never explored in *The Hobbit*. It is simply described as an artefact that bestows invisibility upon its wearer. Still, Bilbo gains a startling insight into the nature and misery of Gollum's existence:

> A sudden understanding, a pity mixed with horror, welled
> up in Bilbo's heart: a glimpse of endless unmarked days
> without light or hope of betterment, hard stone, cold fish,
> sneaking and whispering.[40]

Bilbo is wearing the Ring at this point, and has a chance to kill Gollum, who is definitely trying to kill him. It is this impulse of mercy, Bilbo's first ethical choice while wearing the Ring, that explains how little harm the Ring causes him in the end. This act of mercy has profound implications for the story of *The Lord of the Rings*, and for the ultimate fate of the Ring. Always perceptive, Gandalf sees what Frodo cannot as he describes Bilbo's actions. Frodo is repelled by the very thought of Gollum, and remarks that it is a pity Bilbo did not stab him when he had the chance. Gandalf replies:

'...[Gollum] is bound up with the fate of the Ring. My
heart tells me that he has some part to play yet, for good
or ill, before the end; and when that comes, the pity of
Bilbo may rule the fate of many – yours not least.'[41]

Gandalf's remarks are deeply prophetic, as we find near the end of
the story. This is one of the moments when one of the Wise
receives an insight into the future of Middle-earth.

As we have seen, the One Ring was forged as an instrument of
domination, and contained a great part of Sauron's essence. The
Ring's power is to subvert the hearts of those that possess it, or even
desire it. Against the advice of Elrond, Isildur takes up the Ring on
the grounds that it is recompense for the death of his father. Sméagol
justifies the murder of Déagol and the theft of the Ring on the
grounds that it was his birthday and that the Ring was due to him
as a present. Boromir is driven mad by the thought of the Ring, and
how, against the advice of the Council of Elrond, he might use it to
save Minas Tirith and Gondor. During the brief period that Sam
bears the Ring, he also is tempted to use it to do good:

Already the Ring tempted him, gnawing at his will and
reason. Wild fantasies arose in his mind; and he saw
Samwise the Strong, Hero of the Age, striding with a flaming sword across the darkened land, and armies flocking
to his call as he marched to the overthrow of Barad-dur.[42]

It is Sam's love for Frodo that allows him to weather this temptation that strikes almost to the very core of his being. It is the nature
of the Ring to base its temptation on the very things those that
would use it care most deeply about. For Boromir, this is the desire
for the power to protect the country he loves. For Sam, it is the simple gardener's desire to make barren things fertile.[43]

Even Bilbo was not entirely truthful with the Dwarves when he
first described how he came by the Ring, claiming that he won it in
the Riddle game with Gollum. The Ring has the most painful effect

on Frodo, who bears it for most of *The Lord of the Rings*. Physically the effects are profound, and become more serious the further Frodo carries the Ring towards and finally into its maker's realm. Frodo at the last is so weary with the burden of the Ring that he can no longer walk, and Sam must carry him on his back. And yet the Ring has a more profound internal effect upon him. Sam finds Frodo a prisoner in the tower of Cirith Ungol, in despair because he believes the Ring has been taken from him, and the struggle is all over. Sam reveals that he has carried the Ring for Frodo. Frodo's reaction is extreme. Suddenly, he can no longer see his most faithful friend and follower, merely:

> ...an orc... leering and pawing at his treasure, a foul little creature with greedy eyes and a slobbering mouth.[44]

The Ring tempts even the greatest of the Wise, and though they are wise enough (save Saruman, and possibly Denethor) to recognise the danger of that temptation, it proves to be a sore trial for them. Near the beginning of *The Lord of the Rings* Gandalf informs Frodo of the peril that the Ring represents to him, the Shire, and the free peoples of Middle-earth. Frightened by the responsibility of possessing it, Frodo asks Gandalf to take the Ring:

> "No!' cried Gandalf, springing to his feet. 'With that power I should have a power too great and terrible. And over me the Ring would gain a power still greater and more deadly.'[45]

Gandalf knows the power of the Ring is to play on and subvert the virtues of its bearer. For Gandalf these virtues are those of pity and mercy. Galadriel, also, has to face this test of character. In Lothlórien, after the episode where Frodo and Sam are given the privilege of gazing into the Mirror of Galadirel (a powerful scrying device), Frodo offers the Ring to her. Galadriel reveals that she has for a long time thought about all the good that she might achieve with the Ring:

'I do not deny that my heart has greatly desired to ask
what you offer. For many long years I had pondered what
I might do, should the Great Ring come into my hands,
and behold! it was brought within my grasp.'[46]

Galadriel understands the nature of the Ring, and the nature of
Sauron's evil:

'The evil that was devised long ago works on in many
ways, whether Sauron himself stands or falls. Would that
not have been a noble deed to set to the credit of his Ring,
if I had taken it by force or fear from my guest?'[47]

Galadriel's tone is ironic: she recognises the inherent evil in taking
something by force in order to achieve a greater good, indeed the
danger within the whole 'end justifies the means' utilitarian argu-
ment. But this is not her greatest temptation. Frodo has offered her
the Ring of his own free will.

'And now at last it comes. You will give me the Ring
freely! In place of the Dark Lord you will set up a Queen.
And I shall not be dark, but beautiful and terrible as the
Morning and the Night! ... All shall love me and despair!'[48]

Galadriel passes this test because she understands the fundamental
nature of the Ring. Immediately after she has made the decision to
'diminish, and go into the West, and remain Galadriel'[49] she
explains to Frodo why he cannot use the Ring to know the
thoughts of the bearers of the other remaining Rings. Galadriel
makes it very clear that the Ring has been designed by Sauron for
a specific purpose, and that certain conditions must be met before
it can be used as a source of such power:

'Did not Gandalf tell you that the rings give power according to the measure of each possessor? Before you could

use that power you would need to become far stronger,
and to train your will to the domination of others...'[50]

Sauron designed the Ring to dominate others. Any bearer of the Ring who wishes to use its full powers must develop their personality towards domination. Galadriel has also made it clear that the Ring grants power in direct proportion to the power of its bearer. Herein lies the great danger to the West – and its one desperate hope. During the Council of Elrond, Elrond himself explains to Boromir why the forces of the West cannot use Sauron's Ring against him:

'Its strength, Boromir, is too great for anyone to wield at
will, save only those who have a great power of their own.
But for them it holds an even deadlier peril. The very desire
of it corrupts the heart. Consider Saruman. If any of the
Wise should with this Ring overthrow the Lord of Mordor,
using his own arts, he would then set himself up on
Sauron's throne, and yet another Dark Lord would appear.'[51]

It is clear that the beleaguered forces of the West cannot use this most potent artefact against its creator. Yet neither can they hide it from him indefinitely. Sauron has a strange, symbiotic relationship with the Ring. Even without possessing it, whilst it still exists Sauron retains much of his power. And his personal power is vast, and augmented by the might of his armies. There is, quite simply, no safe place to hide the Ring, no fortress or stronghold that Sauron could not eventually break down. At the Council, Elrond admits that he does not have the strength to withstand the concentrated might of Sauron, and that neither does Galadriel in Lothlórien, nor Círdan at the Grey Havens. These places would be the last to fall to Sauron, but fall they eventually would, and the Ring would be recovered by him.[52] It is clear also that the Ring cannot simply be thrown away. Glorfindel suggests at the Council that the Ring might be cast into the sea and thus lost forever. Gandalf explains to him that the Ring would eventually be found again (we might remember that it languished at the bottom of the Anduin for nearly 2500 years and was found), and Galdor points out that the roads to the sea are fraught with the greatest peril. In the chapter on Gandalf we will look in more detail at the desperate strategy that the West selects – the sending of the Ring into the land of its maker. It is the unique nature of the Ring that dictates this strategy – by its very nature it must not be used, and cannot be hidden.

It is worth considering the actual powers and properties of the Ring. Its most obvious power is that it bestows invisibility on its wearer. This is the power that allows Bilbo in *The Hobbit* to escape from Gollum, to evade the giant spiders, to avoid capture by the Woodelves, and to burgle Smaug's lair. In *The Lord of the Rings* the nature of this power is developed more fully. The Ring removes the wearer from the sight of others by transferring him partly into the realm of shadows – the same realm occupied by the Nazgûl. When Frodo dons the Ring during the Nazgûl attack on Weathertop, he is drawn into their realm and sees them clearly. Conversely, they see him clearly too. The Ring removes its wearer from mortal sight at the expense of making him much more visible to Sauron or his Nazgûl. When Frodo stands looking east on the summit of another mountain, Amon Hen, whilst wearing the Ring:

> ... suddenly he felt the Eye. There was an eye in the
> Dark Tower that did not sleep. He knew that it had
> become aware of his gaze. A fierce eager will was there.
> It leaped towards him; almost like a finger he felt it,
> searching for him.[53]

The power of invisibility carries with it a dreadful peril. And the ultimate fate of any that bears the One Ring for long enough is truly dreadful – to become as the Nazgûl are, a shadow-thing of Sauron.[54] The Ring is also extremely difficult to give up: Isildur refused to do so, in spite of the urgings of the wisest of Middle-earth; and Bilbo, who for reasons already discussed sustained little harm from the Ring, only did so with difficulty. Frodo is ultimately unable to give up the Ring and dons it in the fiery chambers of Mount Doom, intent on challenging Sauron, and claiming the Ring for himself. It is Sméagol who accomplishes the task, biting the Ring from Frodo's finger, and stumbling in his triumph into the Cracks of Doom. The pity that Bilbo showed in not killing Gollum when he had the chance finally leads to the Ring's destruction, and Gandalf's wise words to Frodo on the subjects of pity and fate are vindicated.

So what does the making of the One Ring, its nature and its effects, have to do with the acts of creation described in the previous section dealing with the First Age? In that section we observed the repeated failure of the forces of evil to create anything new or anything with a consciousness of its own. This failure is overcome with the forging of the One Ring. As we have noted, this artefact has a rudimentary consciousness, a deep malevolence, and a rudimentary will. Sauron accomplishes this feat only by placing half of his own essence into the Ring. Still, something new has definitely been created when Sauron does this. The Ring once separated from Sauron is other than Sauron, though they yearn for each other. And the essence of Sauron, evil though it is, still may trace its descent back to its original creation by Ilúvatar. Sauron accomplishes what Morgoth did not: an act of true creation, and he does so presumably without the direct volition of Ilúvatar himself. Like Fëanor he steals something, but he does so only at the expense of dividing, and almost consuming himself. Like the Silmarils, the One Ring is a true creation: a darkness to their light. It seems that in Middle-earth evil must either attempt corruption and have its corruption eventually subverted to good, or attempt to create and so devour itself.

THE THREE ELVEN RINGS

We have already discussed the One, the Seven, and the Nine. However, the Three Rings of the Elves deserve special comment. As mentioned before, they were forged in the Second Age by Celebrimbor in Eregion, and though made with Sauron's lore, were never touched or sullied by him.

Their names were Vilya, the Ring of Air; Nenya, the Ring of Water, or Adamant; and Narya, the Ring of Fire. In appearance each Ring had its own identifying stone. Vilya, the mightiest of the three, though of unspecified powers, was golden and bore a sapphire; Nenya bore a white adamant, and gave power in the arts of concealment; and Narya displayed a ruby, and was associated with fire.

The Elves were unable to make use of the Great Rings whilst Sauron possessed the One Ruling Ring. However, after the Last Alliance and the temporary downfall of Sauron at the hands of Gilgalad and Elendil, the Great Rings were distributed amongst the Wise. Vilya was borne by Elrond, and Nenya by Galadriel, who used it to keep the land of Lothlórien concealed from the gaze of Sauron. The location of Narya, however, was a secret until the final downfall of Sauron and the end of the Third Age. In fact Círdan the shipwright gave Narya to Gandalf upon his arrival at the Grey Havens from the undying lands in around 1050 of the Third Age, with these words:

> 'Take now this Ring... for thy labours and thy cares will be heavy, but in all it will support thee and defend thee from weariness. For it is the Ring of Fire, and herewith, maybe, thou shalt rekindle hearts to the valour of old in a world that grows chill.'[55]

Much of Gandalf's affinity with fire is explained by his possession of Narya.

Yet the fates of the Three Rings were inextricably linked to the fate of the One Ruling Ring, and dependent upon its continued existence for their power. This was the tragedy of the Elves: Middle-earth was lost to them whatever happened. If Sauron were to prevail, the Middle-earth they knew and loved must be destroyed. If Sauron were to be defeated by the destruction of the One Ring, then the power of the Elves too would fade, and they would fade from Middle-earth. Galadriel is well aware of the paradox that faced the Elves:

'... if you fail, then we are laid bare to the Enemy. Yet if you succeed, then our power is diminished, and Lothlórien will fade, and the tides of Time will sweep it away.'[56]

Galadriel is right. After the final fall of Sauron, the Elves (Arwen Evenstar excepted), Gandalf, Frodo and Bilbo depart from Middle-earth and cross the Western Sea to the Undying Lands. The Third Age, the Age of Men and Elves, is over:

But when all these things were done, and the heir of Isildur [Aragorn] had taken up the lordship of Men, and the dominion of the West had passed to him, then it was made plain that the power of the Three also was ended, and to the Firstborn [the Elves] the world grew cold and grey. In that time the Noldor set sail from the Havens and left Middle-earth forever.[57]

CHAPTER THREE

THE LESSENING OF THE AGES

lthough there are many reasons for the enduring popularity of *The Lord of The Rings*, one is undoubtedly the sheer breadth of detail which Tolkien supplies concerning the world in which it is set. As well as breathtaking descriptions of the land and peoples directly involved, there is an ever-present history, and wealth of legend, which surround them. Throughout the book there is a constant reference to events of the past, and of kings and heroes whose epics occurred many thousands of years before. All of this creates a feeling of reality, a feeling that we are reading of a real world peopled by real beings with their own cultures, history and beliefs, that has rarely been matched in a work of fiction before or since. We feel, as we hear of these great heroes of old, that they are more than just names invented for the story. Rather, they seem part of a rich tapestry that we have yet to hear. This is, of course, because they are. Professor Tolkien was not content with just writing a story; he had created a whole world with a complete history from the earliest days, many thousands of years before the events concerning the Hobbits and the Company of the Ring. Every action taken by the characters of Middle-earth is set against a rich, living background of what has gone before.

Some of this history was included in the Appendices at the end of the third volume of *The Lord of the Rings*. With the posthumous publication of *The Silmarillion,* we gained the opportunity to read of the Elder Days, when Men first appeared, the Elves first named all the things of the world and Morgoth, Sauron's dark master, fought to rule it.

But the tales of the First and Second Ages of Middle-earth are more than just stories, or a pre-history to *The Lord of The Rings*. They allow us to see the whole history of the world, the constant struggle between good and evil and in such detail that, as with our own history, we can read the lessons they contain. In this chapter, we will concern ourselves with the whole history of Middle-earth, from its creation and shaping, to the Fourth Age, the Age of Man, with the reign of Aragorn as King Elessar.

There are two main themes embodied in the history of Middle-earth. The first is the lessening of the ages, the constant and inevitable decline of the protagonists, both good and evil, over time. In the beginning this struggle is directly between the gods, or Valar, themselves. After the destruction of the Two Trees, and the theft of the Silmarils, it is the Elves, later aided by Men, who are forced to confront Morgoth. Then, by the time of the events of *The Lord of The Rings*, it is a weakened and disunited race of Men who bear the brunt of the malice of Sauron – a mere lieutenant of Morgoth's in earlier ages, though still terrifyingly powerful to his enemies. Then even Sauron passes away, as do the Firstborn, or Elves, and with them much of the magic and power of the world.

The second theme in the history of Middle-earth is the repetition of key events in the struggle between the two sides. Time and again, we see how disunity and division always spell disaster for Elves or Men, and how both races engineer their own banishment from paradise. The Shadow uses fair words to disguise lies and deceit when force is not enough, but, in the end, this always contains the seeds of its own destruction. Combining these two themes, it is perhaps apt to picture the history of Middle-earth, not as cyclical, but as a downward spiral. The same points are passed with ancient lessons unlearned, but then rediscovered, in a constant deterioration as the world grows older.

MELKOR, THE VALAR AND THE FIRST AGE

Morgoth was originally named Melkor. At first, even Melkor, who becomes the source of all strife and malice in the world, was not evil. The greatest of all the Valar (his name means 'He who Arises in Might'), his pride led him to defy the will of Ilúvatar and attempt to weave his own tune into the Song of Creation. This is the struggle between good and evil in its purest and most spiritual form. As we saw in chapter two, this contest determined the very nature of the elements, with Melkor's bitter cold producing the beauty of snow and frost, his scorching fires producing clouds and rain. The lesson we saw in that section, that acts of evil turn in the end to good, is a major theme of the history of the world (Arda, as Tolkien names it).

After the creation of Arda, or the world, Melkor battles with the other Valar from his stronghold of Utumno. Realising that he is no match for the combined forces of the Valar (despite individually being equal to, or even greater than, Manwë himself), Melkor begins to corrupt other creatures. He entices the Valaraukar or Balrogs, spirits of pure flame, to his service. Sauron, originally a servant of Aulë, is enlisted as his greatest lieutenant. Even Ossë, the Maiar of the wild seas, is briefly corrupted – giving rise to Kraken and other sea monsters – before repenting and being forgiven by the Valar. With these powerful spirits, Melkor wages war on the Valar, in a titanic, elemental struggle, which sees the whole shape of the world transformed.

> ...they built lands and Melkor destroyed them; valleys they delved and Melkor raised them up; mountains they carved and Melkor threw them down; seas they hollowed and Melkor spilled them. [58]

When Melkor casts down the Lamps forged by the Valar to give light to the world, again causing widespread geological destruction, the Valar withdraw to fortify the Undying Lands, abandoning Middle-earth to Melkor's dark influence. Then, when the Elves first awake, the Valar fear for their safety and reluctantly go to war with Melkor once more. Again, as with any struggle between the gods themselves, the impact upon Middle-earth is seismic, with the whole of the North-West of Middle-earth being broken in the battle. In the end, however, the Valar are victorious, defeating Melkor and chaining him in the Void.

Even in these early days of the world we can see the tactics of evil being developed. When force alone is not enough, lies and deceit turn enemies into allies, and divide foes. But evil is also often overconfident, and can be still be defeated, although the cost (here to the world itself) is great.

After the defeat of Melkor, the Valar decide to summon the Elves to Valinor, both fearing for their safety and wanting their companionship:

> and Mandos broke his silence, saying: 'So it is doomed.' From this summons came many woes that afterwards befell.[59]

Remarkably, it is the impatience of the Valar themselves, and their selfishness in wanting the company of the Elves, that begins the chain of tragic events which follows. Here, not for the last time, we can see how evil can spring from decisions even if there are made from seemingly innocent motives. After the Elves are brought to Valinor and shown paradise, Melkor is freed. Despite having convinced Manwë with fair words of his good intentions, Melkor immediately begins to spread dissension in paradise. By the time he and Ungoliant destroy the two trees and steal the Silmarils, the seeds of evil are sown and the Noldor defy the Valar to follow in vengeance. This act of defiance swiftly bears fruit. Fëanor and his followers murder the Teleri for their beautiful Swan Ships – a notorious crime which becomes known as the Kinslaying.

The decision of the Noldor to defy the Valar and pursue Melkor, or Morgoth (the Black Enemy as he is now renamed), is a deeply significant one. By turning their backs on the Valar and paradise they condemn themselves not only to pain and struggle, but also to their own decline. Their defiance of the Valar, and by implication Ilúvatar himself, has inevitable parallels with the expulsion of Adam and Eve from the Garden of Eden. Although the lies and deceit of Melkor are at work, the Noldor consciously reject paradise through their own pride and a desire for kingdoms of their own in the East. The consequence of their fall from grace is their own descent in status and power.

'And those that endure in Middle-earth and come not to
Mandos shall grow weary of the world as with a great
burden, and shall wane, and become as shadows of regret
before the younger race that cometh after.'[60]

Morgoth also is less than he once was. Where once he was a creature of pure spirit, capable of taking any form, he now finds himself tied to the Earth. His 'creation' of Orcs and moulding of the
strongholds of Utumno and Angband means he has put a part of
himself into them, thereby lessening his own power. As detailed in
the earlier chapter on creation, only Ilúvatar has the power of true
creation. Morgoth must put a part of himself into his foul experiments. While he gains vast armies with which to conquer the
world, he makes himself far more bound to it.

Even at Morgoth's supreme moment of triumph, he miscalculates.
Morgoth and Ungoliant, the powerful Maia who appears as a black spider that weaves webs of darkness, destroy the Two Trees and flee.
Ungoliant, swollen to terrible size through draining the light of the
Two Trees but still hungry, threatens Morgoth and seeks to destroy the
Silmarils. Morgoth's fall from near omnipotent figure is shown by his
fear and the need to summon his Balrog servants to force Ungoliant to
retreat. The light of the Silmarils themselves scorches his hands black,
even through the casket in which they are held, marking him forever:

nor was he ever free form the pain of the burning, and the
anger of the pain [61]

It is also in this venture that Morgoth loses his power to shift forms, or
even become pure spirit, and becomes trapped forever in a single shape:

and he put on again the form that he had worn as the
tyrant of Utumno: a dark lord, tall and terrible. In that
form he remained ever after.[62]

It is this more than anything that symbolises Melkor's weakening after his fall from grace. Through his carving of strongholds and his breeding of the Orcs, Trolls[63] and dragons, he binds himself to the world and to a single, terrible appearance. Unfortunately for the Elves, although Morgoth may be weaker than in the earliest days, he is still a God, and as one of the Valar can only truly be defeated by them:

> for the Noldor did not yet comprehend the fullness of the power of Morgoth, nor understand that their unaided war upon him was without final hope.[64]

The Elves' struggle holds no chance of victory. Whereas in the beginning the struggle between good and evil was an equal one, or at least of like with like, now it has become entirely disproportionate. Yet this did not deter the Noldor.

> 'In Aman we have come through bliss to woe. The other now we will try: through sorrow to find joy; or freedom, at the least.'[65]

Despite the initial setback of the death of Fëanor, after his impetuous assault on Angband, the strength and glory of the Elves is enough to besiege Morgoth for hundreds of years. But this is the best the Elves can hope to achieve – an indefinite stalemate. The forces arrayed on both sides are immense in comparison to later ages. As well as vast armies of Orcs and Trolls, creatures such as Werewolves and later dragons all follow Morgoth's commands. The Black Enemy can even call upon a legion of Balrogs, the great Maiar spirits of Flame, with which to assault his foes. But the Elves, also, have hosts of strength and power unimaginable in later days. Fëanor and his bodyguard battle the selfsame Balrogs for a day and night before succumbing. And there are at least two occasions in which Balrogs are slain in single combat with great Elven heroes, although the Elves are also killed.[66] This is in stark contrast to the Third Age, when a single Balrog drives an entire Dwarven House from Moria, and is spoken of in terrified whispers. Gandalf himself, one of the most powerful figures in all Middle-earth in that time, barely defeats the creature – even with the protection of Narya, the Elven Ring of Fire – and his physical form is slain in the battle.

When the stalemate between the Elves and Morgoth is finally broken, as it inevitably has to be, it is Morgoth who emerges the victor. However, the majesty of the Elves is shown again when Fingolfin, the High King of the Elves and greatest warrior of all the Noldor, falls into despair upon seeing Morgoth victorious, and challenges Morgoth to single combat. So terrifying is he in his anger that none of Morgoth's servants dare oppose him and Morgoth is forced, through shame, to confront him:

> though his might was greatest of all things in this world,
> alone of the Valar he knew fear. But he could not now
> deny the challenge before the face of his captains.[67]

The result, again, is inevitable and a metaphor for the whole Elven struggle. Fingolfin wounds Morgoth seven times but is eventually crushed beneath his heel. Thorondor, the King of the Eagles, rescues the High King's body, scarring the Dark Lord's face with his claws at the same time. The assistance of the Eagle is significant – alone the Elves are doomed, no matter how valiant. Hope lies in co-operation with the other races.

The relationship with the race of Men makes this point well. When Men and Elves first meet, there is distrust on both sides, the result of Morgoth's lies. Then, when Morgoth breaks the siege of Angband, it is the treachery of the Easterlings that spells final defeat for the army of Fingolfin.

> [Morgoth's] …design was accomplished in a manner after
> his own heart; for … fear and hatred were aroused among
> those that should have been united against him.[68]

Disunity and mistrust always serve the cause of evil, whether Men against Men, or Men against Elves.

Nevertheless, it is a union of Men and Elves that saves all the peoples of Middle-earth. The Valar had refused the pleas for aid from the Elves, sent with messengers across the Sea, as the Elves had chosen their fate. But Eärendil the Mariner,[69] who comes as a representative of both races, embodies the hope of peace and co-operation between all of Ilúvatar's children. The Valar had intervened once already for the sake of the Elves and subsequently been defied, with the Noldor choosing exile, as the Avari, or unwilling, Elves had before refused the initial summons to Valinor. But the race of Men had been born under the shadow of evil, with Morgoth already at work among them, spreading his lies. Eärendil, symbol of union between the two races, finally convinces the Valar to intervene.

Morgoth himself is a victim of his own evil, as Sauron is to be at the end of the Third Age. In his pride, Morgoth believes himself unassailable, but even more blindly he thinks, unable to understand the concept of compassion, that the Valar have forsaken Middle-earth forever:

> for to him that is pitiless the deeds of pity are ever strange and beyond reckoning.[70]

When the Valar go to war, they precipitate the last great battle of the First Age. It is suggested that the Valar hesitate from fear that the world will not be able to survive the struggle. And again geography itself is the victim, as the whole of Beleriand[71] is sunk under the sea.

So between the Song of Creation and the end of the First Age, we see a clear pattern in the struggle between good and evil. At first good is dominant but, as it grows, evil uses use fair words and deception to turn enemies into allies. Then good and evil are on a more equal footing, where good can win, but only at great cost. Then, as evil's power grows even further, using lies and deception to divide the forces of good, it appears unstoppable but is destroyed at its moment of triumph by an unforeseen intervention – one which evil's own blindness overlooked.

The Second Age

The same pattern in the struggle between good and evil is repeated in both the Second and Third Ages, but on a far lesser scale. Most importantly, the gods withdraw, never again to intervene directly in the affairs of Middle-earth. Morgoth is banished, chained in the void beyond creation, but his legacy lives on. His greatest servant, Sauron, is captured at the end of the First Age, and repents. This repentance may have even be genuine, leaving evil without any great leaders in the world, albeit briefly. But Sauron is commanded to go to the Undying Lands and throw himself upon the mercy of the Valar. A combination of fear, shame and pride causes Sauron instead to slip away to wreak future havoc. Sauron is very powerful. He was once one of Aulë's most learned pupils before his corruption, which then saw him become Morgoth's chief lieutenant. He is still only a Maia, however, and evenly matched against the mightiest of the Elves and greatest of Men.

As with Melkor, thousands of years before, Sauron uses deceit to achieve his ends. Taking on a beautiful disguise and naming himself Annatar, or Lord of Gifts, he goes among the Elves. Although mistrusted by some Eldar, the Elves of Ost-in-Edhil take him in. Celebrimbor, the grandson of Fëanor himself, works with him to create the Rings of Power. It is a combination of their knowledge and power that creates the Nine Rings for Men, whom Sauron then dominates to create his greatest servants, the Nazgûl or Ringwraiths. Celebrimbor and Sauron also create the Seven Rings for the Dwarves. But Sauron has no part in the creation of the three Elven Rings – Narya, Nenya and Vilya – and no power over their bearers. Sauron then creates the One Ring, and is revealed as the Dark Lord. By then he is strong enough to work openly and goes to war against Celebrimbor, destroying his Elven kingdom. However, the Elves are not Sauron's only problem in the Second Age.

The balance of power between Elves and Men is changed greatly at this time. With the defeat of Morgoth, many of the Noldor who had defied the Valar return to the Undying Lands, leaving only a few who will not abandon Middle-earth. While figures such as Galadriel,

Elrond, Círdan, Gil-Galad and Celebrimbor are certainly among the most powerful in Middle-earth in the Second Age, the Elves are still just a shadow of the host that besieged Morgoth in Angband.

Men, on the other hand, are increasing in numbers. Elros was the brother of Elrond, the offspring of the two unions of Elves and Men.[72] While Elrond chooses to live forever with the Eldar, Elros chooses to be mortal and live as a man. He becomes the first of the Dúnedain, the descendants of the three houses of Men who fought against Morgoth. They are rewarded with wisdom and power and life more enduring than any others of mortal race have possessed.[73]

The Dúnedain are given the Island of Númenor as their home, placed between Valinor (the Undying Lands) and Middle-earth, indeed actually closer to Valinor. They become more like Elves than Men in learning, belief and strength. Although at first glance this may appear to contradict Tolkien's overall theme of weakening over time, instead it should be seen as a sign of the union between Elves and Men giving rise to a race lesser than the first, but greater than the second. Like their island home's geographical location, the Dúnedain are neither wholly of one world nor the other, although closer in power and glory to the Undying Lands and the Elves, than Middle-earth and Men.

However, inevitably, the same fall from grace that befell the Elves afflicts the Dúnedain of Númenor. As time passes they become proud and begin to resent the restrictions placed on them by the Valar[74] and the will of Eru[75] himself. Their havens in Middle-earth, previously areas where they spread knowledge and wisdom among the lesser races of Men, become colonies and fortresses.[76] Eventually, their Kings hold on to the throne until senility and death overtake them, abandoning the original custom of handing over the reins of power when their children reach their prime. They begin to grow obsessed with death and ways to prolong life.

All the Númenoreans' defiance and pride achieve is a lessening of their life span, causing greater fear and insecurity and quickening a vicious circle. By the time of Ar-Pharazôn, the 24th King of Númenor, the Dúnedain are deeply divided between the Elf-friends (the Faithful), who hold to the old ways, and the majority of the people, who have become cruel empire-builders. Ar-Pharazôn takes exception to Sauron's claiming the title King of the World. He raises a huge army and sails to Middle-earth to do battle. Sauron surrenders without a fight. But having learned well the lessons of his master Morgoth, Sauron quickly becomes an adviser to the Númenorean King and poisons his mind even more against the Valar. Within a few short years he convinces the King to abandon all reverence for Ilúvatar and turn to a bloody worship of Melkor:

> and in that temple, with spilling of blood and torment and great wickedness, men made sacrifice to Melkor that he should release them from Death.[77]

Evil can only have one master, however, and Sauron is clearly not one to rule solely from the shadows. Although the Dúnedain have fallen far, Sauron, in his hatred for them, desires their total destruction. He convinces Ar-Pharazôn to go to war against the Valar and seize the Undying Lands, the ultimate blasphemy. This assault upon heaven causes the final, and greatest, geological upheaval in the history of the world. The Valar give up their rulership of Arda to Ilúvatar, who remakes its very nature, removing the Undying Lands from the world of Men forever:

> those that sailed furthest set but a girdle about the Earth
> …and they said: 'All roads are now bent'.[78]

We can deduce from this that the world was indeed flat until its remaking, and that the Undying Lands were only then placed elsewhere, unreachable by men, although the Elves can somehow still travel there. The whole of Númenor is destroyed. Men, women and children die together, save for nine ships carrying the few Dúnedain who had remained faithful, under the command of Elendil and his sons Isildur and Anárion. These remnants of the elf-friends found the Dúnedain kingdoms in exile of Gondor and Arnor.

The sheer scale of this cataclysmic retribution upon the Dúnedain shocks even Sauron, who had expected nothing more than the destruction of the armada. Sauron's fate is an eerie echo of the fate of Morgoth at his moment of triumph, thousands of years before. Morgoth became trapped in a single terrible form after the destruction of the Two Trees and capture of the Silmarils, which caused the fall from grace of the Elves as they defied the Valar to follow him. When Sauron repeats his master's trick by having Men destroy their own Paradise, his body is lost with the sinking of Númenor, and his spirit is forced to flee to Mordor. Like Morgoth, he loses the power to look pleasant or beautiful, although with the power of the One Ring 'he wrought himself a new guise, an image of malice and hatred made visible; and the eye of Sauron the Terrible few could endure.'[79]

The Dark Lord wastes little time in striking again. Once he has reformed in Mordor, he masses his Orcs, Trolls and lesser Men, as well as many Númenoreans, who had survived the fall of their homeland in their tyrannical colonies in Middle-earth.[80] Sauron assaults Gondor. But Sauron here shows himself overconfident. Elendil and Gil-galad realise that Sauron will soon grow too strong and will destroy the kingdoms of the Free Peoples one by one. So they join together in what is known as the Last Alliance of Elves and Men. When the two armies meet it is said that

> All living things were divided in that day, and some of
> every kind, even of beasts and birds, were found in either
> host, save the Elves only.[81]

This, once again, perfectly illustrates that central theme of the battle between good and evil. Evil constantly strives to divide and corrupt those around it, while victory for the forces of good can only come when such differences are put aside. The Last Alliance is victorious but at a great cost. Sauron, who in turn is defeated by Isildur, kills both Gil-galad and Elendil. Although the alliance against Sauron is led by the Elves, the one who casts down Sauron and cuts the Ring from his finger is a Man, a Dúnedan. This is a powerful symbol of the waning of the Elves and the ascendancy of Men.

And it is, in turn, Isildur who makes the fatal mistake of taking the One Ring as compensation or booty from Sauron (Tolkien uses the Anglo Saxon term weregild), refusing the advice of Gil-galad's herald Elrond to destroy it. This allows Sauron the opportunity to return. In another echo of ancient times, just as Morgoth was burned by the light of the Silmarils but could not give them up, so Isildur is burned by the evil of the One Ring, but cannot bring himself to part with it. As one was burned by good, the other is burned by evil. As Isildur writes in a scroll, discovered by Gandalf some three thousand years later:

> my hand was scorched, so that I doubt if ever again I shall be free of the pain of it.[82]

The Third Age

As we enter the Third Age, the main protagonists of good and evil are weakened still further. Although Sauron returns, he is without the One Ring. However, so long as the Ring survives, he also cannot be truly vanquished. He has once again to build up his strength in secret and use the ancient tactics of divide and rule against the forces of Elves and Men.

These tactics work most successfully against the remnants of the faithful Númenoreans; the Dúnedain. Arnor, the kingdom of the Dúnedain to the north, was originally founded by Elendil at the end of the Second Age. Within less than a thousand years, a quarrel over the line of succession means that the realm is split into the three squabbling petty kingdoms of Arthedain, Cardolan and Rhudaur. These prove easy prey when Sauron's most powerful Ringwraith, the Witch-king, becomes ruler of the realm of Angmar several centuries later.

Sauron himself is still hidden at this time, but his foremost servant does him proud. First Rhudaur, then Cardolan fall to the Witch-king's armies and malign influence. Arthedain holds out for more than five centuries, but is eventually crushed in the twentieth century of the Third Age. An Elven army from Rivendell[83] and a mighty fleet from

Gondor arrive too late to save the Dúnedain of the North, although their vengeance on Angmar is total, obliterating all its armies. The Witch-king, however, escapes and Sauron is well pleased with the exchange. All remnants of the original Arnor are destroyed, gone for the duration of the Third Age, while Orcs can always be replaced. Only a handful of the Dúnedain survive as the Rangers of the North, patrolling the whole of Northern Eriador as mysterious green-clad wanderers. Their leader at the time of *The Lord of the Rings* is Strider, later revealed to be none other than Aragorn, descended directly from the last King of Arthedain and, through him, Elendil himself, making him the rightful High King of all the Dúnedain.

Gondor itself fares somewhat better than its Northern counterpart. At the time of the War of the Ring it is still the mightiest nation of Men and the foremost bulwark against the threat of Sauron. A mighty seafaring country, it keeps watchful guard against Mordor and Sauron's wild subject peoples of the South and East.[84] But Gondor has also diminished since its founding, some three thousand years before, and its history had not been untroubled. The kinstrife of the fifteenth century and the defeat of Castamir the Usurper[85] leads to the defeated nobles becoming the Corsairs of Umbar. Umbar is a constant thorn in the side of the Dúnedain and, by the time of *The Lord of the Rings*, another vassal of Mordor.

Before Sauron declares himself openly his servants, the Nazgûl, have been working against Gondor, as the Witch-king had against Arnor. Issuing from Mordor in the year 2000, they capture the ancient stronghold set to watch the East; Minas Ithil. Renamed Minas Morgul, the city is a spearhead for Sauron's forces in Gondor and constantly threatens the whole of Ithilien, that part of Gondor closest to Mordor. The Royal capital of Osgiliath has to be abandoned and a new capital declared at Minas Anor, now renamed as Minas Tirith.[86] More seriously, the Nazgûl invasion ends the Gondorian monarchy as, fifty years later, King Eärnur, foolishly accepting the Witch-king's challenge to single combat, is betrayed and killed. The rulership of Gondor is taken over by the line of Ruling Stewards.

Gondor's constant wars against the Easterlings and other pawns of Sauron are not wholly without hope, however, as they also lead to an alliance with a group of Northmen later known as the Rohirrim. These people, led by King Eorl, are expert horsemen and unparalleled cavalry. They ride to the rescue of the army of Gondor at the Battle of the Field of Celebrant, some five hundred years after the capture of Minas Ithil. In gratitude, Cirion, the Steward of Gondor, gives the lands between the rivers Isen and Anduin to his saviours, and Rohan is born. This is a bargain for Gondor, and the whole of the West. Great aid is rendered by the Rohirrim cavalry at the battle of the Pelennor Fields. Moreover, the destruction of the chief Nazgûl, the Witch-king, is achieved by the disguised shield maiden, Éowyn.[87] Although Gondor is certainly weakened by the end of the Third Age, it is still defiant and the alliance with Rohan remains strong.

More serious is the spiritual decline of Gondor, its ruling Dúnedain and the line of Stewards. The constant spectre of destruction at the hands of an ever-growing Mordor leads to Gondor feeling increasingly isolated and threatened. The Men of Gondor are a proud people, seeing themselves as the only force standing between Sauron and the subjugation of all Middle-earth. When Boromir, the son of Denethor, the 26th ruling Steward of Gondor, comes to the Council of Elrond, he is haughty, saying that he does not come to beg for help, only to seek advice. When Boromir learns of the existence of the Ring – also known as Isildur's Bane – he can see it only as a weapon to be wielded against Sauron:

> 'Why do you speak ever of hiding and destroying?... Let the Ring be your weapon.... Take it and go forth to victory!'[88]

Despite the words of the wise, warning him of the threat of the Ring to corrupt any who use it, Boromir falls under its evil influence. Although his original motives may have been noble – trying to gain aid for Gondor and save it from apparently inevitable defeat – he is tempted to greed and violence and tries to take the Ring from Frodo by force. It is this act which breaks the Fellowship of the Ring and causes Frodo to slip away, with Sam, to continue his journey to Mordor and Mount Doom alone.

Although Boromir's fall is clear, it is far from total. The warrior partly redeems himself in his, admittedly fruitless and ultimately fatal, defence of the other Hobbits, Merry and Pippin, against the Orcs sent to capture them. It is also likely that, without his moment of weakness, Frodo and Sam would have been unable to break so completely from the Company of the Ring and travel to Mordor alone. Had they not, it is possible that the encounter with Gollum and the journey to Mount Doom would have gone differently, with the eventual destruction of the Ring being prevented, leaving Sauron triumphant. As we have seen, time and again, the acts of evil can often ultimately come to good.

Spiritual corruption or decline can also be seen in the rulers of both Gondor and Rohan. King Théoden of Rohan falls under the influence of Saruman, through his servant Gríma Wormtongue. A frail and suspicious old man when Gandalf encounters him before the Battle of Helm's Deep, he is restored by Gandalf's counsel, and the power of the Elven Ring Narya,[89] and leads the Rohirrim into battle once more.

Unfortunately the decline of Denethor, the ruling Steward of Gondor and Boromir's father, is not so easily reversed. Concerned for the future of Gondor, he succumbs to pride and pits his will directly against Sauron, by using the Palantír, or seeing stone, of Minas Tirith. As Sauron has captured the Palantír originally housed in Minas Ithil after its fall, this proves a very costly gamble. Although Denethor gains much knowledge from using the stone, Sauron twists what the Steward sees to emphasise the unstoppable might of Mordor, and accentuate the weakness of Gondor. The battle of wills between the two takes its toll on Denethor's mind until

> pride increased... together with despair, until he saw...
> only a single combat between the Lord of the White Tower
> and the Lord of Barad-dûr, and mistrusted all others who
> resisted Sauron, unless they served himself alone.[90]

Denethor is never entirely seduced by evil, unlike Saruman or Ar-Pharazôn, the last King of Númenor. He never becomes a servant of Sauron, although he is a pawn. His corruption is merely the latest in a long line of Elves and Men who succumb to pride, despair and hubris – beginning with Fëanor himself. Because of the detail used in *The Lord of The Rings*, as opposed to the sweeping, epic style of *The Silmarillion*, we have in Denethor an opportunity to examine more closely just how the Shadow works to turn a strong and good mind into a broken one. Call it a character study in corruption, if you will.

Like his son Boromir, Denethor's motives are at first pure and arise from a desire only to protect Gondor and defeat its rival and enemy, Mordor. We know, sadly, that pure motives alone are not enough to resist corruption by Sauron. Denethor is described as both a strong and wise man, but in a contest of wills with a Maia of Sauron's power there can be only one outcome. But Denethor is not so easily forced into obeying the Dark Lord.

Firstly, Sauron plays upon their struggle itself, to make it overshadow all others. He wishes to turn Denethor's attention solely to the military struggle between Gondor and Mordor. This view, it should be said, is not entirely unrealistic. Gondor is the guard upon Mordor's gates and, especially with the Elven kingdoms hidden from Sauron's Eye, it is Gondor that is destined to suffer the Shadow's first overwhelming assault. But this single-minded obsession does mean that Denethor thinks only of war and his own strength, so that he dismisses all other options and mistrusts all other enemies of Sauron, even Gandalf:

> **'Pride would be folly that disdained help and counsel at
> need; but you deal out such gifts according to your
> designs. Yet the Lord of Gondor is not to be made the tool
> of other men's purposes, however worthy.'[91]**

Denethor chastises his own son, Faramir, for allowing the One Ring to slip through his fingers. Faramir's respect for Gandalf is, to Denethor, nothing less than a personal betrayal and he even wishes at one point that Faramir had died in his brother's place.

> 'Boromir was loyal to me and no wizard's pupil....he
> would have brought me a mighty gift.'[92]

Denethor's mistrust of Gandalf can also be seen clearly here. Not understanding the wizard's motives, and not being possessed of Gandalf's wisdom, he distrusts his meddling. As Gandalf himself says:

> 'You think, as is your wont, my lord, of Gondor only....
> Yet there are other men and other lives, and time still to
> be. And for me, I pity even his slaves.'[93]

Denethor can now only think in terms of contests, viewing Gandalf as a rival to be mastered in a bitter war of wills.

> Pippin felt once more the strain between their wills; but
> now almost it seemed as if their glances were blades from
> eye to eye...[94]

Gandalf's wisdom enables him to see even the war between Gondor and Mordor as part of a greater design, as part of the struggle between good and evil. Denethor's blindness to this means that he dismisses all thought of aid that does not serve Gondor and himself alone. Although he hopes desperately for the arrival of the Rohirrim in Gondor's hour of need, like Boromir, Denethor mistrusts the wisdom of the Elves, and dismisses the contribution of Pippin, even after the Hobbit has sworn his loyalty.

As we have seen, time and time again, it is disunity that evil seeks and it can only be bested when all its foes work together. Denethor's pride is so great, and so closed, that he can see Gandalf only as a rival and usurper, come to supplant him in his own hall. When, in his final madness, Denethor tries to burn himself and his son Faramir, he is confronted by Gandalf for the last time.

> 'Do I not know thee, Mithrandir? Thy hope is to rule in my
> stead, to stand behind every throne, north, south or west?'[95]

Sauron also preys on Denethor's hubris or pride. Believing that only the might of Gondor can stop Sauron – and seeing that might to be insufficient – Denethor falls into despair. By keeping the focus of Denethor and the Palantír on Mordor and its military strength, Sauron slowly but surely drives Denethor to hopelessness. As time goes on, he speaks in increasingly defeatist terms of the war against the Shadow:

> 'let all who fight the enemy in their fashion be at one, and keep hope while they may, and after hope still the hardihood to die free.'[96]

Upon learning of the arrival of the Witch-king at his gates, Denethor laughs in bitterness at Pippin's misapprehension that Sauron himself is come.

> 'Nay, not yet, Master Peregrin! He will not come save only to triumph over me when all is won.'[97]

The use of 'me' here is significant. Denethor can only see the struggle as one between himself and Sauron, and it is a struggle he is coming to believe cannot be won. Then, when Denethor finally descends into madness:

> 'Why do the fools fly?... Better to burn sooner than late, for burn we must... The West has failed.'[98]

Despair has taken him entirely and – to Denethor – Gondor and the West are one and the same. Denethor's choice of a pyre as the manner of his death is important too, as Dúnedain Lords were always entombed. He himself refers to it as a heathen death, while Gandalf goes further:

> 'only the heathen kings, under the domination of the Dark Power, did thus, slaying themselves in pride and despair, murdering their kin to ease their own death.'[99]

It is clearly a sign of how far the great Lord of Gondor has fallen that he chooses to meet his end in this way[100] instead of following Gandalf's advice:

> 'your part is to go out to the battle of your City, where maybe death awaits you. This you know in your heart.'[101]

The role of the Palantír in Denethor's downfall reveals another side of Denethor's fatal pride. The seven seeing stones, or Palantíri, carried to Middle-earth from Númenor, were created as powerful magical tools, each linked to the others, allowing instant communication between those wielding them. They also act as 'crystal balls', granting the user the ability to see places and events many miles away. The Palantíri had been perilous to use since the fall of Minas Ithil, when Sauron captured the seeing stone of Isildur. Anyone using them would come into direct conflict with the will of the Dark Lord. Denethor, in his pride, chooses to take this risk and place himself in peril, in return for the knowledge the stone grants him. On several occasions he refers to his 'secret' knowledge as he matches wits with Gandalf:

> 'Counsels may be found that are neither the webs of wizards nor the haste of fools. I have in this matter more lore and wisdom than you deem.'[102]

Then later:

> 'Some have accused you, Mithrandir, of delighting to bear ill news... but to me this is no longer news: it was known to me ere nightfall yesterday.'[103]

It is worth noting that Denethor's words here are reminiscent of Théoden's mockery of the wizard as 'Gandalf Stormcrow'.[104] This is clearly one of the lies spread by Gandalf's enemies against him, and a sign of the Shadow at work, wherever it is heard.

After a final vision in the Palantír that breaks his spirit, Denethor is lost:

> 'Didst thou think that the eyes of the White Tower were
> blind? [There] wafts up [the] Anduin a fleet with black
> sails. The West has failed.'[105]

It is precisely this lust for knowledge and information, albeit to protect Gondor, which proves Denethor's undoing. The ships which Denethor sees as the black sails of the Corsairs of Umbar actually bear Aragorn, Gimli, Legolas, the Rangers of the North and many soldiers of Southern Gondor. Aragorn has already led the Shadow Host, the Dead Men of Dunharrow, against the Corsairs and routed them, but by this time Denethor sees only what Sauron wishes him to see. The Steward is ultimately doomed through the Shadow's twisting of his perceptions. The constant struggles with his enemy have coloured his vision and ruined his judgement. In a telling speech just hours earlier, as he prepares the pyre for himself and Faramir, he talks of the enemy:

> 'he sees our very thoughts, and all we do is ruinous.'[106]

Although the Palantír allows Denethor to see much that is hidden, it also allows Sauron to see into Denethor's mind, and to manipulate it. Gandalf realises this only after Denethor's death, observing that

> 'He was too great to be subdued … [but] he saw … those
> things which that Power permitted him to see … [which]
> fed the despair of his heart until it overthrew his mind'[107]

Although never 'turned', the Steward is slowly twisted and destroyed by a foe far more powerful than he is. It is entirely appropriate that, in his final moments atop his pyre, the Steward clutches the Palantír, so that:

> 'it was said that ever after, if any man looked in that
> Stone, unless he had great strength of will… he saw only

two aged hands withering in flame.'[108]

Denethor's final act leaves a permanent memorial to yet another great figure brought low by the Shadow, and an eternal warning to others of the dangers of hubris and the perils of trusting too much in one's own strength.

While Denethor, the Lord of Gondor, and his increasingly desperate attempts to save his country from the Shadow, are a powerful symbol of the decline of Men in the Third Age, it is not only the Dúnedain who are affected. The Elves are truly a shadow of their former strength. Their three strongholds – Lórien, Rivendell and the Grey Havens – are, in fact, secret sanctuaries which provide succour and support for the few who know of them. None are strong enough to contemplate open war. Even the power of the Three Rings, which can now be used with Sauron's loss of the Ruling Ring, is founded in secrecy. Nenya and Vilya, the Rings of Water and Air, held by Galadriel and Elrond, respectively, spend their power keeping the lands of their bearers hidden from the eyes of Sauron and his servants. Although Rivendell proves an invaluable haven, providing respite and support for many – including the Rangers of the North – none of the Elven kingdoms march openly against Sauron. Even in the final battles of *The Lord of the Rings* the only Elves present – except for Legolas – are Elrond's sons, Elrohir and Elladan, who travel with the Rangers of the North. For the first time, there are no Elven hosts fighting in a great war. The contribution of the Elves is in their wisdom, and in their secret aid and succour to pivotal figures such as Aragorn and Gandalf.

Although the folly of the Elves dominated the First Age, it appears that the few Elven Lords and Ladies who remain in the Third Age have learned the lessons of the past. Galadriel, the Queen of Lothlórien, is the only remnant of the Noldor who defied the Valar to fight Morgoth in Middle-earth, and her advice and succour to the Company of the Ring is without flaw. It is also said that Galadriel wished Gandalf to be head of the White Council, rather than Saruman the White; a slight Saruman never forgives. Círdan, Lord of the Grey Havens, plays a small part in the War of the Ring, but we should not forget also that it was he who gave Gandalf Narya, the Elven Ring of Fire, after seeing, in his wisdom, that this was where it would do the most good.

Elrond is the son of that joining of Elves and Men, Eärendil, who proved to be the saviour of the world in the First Age. Elrond embodies the best of both peoples and, although the Lord of Imladris, or Rivendell – an Elven haven – he never abandons his mortal lineage. It was Elrond's brother Elros who founded the Dúnedain line. And so we see Elrond act always as a wise counsel to his brother's descendants. It is Elrond who advises Isildur to destroy the Ring at the end of the Second Age, and Elrond who provides succour, refuge and hope to the Rangers of the North after the fall of Arthedain. Aragorn himself is brought up by Elrond and loved as his own son, eventually marrying Arwen Evenstar, Elrond's daughter.[109] This union closes perfectly the history of Elves and Men, harking back to the very first union of Elves and Men in the First Age, Beren and Lúthien.

While Men and Elves are both lessened in the Third Age, they are not entirely alone. When Sauron's power grows once again, the Valar fear for Middle-earth. They know that the strength of Men and Elves has waned still further since the Last Alliance, but they cannot intervene directly. Sauron is merely a Maia. For the Valar to act in person would have been an entirely disproportionate response. Instead, when around a thousand years of the Third Age have passed, they send five Maiar from the Undying Lands to combat Sauron: the five wizards or Istari.[110] The arrival of the Istari shows that the Valar have not entirely abandoned the peoples of Middle-earth, but are forced to act through proxies. The time for the gods to exert their power directly in Middle-earth is long past.

The two greatest of the Istari are said to be Curunír and Mithrandir – Saruman and Gandalf. Saruman is the eldest and first to arrive. Most closely linked with the race of Men, he is destined to fall and become nothing more than a pale imitation of Sauron, envying the enemy he once hated. The domain of Radagast the Brown is the beasts and birds of Middle-earth. Although he proves naïve, and is an instrument of the treachery of Saruman, Radagast is never actually corrupted. Two Blue wizards are also mentioned: they are said to have travelled to the East and are never heard from again.

The sight of Saruman, once the greatest of the Istari and then the Lord of Isengard, reduced to leading a handful of brutal men in the destruction of the Shire, is a perfect illustration of the decline of the wise and powerful. Saruman takes a petty revenge on the Hobbits, blaming them for his downfall, by attempting to destroy the Shire they saved the world to protect. Although devastating for the Hobbits upon their return, the sight of a figure who once held the fate of nations in his hands reduced to a petty tyrant in Hobbiton illustrates Saruman's own fall perfectly. Then he falls even further, defeated by the Hobbits with no outside help from Elf or wizard. The Hobbits do not even bother to kill him, but merely send him on his way. Saruman's final humiliation is his murder by his own abused servant, Gríma Wormtongue.

Last but not least of the Istari is Gandalf. Gandalf, closest to the Elves, is, without doubt, the chief architect of Sauron's downfall. Gandalf's role in the War of the Ring, and for many centuries before, is so important that we have devoted an entire chapter to the Grey Wanderer. It is worth mentioning here that Gandalf's wisdom is in never pitting himself directly against Sauron, never attempting to match his power against the Dark Lord's, even while ceaselessly working against him.

Although it may not seem so to the peoples of the West, Sauron too is greatly diminished in the Third Age. As we saw in the chapter on Creation, Sauron put a great part of himself into the One Ring, never contemplating that he would lose it. He is reduced to a mere spirit after his defeat by Isildur. However, it is this selfsame mistake that allows him to return over the next thousand years, as he could never be finally vanquished until the Ring itself was destroyed.

Over time Sauron grows again, along with his Nazgûl servants, until he threatens the whole of the West. But he still has to return in secret, slowly marshalling his power and forces. In this he is very successful. He first appears in Dol Goldur,[111] where his shadow touches the home of King Thranduil and the forest Elves in Greenwood the Great, slowly leading to it being renamed Mirkwood. Even when the Elves and Istari realise the danger, they believe the presence in Dol Goldur is merely one of the Ringwraiths. It is not until a staggering 1700 years later, when Gandalf finds the Dwarf Lord Thráin captive in the dungeons of Dol Goldur, that Sauron's existence is uncovered for sure.

In his weakness Sauron is forced to use his servants, the nine Ringwraiths, for his public assaults. As we have already seen, they prove highly successful in destroying Arnor, through the Witch-king's realm of Angmar, and in threatening Gondor, after the capture of Minas Ithil. Sauron does not declare himself openly until the year 2951, almost two thousand years after his return, and less than 30 years before the War of the Ring. Even at this point, when his military strength is the greatest in Middle-earth, Sauron is still a Maia, a shadow of the strength of his master, the Valar Morgoth. Where once Morgoth had ruled over entire legions of Balrogs, only one remains in Middle-earth by this time, in Moria. Also a Maia of great power, it is unclear whether the Balrog actually takes any direction from Sauron or considers himself the Dark Lord's equal – even though Sauron had once been chief of Morgoth's lieutenants.

It is a similar story with the other great creatures of evil in the Third Age, the dragons. Gandalf introduces Bilbo to the Dwarves – and aids and abets the whole enterprise recounted in *The Hobbit* – to destroy Smaug, fearing the devastation the dragon could wreak in the North when Sauron declares war.[112] But, again, where Morgoth had bred the first dragon and commanded a whole flight of the beasts in the War of Wrath, there is no direct evidence that Sauron is their master. It is probably safe to assume that Sauron could have had some way of coming to an agreement with dragons, probably by offering plunder and loot in return for their power to wreak utter devastation. Great though this power might still be, it is nevertheless only a pale shadow of the power of the dragons of the First Age, who drove back the army of the Valar themselves in the War of Wrath.

Another powerful and evil Maia lurking in the Third Age is Shelob, a child of Ungoliant, the dreadful spider of darkness that destroyed the Two Trees of Valinor. Shelob guards the entrance to Mordor at Cirith Ungol, shown by Gollum to Frodo and Sam.

However, Shelob is an ancient evil:

> who was there before Sauron... and she served none but her-
> self... weaving webs of shadow... and her vomit darkness[113]

Sauron knows of Shelob's presence and approves, considering her a better guard for his borders than anything he might come up with himself. But Shelob is entirely independent of Sauron and cares little for precious things, even the One Ring.

There are two important exceptions to the lessening of the creatures of darkness in the Third Age: the appearance of new types of Orcs and Trolls. While Morgoth bred the race of Orcs in the First Age, in *The Lord of The Rings* we see a new breed – the Uruk-hai – in both the armies of Sauron and Saruman. These creatures are larger and stronger than their predecessors and, most dangerously, are not afraid of the sun. While the details of their origins are not known, it is likely that they are the result of experiments upon Orcs and Men, melding the two races to add hardiness and stature to Morgoth's original breed. Certainly Saruman has half-orc spies, said to be of Dunlending stock on the human side, and it seems probable that the Uruk-hai are another variation of this cross-breeding. While this may seem at first to contradict the general rule of a weakening of all the races over time, another way to view it is to think of the addition of human blood to the orc stock, making the result a hybrid of the two, lesser than Men but greater than the Orcs.[114]

Similar experiments upon the Trolls, great powerful creatures but dull witted[115]and turned to stone by daylight, produce the Olog-hai. These creatures are truly fearsome, wielding great hammers and bearing shields. They, like the Uruk-hai, can bear the Sun, and seem far more intelligent than normal Trolls. It is unclear, however, how dependent on the constant controlling will and power of Sauron they are. Upon the destruction of the One Ring, and its master, they are rendered witless:

> some slew themselves, or cast themselves in pits, or fled
> wailing back to hide in holes and dark lightless places

far from hope.[116]

Although Sauron cannot create new races, being only a Maia, he is a great servant of first Aulë, then Morgoth. His skill and talent produce not only the Rings of Power and the Uruk-hai and Olog-hai, but also the Black Speech of Mordor. Unhappy with the different dialects and guttural variations of Westron spoken by the different tribes of Orcs, who have trouble communicating with those from another group, Sauron creates a new language. An evil sounding tongue, it is spoken among his armies, to allow communication between various tribes.[117] However, none of Sauron's acts, save the forging of the Rings, are truly acts of creation like those of the First Age, but merely refinements and improvements on existing things. In this Sauron can be said to be 'standing on the shoulders of giants', only able to improve and experiment on the material already present.

In the end, Sauron's evil contains the seeds of its own defeat. Just as Morgoth could not envisage the return of the Valar to stop him, understanding nothing of pity, so Sauron has no concept of selflessness. Knowing that the One Ring is in the hands of his enemies, he fears only the rise of a terrible rival, of one of the Great using the Power of the Ring – his power – against him. It is this blindness that allows the army of the West to distract his attention at the Gates of Mordor, while Frodo and Sam journey to Mount Doom.

'His doubt will be growing, even as we speak here. His Eye is now straining towards us, blind almost to all else that is moving. So we must keep it. Therein lies all our hope.'[118]

As we have seen, it is only through unity and co-operation between the Free Races that evil can be defeated. Although many underestimate the Hobbits, Gandalf sees their inner strength of purpose and physical hardiness. Bilbo resists being corrupted by the Ring for 60 years while Frodo, until the last moment, carries the burden under the continual searching of the Eye of Sauron. Elrond, in his wisdom, sees this also, comparing Frodo to the greatest mortal heroes of the First Age:

'and though all the mighty elf-friends of old, Hador, and
Húrin, and Túrin, and Beren himself were assembled
together, your seat should be among them.'[119]

Elrond's words are highly significant. It was only through the
friendship of Men and Elves that Morgoth was finally defeated.
Sauron also fell to a great alliance of Elves and Men in the Second
Age. At the end of the Third Age, just as in the First Age, evil cannot be defeated by force of arms. Even if the One Ring is used to
defeat Sauron, another Dark Lord will inevitably be created.

History repeats itself, with the only hope for the West lying in
evil's own folly and the unity of Sauron's enemies. It is no coincidence that the Company of the Ring is made up of members of
every race of Free Peoples – Man, Elf, Dwarf, Hobbit and even a
Maia! This symbolic gesture shows an understanding of the history of Middle-earth and the only hope for the West. While Sauron
can think only in terms of war and power, the salvation for good
lies in hope and trust. When the Istari are despatched to fight the
growing Shadow, they are forbidden to match power with power –
an edict Saruman breaks, causing his own downfall.

But, most important of all, is the impulse that prevented Bilbo
from killing Gollum when he had the chance, upon his first gaining
the Ring. Frodo, in anger and fear, tells Gandalf that it was a pity
Gollum was not killed. Gandalf, in one of the most important state-
ments in *The Lord of the Rings*, replies:

'Pity? It was Pity that stayed his hand.... Be sure that he
took so little hurt from the evil... because he began his
ownership of the Ring so.'[120]

It is that selfsame virtue, the pity felt by the Valar, that causes the downfall of Morgoth in the First Age. Pity is, in turn, ultimately responsible
for the destruction of his greatest servant and agent of evil, Sauron.
When Frodo balks at the last and refuses to throw the Ring into the

Cracks of Doom, to unmake it in the fire in which it was born, it is Gollum who bites off Frodo's finger and falls, with the Ring, into the flames. This poignant, powerful and elegant conclusion to Tolkien's tales of Middle-earth makes two crucial points. Acts of evil will, in the end, turn to good through Ilúvatar's will. Furthermore, the events of the past are echoed down the Ages, as Morgoth and Sauron are both undone by the co-operation of the Free Peoples and, despite their skills at corruption, their own incomprehension of the good in others.

It remains only to say a brief word about the Fourth Age. Although most of the events of this time are beyond the scope of Tolkien's work, we know that it is also known as the Age of Men. The Elves finally depart for the Undying Lands, their time at an end:

> 'when the One has gone, the Three will fail, and many
> fair things will fade and be forgotten.'[121]

Men too are destined to fade in power, although Aragorn begins a new line of Kings ruling both Gondor and Arnor.[122] With the passing of the Elves,[123] much magic is gone from the world and all contact with the Valar and the Undying lands is ended. But although the world has grown still older, and weaker, the battle between good and evil is not over. It will continue to be fought, along the same pattern, until the end of the world. No Dark Lord as great as Sauron may ever rise again but, as Gandalf foresees:

> 'Other evils there are that may come; for Sauron is himself
> but a servant or emissary.'[124]

The battle between good and evil is eternal, and will be played out until the end of time. But the details of that struggle, and whether the lessons of the past are learned or have to be found again and again, not even Tolkien can tell us.

CHAPTER FOUR

FOUL AND FAIR: THE CAST OF THE LORD OF THE RINGS

THE VALAR

The Valar are the gods, or Angels, depending on your point of view, of Middle-earth. Ilúvatar, or Eru, created them from nothingness, at the beginning of the Universe. It is Ilúvatar who is the One True God, and the ultimate source of creation and life,[125] but the Valar are his agents and it is between them that the struggles of good and evil originally occur.

Each Vala has their own area of authority, just like any pantheon of gods from Greek to Norse to Egyptian. The most important difference between the Valar and their pagan equivalents is that the enlightened peoples of Middle-earth, whether Elves or Men, revere them as servants of a higher power, rather than worshipping them as their creators. Manwë is acknowledged as the Lord of Arda, Ulmo is respected by sailors everywhere and Varda is especially revered by the Elves as the creator of the stars. But it is Ilúvatar that is worshipped as the creator of the universe and the highest god of all peoples.

There are 14 Valar and, although they take on male and female forms when they descend into the world, they are by no means limited by such material appearances. Each Vala, at least in the beginning, had the power to take on any form they pleased and even become pure, invisible spirit. The eight Aratar, or greater Valar, are Manwë and Varda, Ulmo, Yavanna and Aulë, Mandos, Nienna and Oromë. The six remaining, or lesser Valar, are Tulkas, Estë, Vairë, Vána, Nessa and Lórien. Melkor, the dark god who tried to take the world for his own, is no longer counted among their number.

Chief among the Valar is Manwë, Lord of Arda. He is the closest in understanding and thought to Ilúvatar, and was second only to Melkor in power in the beginning. Manwë is the god of the sky, and rules all the creatures of it. It is Manwë who sends the mighty Eagles to Middle-earth to aid the Elves against the enemy. When Melkor first claimed the whole of the world as his own it was Manwë who called the other Valar and the Maiar, the lesser spirits of Ilúvatar, to oppose him. Manwë loved the group of Elves known as the Vanyar[126] best, because of their love of words and poetry. Known also as the vice-regent of Ilúvatar, Manwë sits on a huge throne on Taniquetil, the highest mountain of the world, where he surveys his domain. All the birds and creatures of the air bring him news from across the world, allowing him to see and hear to the ends of the earth. Manwë is the holiest of all the Valar, and it fell to him to hallow the Lamps that first brought light to Middle-earth, as well as the vessels that were to carry the fruits of the two trees, the Sun and the Moon. While it was a host of all the Valar who defeated Morgoth at the end of the First Age, it was Manwë, Morgoth's brother in the beginning, who finally thrust him outside the walls of the world to leave him chained forever in the Void.

While Manwë is the King of the Skies, his wife Varda is the Queen of the Heavens, the Lady of the Stars. Words, even those of the Elves, cannot describe her beauty, as the light of Ilúvatar shines in her face. She knew Melkor before the Song of Creation that made the world and spurned him, which is why he hated her more than any of the Valar. It is Varda who created the stars,[127] the first things seen by the Elves as they awoke. Because of this the Elves, and many other peoples of Middle-earth, revere her above all other Valar. It is her authority over the heavens that is used to give the Sun and Moon the power to travel them, and she who determines their course of day and night. It is also Varda, rather than Manwë, who hallows the Silmarils, giving them the power to burn evil at their touch, as Morgoth discovers to his cost when he steals them.

Varda's pre-eminence in the hearts and minds of the Elves and other peoples of Middle-earth, and her power to drive off the unholy creatures of evil, is shown clearly in the *The Lord of the Rings*. Where the other gods are scarcely mentioned at all, Varda, under the title of Elbereth Gilthoniel, is the subject of many songs by the Elves in Rivendell and elsewhere, and her name is used as a blessing.[128] Her power is also invoked on at least four occasions. Her name alone proves more power-ful than Frodo's sword against the Nazgûl on Weathertop, while Legolas calls upon her before shooting the flying mount of another Ringwraith. Later, when Sam kindles the Phial of Galadriel in his struggle with the Shelob in Cirith Ungol,[129] the Elvish verse he recites, without even knowing the language, calls upon the Queen of Stars to watch over him. Finally it is the name of Elbereth, combined again with the light of the Phial of Galadriel, which breaks the power of the terrible stone Watchers when Sam enters the Tower of Cirith Ungol in Mordor.

Ulmo is the next most powerful Vala after Manwë. The Lord of Waters, he lives alone in the Outer Sea, only rarely coming to the councils of the Valar. His appearance is terrible and his voice is as deep as the oceans he commands. Assisted by his Maiar, Uinen and Ossë,[130] Ulmo has authority over every aspect of water. His power extends through every ocean, stream, river and fountain in Middle-earth and the Undying Lands, giv-ing him influence and knowledge of events hidden even from Manwë.

Ulmo actually argues against summoning the Elves to Valinor, believ-ing that they should be left to roam free. Ulmo never abandons the Elves, even after they are banished from the Undying Lands. He defies his fel-low gods and intervenes directly to aid the struggles of the Elves against Morgoth in *The Silmarillion*. The King of the Sea, he appears to both Finrod and Turgon, in person and in their dreams, and persuades them to found the hidden strongholds of Nargothrond and Gondolin. It is also Ulmo who guides the human hero Tuor to Gondolin, setting in motion the chain of events that eventually lead to the salvation of Middle-earth.[131] Despite the exile of the Noldor, Ulmo uses Tuor as his messen-ger, warning King Turgon to abandon his precious city before it falls.

> 'So it shall be while I endure, a secret voice that gainsayeth,
> and a light where darkness was decreed.' [132]

But the Doom uttered by Mandos is too strong. Turgon ignores the wis-dom of Ulmo and refuses to abandon the city he loves, dying in its betrayal to Morgoth by Maeglin. But Tuor is still welcomed as a messenger of Ulmo and marries the King's daughter Idril. Their son Eärendil becomes the Mariner who, representing the union of Elves and Men, sails to the Undying Lands and petitions the Valar to ride to war and defeat Morgoth. [133]

Despite the continuing folly of the Elves, Ulmo refuses to desert them. When Gondolin falls to the enemy, it is his power in the waters of the Vale of Sirion that protects and hides their flight from the city.

While Manwë and Varda are closest to the Vanyar, Ulmo is, unsurprisingly, closest to the Teleri, the Sea Elves. The Teleri learn the craft of sailing and the art of building their treasured White Swan ships from Ulmo and his servants. It is also Ulmo who places the 'sea longing' in the hearts of Elves, filling them with a love of the sea and the Uttermost West. This gift Ulmo also gives to Men, and Ulmo is revered by the Dúnedain of the Isle of Númenor, at least before they are turned by Sauron to the worship of Morgoth.

Although never mentioned explicitly in the events of *The Lord of the Rings* as Elbereth Gilthoniel is, we can see Ulmo's influence at work on at least two occasions. When Elrond uses the river at Rivendell to destroy the Nazgûl as they pursue Frodo, the power of the water almost certainly derives from Ulmo. Also the sea longing that comes upon Legolas, after sailing with Aragorn to the rescue of Minas Tirith, is a sign of Ulmo's continued influence.

Aulë is the next of the Valar in power to Ulmo. He is the smith of the Valar, the Lord of all substances of the Earth. His authority is not only in crafting the treasures of the world – gems, gold and the like – but in carving the very mountains and valleys themselves. It is Aulë who struggles most directly against Melkor in the moulding of the world, with the Dark Lord constantly striving to unmake and destroy the lands Aulë has crafted. Aulë is known as the 'friend of the Noldor' because of his special kinship with that group of Elves, who share his love of smithcraft and learn all they can from him. It is Aulë who makes the Lamps that Melkor destroys, as well as the vessels that carry the Sun and the Moon. When Ossë raises the Isle of Numenor from the Sea, at Ulmo's command, it is Aulë who fixes it fast.

Although Aulë always remains faithful to Ilúvatar, it has to be said that those of his domain have a decidedly poor track record in the history of Middle-earth. Aulë's creation of the Dwarves[134] is in defiance of Ilúvatar's will. Although it was done without malice or lust for power, the resulting race are insular, secretive and sometimes prone to greed. The Elves closest to Aulë in thought and judgement, the Noldor, are the very ones who defy the Valar and pursue Morgoth in anger and vengeance, leading to a litany of evils and wrongs. And it is no coincidence that the two enemies of the West in *The Lord of the Rings*, Sauron and Saruman, were both originally Maiar servants and apprentices of Aulë. There is a clear warning here against the love of the creation of material things, which can all too swiftly become the love of the things themselves, giving rise to greed, avarice and envy.

Aulë's partner is Yavanna, the giver of fruits. Where Aulë is the Lord of the substance of the earth, Yavanna is the goddess of all growing things from trees to flowers or plants. Also known as Kementári, the Queen of the Earth, she is described as tall and robed in green. In the time of darkness, before the creation of the stars and the awakening of the Elves, she is said to have frequently travelled to Middle-earth to tend the hurts of Melkor, who then ruled it unopposed. It is Yavanna who sings a song of power to grow the Two Trees[135] of Valinor. Later, when Melkor and Ungoliant destroy them, it is Yavanna who who coaxes the two last fruits that are then sent heavenward, to become the Sun and the Moon.

The Ents, the spirits who take the form of huge, walking trees and protect the forests from the axes of Orcs, Dwarves and Men, are one of Yavanna's contributions to the great Song of Creation at the beginning of time. Like Ulmo, although not mentioned explicitly in *The Lord of the Rings*, her influence can still be seen. The White Tree of Gondor, the symbol of the Dúnedain realm's fortunes, comes originally from Númenor. This tree in turn came from the fruit of a tree in the Undying Lands, which was itself an image of the Two Trees of Valinor. Its holy status is a result of Yavanna's authority and blessing.

Námo is more commonly known as Mandos, the Keeper of the Houses of the Dead. He and Irmo, his brother, are known together as the Fëanturi, or Masters of Spirits. Although the Elves are immortal and do not age, they can be killed by weapons or even weariness and hurt. Then their spirits travel to the Halls of Mandos. The fate of Men is not so clear. When they die, they are believed by some also to travel to the Halls of Mandos, but whether they stay there forever in a place apart from the Elves or whether their souls go on somewhere else, only Mandos and Manwë of the Valar know.

Mandos is also known as the Judge, the Doomsayer of the Valar. He forgets nothing and actually knows the future. He speaks rarely and when he does it is normally to pronounce a Doom of one sort or another. It is Mandos who foretells that the fate of the Silmarils will be bound up with the Air, Earth and Sea.[136] He also pronounces the Doom of the Noldor as they force their way out of the Undying Lands. Only once is Mandos ever moved to pity, upon hearing the song of Lúthien Tinúviel, the saddest and most beautiful song ever sung.[137] He is so moved that he allows the soul of Lúthien's mortal husband Beren to return to Middle-earth. On one other occasion the power to judge the fate of the peoples of the world is actually taken from Mandos by Manwë. The Chief of the Valar grants a special fate to the Peredhil, or half elven. Eärendil and his wife Elwing, and their sons Elros and Elrond, are all allowed to choose whether they wish to live as Men or Elves. Elrond chooses the latter, and plays a vital role in the events of *The Lord of the Rings* thousands of years later. His brother Elros chooses to be mortal and founds the race of the Dúnedain. Aragorn is his direct, if distant, descendant.

Nienna is the sister of the Fëanturi, Mandos and Lórien. She is the Lady of sorrow and pity.[138] She mourns for all the hurts of the world and waters its wounds with her tears. Even during the great Song of Creation, when the Universe was created, she mourned for the hurts to come.

It is perhaps easy to dismiss the importance of Nienna amidst all the power and splendour of the other Valar, but this is to misunderstand the nature of the struggle between good and evil. Those that listen to Nienna gain endurance in hope and learn how to turn sorrow to wisdom, a gift of infinite value to the immortal Elves. The Noldor Elves of the First Age are rash, quick to anger and overconfident in their strength of arms. This is in stark contrast to the less warlike figures of, say, Elrond and Galadriel in *The Lord of the Rings*, whose eyes bear the sorrow, and wisdom, of ages. The strength to bear the burden of thousands of years of pain and suffering, and turn it to sage advice, is a gift of Nienna. Age by itself is no sign of wisdom, as Saruman's corruption shows – he was a Maia many thousands of years in age before he journeyed to Middle-earth to battle Sauron.

The most important figure in the struggle against Sauron in *The Lord of the Rings*, Gandalf, learned pity and patience from Nienna in the Undying Lands. It is these strengths that give him the wisdom to resist the corruption of Sauron and lead the West to freedom. It is also pity that moves the Valar to forgive the Noldor Elves their hurts and wrongs and march to war against Morgoth at the end of the First Age.[139]

Oromë is the great hunter of the Valar and his wrath is dreadful to behold. He always loved Middle-earth and even when the Valar abandoned that land for Valinor he returned often to hunt the evil monsters of Morgoth. His name means 'sound of horns' and all creatures of evil fear his horn, the Valaróma. It is Oromë who was sent to summon the Elves to Valinor, and it is he who named them Eldar, people of the stars. Oromë especially loves hounds and horses. His own steed, Nahar, is the ancestor of the magnificent horses of the Rohirrim. King Théoden, when he charges down upon the enemy in a terrible battle fury at the Battle of the Pelennor Fields, is described as resembling the mighty Oromë.[140]

Manwë, Varda, Ulmo, Yavanna, Aulë, Mandos, Nienna and Oromë are the eight greater Valar, or Aratar. The remaining six play a far smaller part in the events of the world.

Vairë is the wife of Mandos. Known as the Weaver,[141] she places all the events of the world in her tapestries, which line the halls of her husband. But she seems to play no direct part in any of the events of the history of the world and is not mentioned again after her description as one of the Valar.

Irmo is the brother of Mandos and Nienna. He is the Master of Visions and Dreams. He, like Mandos, is more commonly known by the name of his home, the gardens of Lórien,[142] which are said to be the most beautiful place in the world. Lórien plays a far lesser part in the history of Middle-earth than his brother, although two of the most important Maiar of the First and Third Ages, Melian and Olórin, later known as Gandalf, originally lived in his gardens.

Estë, the partner of Lórien, is called the Gentle. She is the goddess of healing and rest. She is said to dress in grey and sleep by day, being active with her powers and gifts at night. When the Sun and the Moon first crossed the heavens Estë, and her husband, beseeched Varda to change their course as they were always shining, disrupting the sleep of the world.

Vána, the Ever-young, is Oromë's wife and the younger sister of Yavanna. All that we know of her is that flowers are said to open as she passes, and birds to sing at her approach.

Tulkas is physically the strongest of the Valar. He was the last of the gods to arrive in Arda, coming to help the others in the war against Morgoth. With a golden beard and hair, he is slow to anger and swift to laugh, even in combat. The champion of the Valar, he uses no weapons but his hands and can tirelessly outrun any mount. It is Tulkas who physically defeats Melkor when the Valar go to war. Although a steadfast friend and ally, Tulkas is not considered the greatest of counsellors, giving little thought to anything but the moment.

Nessa is the spouse of Tulkas and the sister of Oromë. Little is said of her except that she delights in dancing, is swifter than an arrow and is loved by deer.

And last, but unfortunately not least, is Melkor, or He Who Arises in Might. No longer numbered among the Valar, he was renamed Morgoth, the Black Enemy, by Fëanor, after the theft of the Silmarils.[143] Melkor was originally the most powerful of the gods, equal in status to Manwë but having some of the knowledge and powers of all the other Valar. But he grew proud and attempted to weave his own tune into the Song of Creation.[144] When the Valar descended into Arda to form the world, Melkor fought them, attempting to have it all for himself. Defeated twice by the Valar, Melkor is the source of all strife and malice in the world. The evil races of Orcs and Trolls were bred by him,[145] the Balrogs and Werewolves are Maiar he corrupted to his service. Sauron was his chief lieutenant and it is Morgoth's lies and deceit that led to the fall of both Men and Elves[146] from grace.

The original Dark Lord, Morgoth spends his power in carving his underground strongholds of Utumno and Angband, and loses a little of himself in each of his evil creations. Although he is chained and thrust out into the Void, part of him – evil – will forever be part of the world, among every race and nation.

The Maiar

The Maiar are the lesser Ainur, or spirits, of Ilúvatar the Creator. The greater Ainur are the Valar, the gods of Middle-earth, immensely powerful figures who each have authority over a particular domain. Manwë is the Lord of the Sky, Ulmo the King of the Sea, Aulë has power over the Earth itself and the precious metals and gems it contains. The Maiar in their turn are often associated with, or even servants of, a particular Vala.

Although weaker than the Valar they serve, the Maiar can still be tremendously powerful. They often exert control over a particular element, such as fire or the land around them. As spirits, they often have the ability to change shape and take on powerful physical forms. However, the act of taking on a physical form has its own risks and dangers. Although the form itself gives the Maia in question greater power over their surroundings, it can also tie them to the world, imprisoning them in the body they have chosen. Taking on a physical form also makes them susceptible to physical dangers, such as an enemy's weapons. It can also expose them to the physical frailties and weaknesses associated with the material world, such as tiredness or emotions such as pride or greed.

Sauron was one of the most powerful Maia of all, and certainly the most notorious. Originally a servant of Aulë, from whom he learned the skills to create the Rings of Power, Sauron was corrupted by Morgoth and became his chief lieutenant. He was also known as Gorthaur the Cruel in the First Age, when he served Morgoth. Sauron took the name Annatar, Lord of Gifts, in the Second Age, when he tricked the Elves into helping him to forge those selfsame Rings.[147] The One Ring Sauron used to increase his own power and the Nine Rings for Men he used to create his Nazgûl servants, the Black Riders.[148]

Once Morgoth is defeated and chained in the void, Sauron proves himself a worthy successor to the title of Dark Lord. Although Sauron repents, at least publicly, when captured by the Valar after the defeat of Morgoth, he is too proud to go to the Undying Lands and seek forgiveness. Instead, he hides himself away, condemning himself forever to evil. In the Second Age he destroys the Elven realm of Eregion, killing their leader Celebrimbor, the grandson of Fëanor himself. He engineers the downfall of the Dúnedain of Númenor, and enslaves all the kingdoms of Men in Middle-earth to the East and South. Only in the North West do the remaining Elven kingdoms and Dúnedain realms resist him. The Land of Mordor is his stronghold. He is defeated by the Last Alliance of Elves and Men, led by Gil-galad and Elendil, both of whom he kills in their final battle. However Sauron himself falls at the hand of Isildur, Elendil's son. But Isildur refuses to destroy the Ring, allowing Sauron to return in the Third Age.

Mordor is again Sauron's base in the Third Age, although he returns first to Dol Guldur in Greenwood the Great. It is Sauron's power and influence that lead to it being renamed Mirkwood. A complete list of Sauron's crimes, details of his search for the One Ring, and the events of his eventual defeat would be far too lengthy to go into here.They are dealt with extensively elsewhere in this book.[149] For now, it is sufficient to say that where Morgoth led, Sauron follows. Where Morgoth carved out the black and flaming pits of Utumno and Angband, Sauron makes Mordor into a barren and terrible place. Morgoth created the Orcs and Trolls in twisted mockery of Elves and Ents. Sauron continues his vile experiments, cross-breeding the Orcs with Men to produce the Uruk-hai, soldier Orcs unafraid of the sun.

Perhaps the main difference between Sauron and his master is that Morgoth hated everything that was not his own creation. With his fall from grace, Morgoth lost the power to make anything new and, although he fought to enslave all of Middle-earth, he truly wished to destroy all of Creation in his anger and malice. Morgoth would never have rested until the whole world was broken. Sauron, on the other hand, wishes only to rule Middle-earth, subjugating all the races that oppose him.[150]

But Sauron is not the only Maiar corrupted into the service of Morgoth. The Valaraukar, or Balrogs, were originally flame spirits who joined the Enemy and took on hideous forms. They are huge in size, creatures of shadow and fire, with great wings and flaming swords and whips. The Balrogs were the shock troops of Morgoth's armies and always led his great assaults. It was a legion of these monsters that killed Fëanor and his bodyguard, and they were in the forefront of the invasion of the hidden Elven city of Gondolin. Gothmog was their chief, who eventually fell in single combat with Ecthelion of the Fountain, Gondolin's captain of the guard. The Balrogs are thought to have all been destroyed in the final battle of the First Age, the War of Wrath, when the Valar defeated Morgoth and crushed his armies.

Unfortunately for the free peoples of Middle-earth, and especially the Dwarves, a single one of these dreadful monsters hid itself deep in the earth to escape destruction. Known as Durin's Bane, it is awoken by the Dwarves of Khazad-dûm in the Third Age, as they dig too deeply for the precious metal, mithril. A terror of power almost unmatched in the First Age, the Balrog is almost unstoppable in the Third. It kills the Dwarven King and forces his people into exile, attracting hordes of Orcs and Trolls to its evil presence. Before long the Dwarven mansions are renamed Moria, the Black Pit.

When Gandalf and the Company of the Ring attempt to travel through Moria, they fight with the Orcs before encountering the Balrog itself:

> like a great shadow, in the middle of which was a dark form,
> of man-shape maybe, yet greater; and a power and terror
> seemed to be in it and to go before it.[151]

Even with Narya, the Elven Ring of Fire, to protect him from the Balrog's flames, Gandalf barely defeats the creature, losing his own life in the process. The Balrog, however, is gone forever, while Gandalf is granted leave to return for a short time to finish his mission and defeat Sauron.

The exact relationship between the Balrog in Moria and Sauron in Mordor is unclear. Although Sauron was the greatest of Morgoth's Maiar and his chief lieutenant, he does not seem to exert any control over the Balrog. While the two would certainly find common cause against the West, the Balrog shows no sign of threatening anyone outside of its personal domain, and appears content to rule Moria. Any pact with Sauron would almost certainly have meant the Balrog actively threatening those outside its own realm.

Moreover, when the Company of the Ring finally encounters the Balrog, it shows no sign of targeting Frodo in particular, and makes no effort to use its powers to find the One Ring. Instead, it seems to react solely to invaders in its realm, and immediately attacks the most powerful of the threats, Gandalf. We can safely assume that if such an awesome evil knew of the existence of the Ruling Ring and Sauron's search for it, like the Nazgûl, it would be pursuing the prize. We can also assume that it would be seeking such a treasure for itself. If Sauron feared the Wise would use the Ring against him, an evil Maia with the power of the Balrog would show no hesitation.

Although far less powerful than the Balrogs, the Werewolves of the First Age were also spirits corrupted by Morgoth. Sauron ruled Tol-in-Gaurhoth, the Island of Werewolves, and commanded these creatures. The Werewolves had the shape of huge, terrifying wolves. They dwarf even the largest Wargs, wolves large enough to be ridden like horses by Orcs, and also possess a malicious cunning and the power of speech. Draugluin was the name of the oldest of their kind, and was the Sire of the Werewolves. Carcharoth, however, was the greatest of his kind.

Raised by Morgoth himself, and fed with some of the dark god's own power, Carcharoth bit off the hand of the mortal hero Beren, while he was holding the Silmaril cut from Morgoth's crown. The Silmarils burn the flesh of anything evil. This one, swallowed, sears the belly of the wolf. Carcharoth goes mad with the pain and runs wild, laying waste everything in his path. In his madness he becomes the most terrible monster that has ever been in Middle-earth, because the power of one of the Silmarils is in him, turned to pain and fury. Huan, the wolfhound, eventually kills him. Huan was originally a hound of the Valar Oromë himself, from the Undying Lands, and it had been foretold that Huan would die fighting the greatest werewolf that had ever been. Huan had already defeated Sauron himself in the shape of a wolf, while helping the lovers Beren and Lúthien, but he is mortally wounded in the battle with Carcharoth. The Werewolves still appear to exist in the Third Age, serving Sauron. Gandalf lists them among the Dark Lord's servants as he speaks to Frodo in Rivendell, but none are ever seen or mentioned, so their number and power cannot be estimated.

Far less is known of the so-called Vampires of Morgoth. Only one is ever named, Thuringwethil, the messenger of Sauron, who takes the shape of a vampire to fly between Sauron and his master, Morgoth.

Sauron also takes the shape of a vampire to escape after his defeat by Huan, the wolfhound. Whether there are others, or whether 'vampire' is used merely to indicate the form of a giant bat, is never explained.

Possibly the most fearsome Maia of the First Age is the dreadful spider demon Ungoliant. Although originally a spirit corrupted by Morgoth, she forsook even him, living alone in the darkness. Ungoliant is always hungry, consuming light itself and producing webs of Unlight, an utter darkness that not even the sight of the chief of the gods, Manwë, can penetrate. Ungoliant's greatest evil is the destruction of the Two Trees of Valinor, which lit the Undying Lands.

Persuaded by Morgoth with the promise of so much light that even her hunger will be filled, she accompanies the dark god in his raid on the home of the Valar. Morgoth puts some of his own power into her and then, hidden by her webs of total darkness, Morgoth wounds the Two Trees with his spear and Ungoliant sucks them dry, destroying two of the greatest glories in the whole history of the world. In the ensuing darkness, Morgoth steals the Silmarils and the two flee back to Middle-earth. However, Ungoliant is still thirsty and demands the jewels Morgoth is carrying. When he refuses, she attacks him.

> Ungoliant had grown great, and he less by the power that had gone out of him; and she rose against him, and her cloud closed about him…[152]

Morgoth's own fall from his position as greatest of the Valar is highlighted by his fear and the fact that he calls on his Balrogs for help. Fortunately for Morgoth, the flames of the Balrogs tear apart the webs of Ungoliant and force her to retreat. She flees south where, in her hunger, she eventually devours herself, but not before spawning the whole race of evil spiders. Her greatest descendant is the spider guardian of Cirith Ungol, Shelob.

Shelob lives under the borders of Mordor, protecting one of the entrances to Sauron's realm. The evil giant spiders of Mirkwood and the Ephel Duath are her offspring. Shelob does not serve Sauron. She serves no one but herself, but Sauron knows she is there:

...hungry but unabated in malice, a more sure watch upon .
that ancient path into his land than any other that his skill
could have devised. [153]

Shelob feeds on unwary intruders: Orcs and prisoners of Sauron. She
has a pact with Gollum. Unpalatable in himself, he leads tastier food to
her, in return for passage. It is through Cirith Ungol and past Shelob
that Gollum comes and goes from Mordor. He leads Frodo and Sam to
Shelob, planning to take the One Ring from their corpses. Shelob cares
only for food. Man-made things, even as powerful a creation as the
Ring, are of no interest to her.

Shelob comes upon the Hobbits as planned and paralyses Frodo, but
Sam proves far more troublesome than expected. Sam manages to
wound one of Shelob's eyes before she drops on him, as he is holding
up the aptly named Elven blade Sting. Shelob skewers herself on its
point. Not even the strongest mortal or Elven hero could have hoped to
wound her, but Shelob's own strength is her undoing. Even then she
would have killed Sam, if he had not prayed to Elbereth Gilthoniel, the
holy Queen of the gods and creator of the stars, and invoked the power
of the Phial of Galadriel. The light of the Phial blinds Shelob and forces
her to retreat, allowing Sam to escape and go on to rescue Frodo from
the Orcs. Whether Shelob bled to death, or recovered to feast on more
unwary morsels in future years, is not said.

These are the most important examples of the Maiar corrupted by
Morgoth, but the Majority of the Maiar fight against the Dark Lord and
faithfully serve the Valar. Of these the most powerful in battle is
Eönwë, the herald of Manwë. Eönwë leads the armies of the Valar to
war, and is the mightiest warrior in the entire world, greater in skill
with his weapons than any of the gods.

Ossë and Uinen are the chief Maiar of Ulmo, the King of the Seas.
Ossë is a Maia of the coasts and islands of the world, who loves storms
and wild tempests. He was corrupted briefly by Morgoth, who promised to give him Ulmo's throne. Between them they created the sea
monsters of Middle-earth, like the Kraken found outside the gates of
Moria. But Uinen, Ossë's wife, convinces him to repent and Ulmo for-

gives him. This story shows that Sauron himself could truly have been forgiven after the defeat of Morgoth, if his own pride and fear had not overcome him. Uinen is the opposite of Ossë. She brings calm to the wild waters of her husband and is loved by sailors, especially the Dúnedain of Númenor, who worship her alongside the Valar.

Of all the Maiar, Melian was the most important enemy of Morgoth in the First Age. Among the Valar, she was the most closely connected with Lórien and Yavanna. She originally lived in the gardens of Lórien and was the wisest, most beautiful and most powerful of all his servants. But Melian was also close to Yavanna and loved the trees of the forests. Nightingales always accompany her, and her singing is so beautiful that the Valar would stop whatever they were doing to listen to her.

When the Elves awake, Melian travels to Middle-earth and meets Elwë, the first Lord of the Teleri, better known as King Thingol Greycloak of Doriath. They fall in love instantly and spend so long wrapped up in each other that the Teleri are forced to choose another King, his brother Olwë, and continue their journey to the Undying Lands. Many of the Teleri, however, refuse to abandon their search for Thingol and remain in Middle-earth, becoming known as the Sindar Elves.[154]

When Melian and Thingol finally emerge, they are taken as King and Queen of the Sindar, and found the realm of Doriath. The marriage of Melian and Thingol is the only union ever between the Maiar and another people and produces some of the most important figures in the history of Middle-earth. Their daughter is Lúthien Tinúviel, the most beautiful creature, and most powerful singer of spells, ever to live in Middle-earth. Not only does Lúthien successfully enchant Morgoth himself, but she moves the Vala Mandos to pity to save her mortal husband Beren. Melian is also the great grandmother of Elros, the first of the mortal Dúnedain, and Elrond, the Lord of Rivendell. This means that Elrond carries the blood of not only Elves and Men, but also the Maiar.

Melian is the wisest figure in Middle-earth. As a Maia of the Vala Lórien, the Master of Visions and Dreams, she can see the future and foretells many of the things that are to happen in Middle-earth. It is Melian who persuades Thingol to hire Dwarves to build Menegroth, the Thousand Caves. The most beautiful place ever built in Middle-earth, it is also a stronghold against Morgoth in the wars to come. Melian also suspects the real reasons for the coming of the Noldor to Middle-earth – that they are exiled by the Valar - and advises Thingol not to trust the sons of Fëanor. These are wise words, as it is the self-same sons of Fëanor who will later destroy Doriath.

But Melian's influence is also seen thousands of years later in the events of the Third Age and *The Lord of the Rings,* through her role as mentor and teacher to Galadriel, who becomes the Queen of Lothlórien.

Galadriel lived in Doriath with Melian and Thingol when she first came to Middle-earth and it was there that she met her husband Celeborn, a Sindarin prince. Melian taught Galadriel about Middle-earth, and they were close confidants. The woodland kingdom of Lothlórien that Galadriel rules in later ages resembles Melian's Doriath far more than the mountain stronghold Nargothrond built by her brother Finrod, or the secret city of Gondolin, founded by her cousin Turgon. Similarly, the form that Galadriel's power takes, expressing itself in wise advice and healing while resisting and hiding from Sauron, rather than aggressively threatening him, are all hallmarks of Melian's power. In her actions, advice and personality, Galadriel resembles her friend and mentor Melian far more than her own Elven brothers and cousins, especially when we compare the protected and hidden nature of Lothlórien with the Girdle of Melian.

As well as the wisdom and vision that come from her connection to Lórien, Melian also has power over the kingdom of Yavanna, the things of the earth. This is shown most clearly when, threatened by the armies of Morgoth before the coming of the Noldor, Melian puts her power into the forests around Doriath.

She creates the Girdle of Melian, hiding the woodland realm from enemy eyes and barring entry to anyone without the permission of Melian or Thingol. The power of the Girdle is so great that even Ungoliant, fleeing the flaming whips of the Balrogs, is forced to avoid Doriath. Considering Ungoliant is so swollen with power at that stage that Morgoth himself fears her, Melian must be the most powerful figure in all of Middle-earth at that time, except for the dark god.

Only once is the Girdle of Melian breached. Melian herself knew it would be, through her wisdom and power over visions. She tells Galadriel:

> 'one of Men... shall indeed come, and the Girdle of Melian
> shall not restrain him, for doom greater than my power
> shall send him' [155]

That man is Beren, the mortal hero fated to love Melian's daughter Lúthien. Thingol demands a Silmaril as dowry for his daughter, expecting Beren to die trying to cut one from Morgoth's crown. Melian, however, knows the doom that will come to Doriath as a result of Thingol becoming involved, even in this indirect way, in the war with Morgoth. Beren and Lúthien defeat Sauron and his werewolves and trick Morgoth himself to gain the Silmaril. Unfortunately, Thingol orders some Dwarven craftsmen from Nogrod to place the Silmaril on the Nauglamír,[156] the great Dwarven necklace. Filled with a lust for the jewel, part of the Curse of the Silmarils, they take it, murdering King Thingol in the process.

Melian remained in Middle-earth only through her love for Thingol, tying herself to a physical form to love him, protect Doriath and give birth to Lúthien. Upon his death she withdraws her protection from her former realm, and leaves in mourning for the Undying Lands. The withdrawal of the Girdle of Melian allows a Dwarven army from Nogrod to sack Menegroth. Later, the sons of Fëanor finally destroy Doriath completely.[157]

The very first Ents were also Maiar. They were spirits who answered the prayer of Yavanna, the Queen of the Earth, to protect her realm.[158] They then became bound to their physical forms and became the eldest of the race of Tree-herds. Thus Treebeard would have been a Maia in the beginning, as the very oldest of the Ents, while Quickbeam, the younger and overhasty Ent who speaks to Merry and Pippin during the Entmoot, would have been born simply an Ent.

One of the most mysterious of all the Maiar is Tom Bombadil. He is obviously a powerful and ancient spirit, and tells the Hobbits that he was:

> here before the river and the trees; Tom remembers the
> first raindrop and the first acorn....He knew the dark
> under the stars when it was fearless – before the Dark
> Lord came from Outside.[159]

This remarkable boast would seem to be borne out by Tom's Elvish name of Iarwain Ben-adar, which means oldest and fatherless. It would mean that Bombadil would have had to have entered the world back at the very beginning of time, as the Valar themselves were struggling with Morgoth to create it. Of course it is possible Bombadil is using poetic license here, to emphasise his own age. We know, for example, that the stars were created long after Morgoth had control of Middle-earth, and the Valar had retreated to the Undying Lands, so there could never have been a time 'under the stars' that Morgoth's malign influence was not known.

Physically Bombadil appears as a short man, though taller than a Hobbit, wearing a blue coat and yellow boots. He is the master of the Old Forest and sings nonsense rhymes that hold great power, even over the Barrow Wights. His power over all things of the forest and its waters suggest he has a connection to Yavanna and perhaps Ulmo, but his origin suggests he serves no one. This would seem to be borne out by his reaction to the One Ring. He is completely unaffected by its power and seems totally disinterested in it, and the struggle with its master. Gandalf says that if Bombadil was entrusted with the Ring he would

> '…soon forget it, or most likely throw it away. Such things have
> no hold on his mind. He would be a most unsafe guardian…' [160]

Bombadil is an enigma. Tremendously powerful, more so than anyone else in Middle-earth in the Third Age except for Sauron, he consciously chooses to limit himself to a tiny patch of land and seems oblivious to the greater questions of good and evil. He bears clear similarities with the Green Man of English folklore, a representation of the power of nature. He appears to care only for the natural world and its seasons, completely oblivious to the struggles of another world, the world of Men, Elves and Hobbits. His partner, Goldberry, is also a Maia, although she appears to be a more straightforward river spirit, connected with the Vala Ulmo.

The five wizards, or Istari, are covered in more detail in the chapter on the wisest of their number, Olórin, better known as Gandalf the Grey. But here it seems fitting to mention that they are Maiar sent to combat Sauron by the Valar, who could not intervene directly against any lesser evil than Morgoth.

The Maiar, while weaker than the Valar, often play a more direct role in the events of Middle-earth's history. The power of Melian is crucial in protecting the Sindar Elves from Morgoth. The Balrogs are the vanguard of Morgoth's armies. It is no coincidence that the final struggle between good and evil in the Third Age is between two of the greatest proxies of the Valar, Gandalf and Sauron. The Maiar who choose to take form and become tied to the conflicts of Middle-earth are central and pivotal figures in its history. Their role is as great, if not greater, than any king or hero of the Elves or Men.

Dragons

The origin of dragons is not a straightforward matter. Creatures so powerful might be thought to be Maiar corrupted by Morgoth, like the Balrogs, but we know for certain that Morgoth bred them in his stronghold of Angband. However, we also know that Morgoth was unable to create true life, a power available only to Ilúvatar himself. Morgoth could only imitate that gift. The Orcs are mockeries bred from captured Elves; Trolls are imitations of the Ents. It is easy then to assume that dragons are mockeries of the mighty eagles of Manwë, Morgoth's brother in the beginning and hated rival. But only the later dragons could fly. The first dragon, Glaurung, had no wings but could breathe fire, making him both lesser and far greater than the eagles. However, as we saw in the chapter on creation, Morgoth always used a part of himself whenever he changed or corrupted the creatures or creations of the world and one thing is clear: the dragons held a great part of his power and evil. This can be seen both in their natural strength and powers, and in their weaknesses.

Whatever the origin of the dragons, one thing is sure, they are one of Tolkien's greatest and most impressive creations. Tolkien describes three types of dragons; those who crawl on their belly like worms, a name sometimes used to describe all dragons, those who walk on legs like lizards, and those with wings. Not all the dragons can breathe fire, but these are the most powerful of their kind, the Urulóki, or Fire

Drakes. All dragons are, however, immensely powerful and difficult to kill. All have their natural weaponry – huge jaws, razor sharp claws and tails stronger than battering rams. The scales covering their backs and heads are stronger than any forged armour, even that of the Dwarves, and their only weak spot is their soft underbellies. A dragon's eyesight is better than even that of the Elves, their hearing is unmatched and their sense of smell is keener than the best trained hound. Physically, a fully-grown dragon is a match for an army of warriors. Even their blood is highly venomous and a danger even after their death.

As well as their natural strength, all dragons have a powerful and malicious will that can enchant anyone who looks directly into their eyes. With a look they can root their enemies to the spot, or cloud and confuse their minds. Their presence and approach cause fear and panic among their victims, and the flames of the Urulóki can turn rivers to steam, and incinerate armies or cities. Dragons are also tremendously long lived, and only grow stronger as they get older.

Dragons are also highly intelligent, speaking many languages and especially enjoying riddle games. Despite their power, intelligence and age they are not considered wise, being greedy, envious and, especially, vain. They can be tricked by a clever enemy, as Bilbo does when he meets Smaug the Golden and convinces him to show off his belly. But this is a dangerous game, as the dragon's own malicious mind and powers can make lies seem like truth. This is clearly shown by the tragic story of the dragon Glaurung and the mortal hero Túrin Turambar.

Although they are the enemies of all the free peoples of the West, Dwarves especially hate the dragons. This is because dragons are lazy, greedy creatures and the easiest way for them to gain a hoard of treasure is to sack an already rich Dwarven mansion. Dragons destroyed many Dwarven Halls, killing the inhabitants and making beds of all the stolen treasure. Of the seven Dwarven Rings made by Sauron and given to the Dwarves, only three are ever recovered by the Dark Lord, four being either destroyed by dragon flame or becoming part of their hoards.

Glaurung, as previously mentioned, was the father of dragons. Morgoth bred him in Angband after the Dark Lord realised his Orcs were no match for the power of the Elves. However, Glaurung was rash and impetuous in his youth and he attacked the besieging Elves when he was barely grown, only one hundred years old. Although terrifying and awesome even then, his armoured scales were still soft and he was driven back into Angband by the arrows of the Elves.

When he next emerges, two hundred years later, Glaurung is fully-grown and a far more terrible creature. He leads the army of Morgoth as it breaks the siege of Angband. In the later Battle of Unnumbered Tears, only the Dwarves of Belegost can withstand him. The Dwarves are naturally resistant to fire, and also wear great war masks to protect their beards and faces.[161] The Lord of the Dwarves, Azaghâl, manages to stab Glaurung in the soft underbelly as he is crushed underneath and, wounded, the dragon flees the battle.

But Glaurung soon recovers and leads the assault on the Elven stronghold of Nargothrond. Only the mortal hero Túrin can resist him, thanks to his Dwarven-made helmet, but Glaurung has more powers at his disposal than flame and claw. Foolishly, Túrin looks into Glaurung's eyes and

> fell under the binding spell of the lidless eyes of the dragon, and was halted moveless... in torment of mind, and could not stir[162]

The malice and intelligence of Glaurung are clearly shown in this tragedy, as he destroys the life of Túrin by subterfuge and deceit, rather than force. Glaurung uses his supernatural powers of persuasion to convince Túrin to abandon his Elven beloved and instead seek his family. But the dragon has cast a spell of forgetfulness on Túrin's sister, Nienor, and when Túrin meets her he does not recognise her. They fall in love and marry, only to have the truth revealed by Glaurung as he lies dying, stabbed from underneath by Túrin. Nienor kills herself, shortly afterwards followed by Túrin. But Glaurung's cruelty has also proved to be his own undoing. If he had merely killed Túrin when he had him helpless, then the hero could not have returned to slay him.

Although Glaurung is the father of dragons, he is not the mightiest. That honour belongs to Ancalagon the Black, the greatest dragon to ever live. In the War of Wrath the Valar march on Middle-earth to destroy Morgoth, and rout his armies of Balrogs, Orcs and Men. Cornered,

Morgoth unleashes his secret weapon, a whole host of winged dragons, led by Ancalagon. The dragons are so powerful that they actually force the army of the gods to retreat! Fortunately for the Valar, Eärendil the Mariner appears in his flying ship Vingilot, along with all the Great Eagles of Manwë. After a tumultuous battle lasting a day and a night, Eärendil finally kills Ancalagon. Ancalagon is so huge and powerful that his dying fall from the sky destroys an entire Mountain range.

In the Third Age, two dragons of note are mentioned. The first is Scatha the worm, killed by the Northman hero Fram. The second is the greatest dragon of his time, Smaug the Golden. It is Smaug who routs the Dwarves of Erebor, the Lonely Mountain, sending Thorin Oakenshield and his father, Thráin, into exile. The story of how Thorin and his Dwarven companions recruit the Hobbit Bilbo Baggins, at the urging of Gandalf, in an attempt to defeat Smaug and recover their lost treasure, is told in *The Hobbit*.

As well as possessing all the powers of a winged Urulóki, Smaug has also taken steps to negate his one weakness – his soft underbelly. By lying on a bed of gems from the Dwarven hoard he presses them into the flesh, giving himself an armoured undercarriage. When Bilbo meets him, he manages to trick the dragon into rolling over to show off his armour, and reveal the one bare patch that is still vulnerable. It is this one unprotected patch that Bard the Bowman, a hero in neighbouring Lake-town, pierces with an arrow to kill Smaug, having been warned of the weakness by a talking thrush.

Although the exact origin of dragons may be a mystery, there is no doubt about their power and usefulness to the forces of evil. However, as we have seen on many occasions in the history of Middle-earth, evil intent may lead to good. It is Gandalf's fear of the devastation that Smaug could wreak on all of Eriador when Sauron goes to war that prompts him to join Thorin in finding a solution.[163] The hiring of Bilbo Baggins as burglar for the expedition leads directly to Bilbo's discovery of the One Ring under the Misty Mountains. This in turn leads to Frodo's journey to destroy the Ring in *The Lord of the Rings*. Without Smaug, Sauron would not have been defeated, and the history of the Third Age of Middle-earth would have had a very different ending.

The Dwarves

The Dwarves are unique in Middle-earth. Unlike the races of Elves or Men, they were not part of the original Song of Creation in which Ilúvatar and the gods vied with Morgoth to produce the world and the creatures of it. However, neither are they merely twisted mockeries or 'copies' of another race, like the Orcs – who are said to be the product of experiments by Morgoth upon the Elves – nor the Trolls, who are poor imitations of the Ents. The Dwarves are, in fact, an act of original creation by a single Valar, or god, Aulë.

Aulë, the great smith of the Valar, was lonely and impatient as he awaited the coming of the Elves and wished for someone to teach his knowledge of the crafts of the earth to. He moulded the Seven Fathers of the Dwarves from stone to make them strong enough in body and spirit to endure all the evils of Morgoth. Ilúvatar appears to him and berates him for his arrogance in attempting something (the creation of life) that is Ilúvatar's province alone. However, as Aulë repents and raises his hammer to destroy the Dwarves, Ilúvatar stops him. As Aulë's act is entirely unselfish, Ilúvatar chooses to give the Seven Fathers life and allow the race of Dwarves to be born. However, he orders them to be placed in sleep beneath the ground until after the coming of the Elves, as the Elves are to be the Firstborn. So, although the Dwarves were actually the first race to appear in Middle-earth, they do not properly awaken until much later, after the Elves have already ventured forth.

This unique origin has profound implications for the nature of the Dwarves. Ilúvatar deliberately gives life to Aulë's creations without change or improvement:

> ' ... in no other way will I amend your handiwork, and as thou hast made it so shall it be.' [164]

This means that the Dwarves, more than any other race upon Middle-earth, reflect a single god and the nature of their creation in temperament and personality – both positively and negatively. The Dwarves, or Khazâd as they call themselves, are smiths and miners with a love of gold and gems.

Created from stone, they are short and broad (thus their Sindarin Elvish name of Naugrim or 'stunted people') but of great physical and mental strength and endurance. They are said to be implacable foes (as well as staunch allies) and deadly in battle, covered from head to toe in mail armour and wielding great axes. They live for hundreds of years but are not immortal like the Elves, and are always described with great beards, of which they are inordinately proud. Dwarvish women are few in number compared to men and rarely leave their mansions. So rare are they, in fact, that only one is known by name: Dìs, the sister of Thorin Oakenshield.[165]

Dwarves reflect the solitary nature of their origin, crafted in secret in a hall under the mountains. Very little is known of their culture or beliefs. Their language, Khuzdul, is not taught to outsiders and is so secret only a handful of words are known. Even their true names are kept secret, and not even engraved on their stone tombs. Each Dwarf takes a name in the human tongue, Westron, for public use, such as Gimli, Gloin's son from the Company of the Ring, or Thorin Oakenshield, the King of the Dwarves in *The Hobbit*. In their writing, the Dwarves use an adaptation of the Elvish runes, refined by the Elven Minstrel Daeron of Doriath. For this the Dwarves held him in greater esteem than did his own people.

Almost the only thing known of the Dwarves' religious or spiritual side is their belief that, when they die, they are gathered in the Halls of Mandos and, after the last battle, they will aid Aulë in remaking the world. The similarity here to the Norse story of Ragnarok and the subsequent rebirth of Midgard could not be more clear and is evidence of the close connection between Tolkien's mythology and that of Norse legend, among others.

The Seven Fathers of Dwarves, the Kings of the Seven Houses, are believed to reincarnate over and over again among their people. Durin the Deathless is the most famous of these, the Lord of Khazad-dûm, greatest of Dwarven mansions. Thorin Oakenshield of the Lonely Mountain is his direct descendant. It is foretold that Durin shall be reincarnated seven times to lead the Dwarves of his House and at the beginning of the Fourth Age his seventh, and last, incarnation is still eagerly awaited by all his folk. Seven is a mystical number for all the Dwarves. There are seven Houses, descended from the Seven Fathers. In turn, the Dwarves receive seven Rings of Power from Sauron.

The Dwarves are great masons and craftsmen of underground halls. The city of Menegroth, or Thousand Caves, the home of King Thingol Greycloak and the Sindar Elves of Doriath in the First Age, is built with the aid of the Dwarves of the Blue Mountains. Lit by lamps under a mountain, it is said to be the fairest city in all Middle-earth at the time. The Dwarves' help is also vital in the creation of Finrod's great stronghold of Nargothrond. It is the Dwarves that give the Elven King Finrod the title Felagund, which means Hewer of Caves.

Superb miners and great smiths, the Dwarves are unrivalled even by the Noldor in the tempering of steel and in the crafting of armour. The Dwarves of Belegost invented ring mail, and it is with the armour and weapons of the Dwarves of the Blue Mountains that Thingol and his people fight against the Orcs of Morgoth.

The Dwarves' strength of spirit is so great that even Sauron fails to corrupt them. Sauron's Seven Dwarven Rings[166] cannot enslave the Dwarves, as the mortal Lords who become the Ringwraiths, or Nazgûl, are enslaved by their Nine Rings. The Dwarves are too strong too bend to Sauron's will. However, Sauron does manage to inflame their natural love of gold and gems into a dangerous greed.

Unfortunately, Dwarves are very suspicious of outsiders and can be quick to judge. Their greed for gold can have tragic consequences, as can be seen from the history of Nogrod, as well as Thorin's own unwillingness to barter with the men of Lake-town and their Elvish allies after the death of the dragon, Smaug.[167] Although they fight against Morgoth, and later Sauron, with an iron will, the Dwarves also often come into conflict with the Elves and the history of the two peoples is littered with tragic feuds and wars.

But the Dwarves greatest foes are the minions of darkness. Implacable enemies of the Orcs, the Dwarves fight many battles against them. Their greatest enemies, however, could be said to be the dragons. These great beasts sack many Dwarven mansions in their prime, having heard of the great wealth within. Most famous is Smaug's occupation of Erebor itself, which gives rise to the events detailed within *The Hobbit*.

The Petty-Dwarves are a group of Naugrim who were banished from the great cities of the east, although their crime is never revealed.

They slowly devolved, becoming shorter and stealthier, while losing their skill at smith-craft. Mîm is mentioned as the last of them, who betrays Túrin Turambar before being slain by the hero's father Húrin.

The three Great Halls of the first Age, during the Time of the Silmarils, are Nogrod, Belegost and Khazad-dûm. Nogrod and Belegost are the sister halls of the Blue Mountains.

The Host of Belegost earns fame and glory in the Battle of Nirnaeth Arnoediad, or Battle of Unnumbered Tears. Glaurung, the first dragon, battles against the Elves and Dwarves and proves unstoppable, through a combination of armour, claws and a terrible fiery breath. But Dwarves of Belegost, as well as being naturally more resistant to flame because of their hardy stone origins, wear great war masks that protect their faces and beards. They hold firm, then surround and attack the dragon. Their leader, King Azaghâl, is crushed beneath the dragon but manages to stab it as he dies. Wounded, Glaurung leaves the battlefield and flees back into Angband. The Dwarven host also leaves the battle, in mourning, carrying their dead lord upon their shoulders.

The History of Nogrod is not so glorious. It is one of the tales of greed and treachery that follow the Silmarils, but with the weakness and greed of the Dwarves playing its own tragic part. The greatest craftsmen of both Nogrod and Belegost produced a great treasure, the necklace Nauglamír – the Dwarves' most famous work of the First Age. It is made as a gift for the Elvish King Finrod Felagund after the building of Nargothrond. This tale, again, has similarities with the Norse Myths, and the creation of the necklace Brisingamen. The hero Húrin later brings the Nauglamír to King Thingol Greycloak and, when Thingol receives the Silmaril from Beren, he calls upon the Dwarves of Nogrod to combine the gem with the Nauglamír.

Unfortunately the Dwarves, influenced by the Curse of the Silmarils, desire the necklace for themselves and, when Thingol demands it, they kill him and flee from Doriath with the treasure. They are swiftly overtaken, killed, and the treasure recovered. However, a few survive and return to Nogrod, with tales of the treachery of Elves. The Dwarves of Belegost refuse to help them but Nogrod goes to war, sacking Doriath and causing bad blood forever between the Elves and Dwarves. The Dwarvish host is, in turn, hunted down by Beren himself and ambushed, with those who flee Beren slaughtered by a forest of Ents[168] and Huorns. The irony of Dwarves invading the very Elven halls they themselves had helped to build, in an early example of the two peoples' co-operation, is clear. The final destruction of the kingdom of Doriath comes soon after, at the hands of the sons of Fëanor driven, again, by the Curse of the Silmarils.

Nogrod and Belegost are both destroyed in the cataclysm that accompanies the defeat of Morgoth in the War of Wrath, at the end of the First Age. Much of the Dwarf population becomes refugees, joining their kinfolk in Khazad-dum. However, some stay and continue to eke out a living in the Blue Mountains, working in the ruins of their ancient halls. When – thousands of years later – Thorin Oakenshield meets Gandalf and hits on a plan to retake the Lonely Mountain from Smaug, Thorin is working in the Blue Mountains.

The Greatest of the Dwarven Halls is Khazad-dûm, ruled by Durin the Deathless, the first and greatest of the Seven Founding Fathers of the Dwarves. By the time of the Company of the Ring, however, Khazad-dûm had become known as Moria, the Black Pit, and sees the death of Gandalf in battle with the Balrog. Little is known of the hall until after the fall of Morgoth, whose eventual defeat saw the destruction of huge areas of Middle-earth, sinking Nogrod and Belegost under the sea.

Situated in the Misty Mountains, the Dwarves of Khazad-dûm not only form a mutually beneficial system of trade and cooperation with the Elven smiths of Ost-in-Edhil, but an actual friendship as had not been seen before. The inscription on the Doors of Durin which is deciphered by Gandalf and the Company of the Ring[169] is not only in the Elvish script but written by Celebrimbor himself – the greatest Elven smith of the Second Age and the creator of the three Elven Rings. It is in these halls only that mithril, or true silver, could be found – a metal more precious than gold, that produced weapons and armour stronger and lighter than steel. The mail coat given to Bilbo as a reward by Thorin after the death of Smaug[170] is made of mithril, and later saves the life of Frodo from an Orc spear in Moria itself. It is described by Gandalf as a gift fit for a king:

' ... its worth was greater than the value of the whole Shire
and everything in it.' [171]

But even in Khazad-dûm a shadow falls upon the bonds between
Dwarves and Elves. When Sauron reveals himself in the Second Age and
makes war upon those selfsame Elves, the Dwarves of Khazad-dûm close
their doors and retreat into the safety of their underground fortress.
However, when Gil-galad and Elendil form the Last Alliance and march
against Sauron in the climactic battle of the Second Age, the Dwarves of
Khazad-dûm fight with them – one of the few Dwarven hosts to do so.

It is the Dwarves' greed which causes the downfall of Khazad-dûm.
They mine too deep in their lust for mithril and awake an ancient evil.
When Morgoth is finally defeated at the end of the First Age, many of
his creatures flee and hide deep underground, to prevent their own cap-
ture and destruction. One of these is a single Balrog. Originally Maiar [172]
of flame and spirit, the Balrogs were corrupted by the promises of
Melkor and became his most powerful servants. The mining of the
Dwarves either breaks the walls of the Balrog's prison, or merely wakes
it up. Either way, a creature of power almost unstoppable in the First
Age emerges in the Third. Known as Durin's Bane, the Balrog kills the
Dwarven king and forces the Dwarves to flee their ancient halls.
Attracted by its evil, a host of Orcs and Trolls take up residence in the
mansion, which becomes known thereafter as Moria.

But, as we have seen elsewhere, calamitous events are often vital points
on the path to the eventual victory of light over darkness. In this case, the
awakening of Durin's Bane leads directly to the meeting of Thorin
Oakenshield and Gandalf, and then to Bilbo's discovery of the One Ring.
Without this chain of events, Sauron would never have been defeated.

The Dwarves are forced to flee Moria and found Erebor, the Lonely
Mountain, beginning a new kingdom there. When that grows too successful and stories of its wealth spread, it attracts the attention of Smaug
the Golden, the greatest dragon of the Age. He sacks the Dwarven Hall
and forces its people into exile once more. Thrór, the King under the
Mountain and grandfather of Thorin Oakenshield, has by now become
an ancient and broken figure. He gives the last of the Seven Dwarven

Rings to his son Thráin II, and journeys, lost in madness, back to his ancestral home of Moria. There he is killed and his severed head branded with the name of Azog, the Orc chief who kills him. The Dwarves are so incensed by the insult to the King of Durin's line, the oldest and greatest of the Seven Dwarven Houses, that they muster all their strength for war and sack every Orc hold in Middle-earth in vengeance. Eventually, the Dwarven Host come to Moria and fight the Battle of Azanulbizar.

It is at this battle that Thorin Oakenshield gains his name, as he uses the branch of a tree to defend himself when he loses his shield. The Orcs are defeated, but almost half the Dwarven Army are also killed. Although Dwarven dead were traditionally placed deep underground in individual stone tombs, the sheer number of casualties suffered means that the Dwarves have no choice but to build a huge pyre and burn the bodies. The Orc leader Azog himself is killed by the young Dáin Ironfoot, the same Dáin who later comes with his troops to help Thorin at the Battle of the Five Armies.[173] Despite the victory, the Dwarves do not dare to enter Moria, out of fear of the Balrog still inside.

Some years later, Sauron captures Thráin and the last Dwarven ring is taken from him in Dol Guldûr, leaving Thorin as the heir to both Erebor and Moria. At this point a chance meeting occurs, upon which the whole history of the War of the Rings turns. Thorin is passing through Bree, when he meets Gandalf on his way to the Shire. Gandalf has been pondering the growth of Sauron's power, and is afraid of the havoc Smaug might wreak if war were to break out. The two make a plan to find a burglar to help Thorin and his companions against Smaug. The burglar is, of course, the Hobbit Bilbo Baggins. After many adventures, during which Bilbo discovers the One Ring and escapes from Gollum in the Misty Mountains, Smaug is slain by Bard the Bowman of Lake-town.

Even here we see the frailties of the Dwarves at work. Thorin is angry when the armies of Lake-town and the Elvish King Thranduil of Mirkwood (who had earlier imprisoned the Dwarves) come to Erebor demanding their share of the dragon's hoard. When Dáin Ironfoot arrives with the Dwarves of the Iron Hills, a battle between them is only avoided by the arrival of a great host of Goblins (Orcs of the Misty Mountains) and Wolves, led by Bolg, the son of Azog. In the subsequent Battle of the

Five Armies, Thorin is killed, along with his cousins Fili and Kili.

The Dwarves also play an important part in the events of *The Lord of the Rings*. It is Glóin, one of Bilbo's companions from *The Hobbit*, who comes to the Council of Elrond with news of the Black Rider at Erebor's Gates asking questions about Hobbits. Glóin's son, Gimli, is chosen as one of the Company of the Ring, and escorts Frodo on his perilous journey to Mordor.

Three events during the journey of the Company of the Ring are worthy of special mention here. The journey through Moria, Gimli's experience of Galadriel in Lórien, and Gimli's discovery at the Battle of Helm's Deep.

The Company of the Ring take the decision to enter Moria after the weather defeats an attempt to scale the mountain Caradhras. Gimli is eager to discover what happened to Balin, another of the Dwarven companions of Bilbo from *The Hobbit*, who some 30 years earlier had returned to Khazad-dûm to reclaim the halls. Unfortunately, the Company discover only Balin's tomb, and a battered manuscript describing his struggles, and eventual destruction, at the hands of the Orcs. It is while fleeing Moria that Gandalf meets Durin's Bane, the Balrog. Gandalf destroys the bridge upon which they battle, and both he and the Balrog are thought to have been slain. Later, however, the wizard returns as Gandalf the White, telling of his titanic struggle against the Balrog, whom he eventually defeated, but at the cost of his own life.

It is in the Forest of Lórien that one of the most remarkable friendships of Elves and Dwarves begins. Despite the initial mistrust of the Elves, Gimli becomes the first Dwarf in many years to gaze upon the beauty of the Golden Wood and its Queen, Galadriel. Galadriel is the only Elf remaining in Middle-earth at this time who has seen the glory of the Two Trees of Valinor, and is probably the most powerful of all those fighting Sauron, save perhaps Gandalf. She is also the keeper of Nenya, one of the three Elven Rings of power. However, even she has to remain hidden from the gaze of Sauron and cannot act against him directly.

When Gimli meets Galadriel, an incredible thing happens. It appears as if:

> ... he looked suddenly into the heart of an enemy and saw
> there love and understanding.[174]

Smitten, the Dwarf praises Lórien as greater than even Khazad-dûm and, when the Company are given gifts by Galadriel to help them on their journey, Gimli asks only for a lock of her hair to treasure. The Dwarf is ever after a staunch defender of the Elven Queen.

Later, Gimli, along with Aragorn and Legolas, is forced to choose to rescue Pippin and Merry after the death of Boromir, and thus journeys into the lands of Rohan. It is at the battle of Helm's Deep, where the Riders of Rohan defeat Saruman's armies, that Gimli discovers the Glittering Caves of Aglarond. After the defeat of Sauron, he returns there with some of his folk to create a new Dwarven mansion.

The most remarkable result of the events told in *The Lord of the Rings*, at least from a Dwarvish point of view, is the relationship that grows between Gimli and Legolas, the Sindarin Elf who also joins the Company of the Ring. Despite their initial mistrust of each other, given the history of the two peoples, they develop a friendship

> ... greater than any that has been between Elf and Dwarf. [175]

After the events of Lórien and Helm's Deep, Gimli and Legolas both agree to visit the other's homes in peace time and when Legolas chooses to sail to the Undying Lands, Gimli goes with him.

This is totally unprecedented. Before the defeat of Sauron, the only soul without Elvish blood allowed to experience the paradise of the Undying Lands had been the great mortal hero Tuor. Tuor was the husband of the Elven Princess Idril Celebrindal and the father of Eärendil, whose intervention on behalf of both the races of Elves and Men allowed the defeat of Morgoth at the hands of the Valar. [176]

Thousands of years later, the Hobbits Bilbo, Frodo and Sam are also allowed to sail into the West because of their unique status as Ring-bearers, having carried the burden of Sauron's Ruling Ring. For any Dwarf to follow them seems incredible. But, as well as the remarkable friendship with Legolas, Gimli wishes to see Galadriel again and it is her intervention that obtains this exceptional grace for him.

As we have seen elsewhere, it is only through the unity and co-operation of all the disparate races that evil can be defeated. Thus it is entirely appropriate, and deliberate, that the long and troubled history of the Dwarves and Elves is finally symbolically reconciled in Gimli's journey – the result of his friendship with Legolas, and his love for Galadriel.

THE GREAT EAGLES

The Great Eagles are the servants and messengers of Manwë, Chief of the Valar and the Lord of Birds.[177] A world apart from their lesser cousins, they are mighty Lords of the Sky, huge in size and preying on sheep and cattle. Able to carry a fully-grown Man or Elf, they are too huge to nest in even the largest trees and their eyries are situated high in the mountains. The wingspan of Thorondor, the King of the Eagles in the First Age, measures 30 fathoms. The Eagles are staunch friends of Elves and Men, and fearless enemies of evil. All are capable of speech, as swift as the wind, and have eyes that can pick out the movement of a rabbit many miles below.

Although the Eagles don't play a central part in the history of Middle-earth, their supporting role is vital. Sent by Manwë to fight Morgoth in the First Age, they act as guardians and watchers over the Elven lands, especially the hidden kingdom of Gondolin, seeing and driving off the vast majority of the Dark Lord's spies. When Gondolin eventually falls, it is only through the treachery of one of its inhabitants, Maeglin, not through the failure of the Eagles.

The Eagles are essential sources of information on the all the activities of Morgoth, carrying news to both Manwë in the Undying Lands and the Elves in Middle-earth. Their eternal vigilance as scouts and messengers means that they are always on hand when most needed. It is Thorondor who rescues the Noldor prince Maedhros, when he has been captured by Morgoth and chained to a mountainside. When the Elven High King Fingolfin lies dead, killed by Morgoth in single combat, it is again Thorondor who swoops and saves his body from mutilation – scarring the face of the dark god in the process.

The Eagles are also fearsome in war. In the final battle of the Valar against Morgoth, the War of Wrath, the host of Eagles fight alongside Eärendil the Mariner in his flying ship Vingilot against Morgoth's flight of dragons.[178] After a day and long, dark night of struggle, Eärendil kills Ancalagon the Black, the mightiest of all the dragons, and the strength of the Eagles prevails. This splendour in battle combines with their role as the messengers of Manwë when the Eagles fall on the treacherous Dúnedain of Númenor. Unfortunately, the warning isn't heeded, and the island is utterly drowned and destroyed.[179]

In the Third Age, the Eagles continue to play a vital role. They intervene to tip the balance in the Battle of the Five Armies[180] and fight against Sauron before the gates of Mordor. Gandalf in particular has reason to be grateful to Gwaihir, the Windlord. The Lord of the Eagles, and the direct descendant of Thorondor, Gwaihir helps Gandalf on no less than three occasions. He rescues Gandalf, along with Bilbo and the Dwarves, from the Goblins, just after Bilbo has discovered the One Ring. He also rescues Gandalf from Saruman's treachery at Orthanc, and from the ruins at the top of Moria's Endless Stair after the defeat of the Balrog. It is also Gwaihir and his Eagles who rescue Frodo and Sam from Mount Doom after the destruction of the Ring.

ELVES

The Elves are the Firstborn, the chosen people of the world. They are the beloved of the gods, and the greatest enemies of Sauron and his predecessor Morgoth. By the Third Age, and the events of *The Lord of the Rings*, the Elves are barely a shadow of their former splendour, but their Lords are still among the most powerful figures in Middle-earth. Their lands too, in Lothlórien, Rivendell, the Grey Havens and, to a lesser extent, Thranduil's woodland kingdom in Mirkwood, are the greatest strongholds of power, wisdom and strength against the Dark Lord in Mordor. But the role they play in Sauron's downfall is a very passive one, offering wisdom, advice, succour and encouragement, rather than mustering armies or forging great weapons of war. This is a lesson the Elves have learned from their mistakes in the past, and a recognition that their time has passed and it is now the Age of Men. But it was not always so.

The Elves first awoke in a Middle-earth under the yoke of Melkor, the original Dark Lord, and Sauron's master in ancient times. To light their way to the home of the gods, the Undying Lands in the West, Varda, the Queen of the Valar, created the stars. The first sight seen by the Elves is the stars above, as the Sun and the Moon are not yet in existence, and the Elves love the stars ever after. Varda herself is especially revered by the Elves under the name of Elbereth Gilthoniel.[181] It is for the sake of the Elves that the gods go to war with Melkor, defeating and chaining him until the Elves have had a chance to journey to the West. Melkor knows the reasons for the war and never forgives the Elves for his humiliation. Much of his effort afterwards is directed against the Elves to punish them.

The Elves strength of spirit is so great that Morgoth can never enslave them. Although Morgoth on many occasions manages to deceive the Elves, or even manipulate and poison their minds so that they do great evil, only one Elf, Maeglin, is known to willingly side with him. Fëanor, the greatest of the Noldor Elves, and the figure responsible for their exile from the Undying Lands, is corrupted and ruined by Morgoth into meeting hate with hate, but his aim remains the destruction of the Dark Lord. Unfortunately, one of the lessons of the history of Middle-earth, as can be seen in the Lessening of the Ages chapter of this book, is that evil cannot be overcome if you become that which you fight.

All Elves are immortal, never growing old and being totally immune to disease. Violence, weariness or a broken heart can still kill them, however. But even then their spirits travel to the Halls of Mandos, the god of the Halls of the Dead, where they reincarnate. This only seems to happen in the Undying Lands, though, as there is no mention of any Elf in the histories of Middle-earth ever having lived before.

As well as immortality, the Elves are blessed with many other fabulous attributes and skills. All are incredibly beautiful, glowing with an inner light and reflecting the light of their beloved stars in their hair. Their faces always look either young or ageless, but the wisdom and weight of their thousands of years can be seen in their eyes. Elves love to sing, and have the most beautiful voices of all the creatures in the world. They delight in all forms of words and language and when they first awoke they began naming everything they saw. It is the Elves that teach the Ents, the Tree-shepherds, to speak and their name for themselves is the Quendi or, simply, those that speak with voices.

Elves have incredibly good eyesight, and can see better in starlight (which they were born under) than a man can see in full daylight. This is one of the reasons that the Elves are such unmatched archers. The Elves that have been in the Undying Lands can also see into the shadow world, which Sauron and his Ringwraiths inhabit, giving them some power against such creatures. The hearing of the Elves is also far better than the mortal races. Although they glow with a beautiful inner light, they can still move completely silently, and are even stealthier than Hobbits. Elves walk so lightly that they can run on snow, they almost never tire and do not even need to sleep. Instead, they seem to meditate in a waking dream, during which their eyes are open and they can still walk or talk.

These features are common to all the Elves, but the Elven race became divided into different groups soon after it awoke. The fault for this lies with the Valar. The gods were impatient to see and talk to the Elves and so they sent Oromë, the Hunter, to summon them to the Undying Lands. It is Oromë who named them the Eldar, or the People of the Stars. But some Elves hid from Oromë and refused the summons. These Elves became known as the Avari, or Unwilling, but are better known as the Silvan Elves, those who never tried to leave Middle-earth.

Most of the Elves answer Oromë's summons and march to the West. Of these the smallest group, at the forefront of the march, are the Vanyar. The second group become known as the Noldor. The third, and by far the largest, are the Teleri. Being so large a group, they lag behind the others and are the last to reach the shores of Middle-earth. Their King, Elwë, meets Melian the Maia,[182] and falls in love. Some of the Teleri take a new King, Elwë's brother Olwë, and continue West. Those that remain until they are reunited with their King – now known as Thingol – are renamed the Úmanyar, meaning those not of Aman, but are better known as the Sindar Elves.

Little is known of the Vanyar, or Fair Elves. They are golden haired and love poetry and singing even more than their cousins. Manwë and Varda, the King and Queen of the gods, especially favour the Vanyar. Their King is Ingwë, held to be the highest Lord of all the Elves. The Vanyar are also the wisest of the Elves and mistrust the evil Vala Melkor, even when he appears to have renounced his crimes. It is because they have no dealings with his lies and deceit that they avoid the dissension and rebellion of the Noldor and thus play almost no part in the history of Middle-earth. The Vanyar only ever leave the Undying Lands once, to march to war at the head of the army of the Valar to finally defeat Morgoth at the end of the First Age. After their victory, they return immediately to the West. However, some of the major Elven figures do carry the blood of the Vanyar, as there is some intermarriage between them and the Noldor. The sign of this is golden hair, as the full-blooded Noldor are always dark haired.

The wife of the first King of the Noldor, Finwë, dies after giving birth to his son Fëanor. Finwë marries again, this time to a Vanyar, Indis. With her he has two more sons, Fingolfin and Finarfin. They and their children all have the golden hair of the Vanyar. Galadriel of Lothlórien, the most powerful Elf of the Third Age, is Finarfin's daughter. This means that she is not only the granddaughter of the first high King of the Noldor, and one of the very few Elves by that time to have actually seen the Undying Lands, but also one quarter Vanyar. Gildor, the leader of the band of Elves who meet Frodo, Sam and Pippin in the Shire, is also golden haired. He is a Noldor, but of the House of Finrod, the brother of Galadriel. And Glorfindel, the mighty Noldor lord who comes to the aid of Aragorn and the Hobbits as they are being pursued by the Nazgûl, is also golden haired and thus related to the Vanyar.

The Noldor, or Deep Elves, play a much larger part in the history of Middle-earth. They are the favourites of the Valar Aulë, and are masters of all crafts involving skill with the hands, from making jewellery to forging weapons or armour. They are always thirsty for knowledge and are the first Elves to invent writing. Their language is Quenya, which by the Third Age and the time of *The Lord of the Rings* is no longer spoken, but only used as a language of scholars and learning, a little bit like Latin in Renaissance Europe.

Fëanor, the eldest son of Finwë, is the greatest of all the Noldor. He forges the Silmarils, which capture the light of the Two Trees of Valinor and are the most beautiful objects ever made. Unfortunately, Fëanor is corrupted by the lies and malice of Melkor and becomes possessive and greedy. When Melkor steals the Silmarils and kills his father Finwë, Fëanor swears vengeance and leads the Noldor to defy the Valar and pursue Melkor to Middle-earth. It is Fëanor who renames Melkor Morgoth, the Black Enemy. And it is Fëanor's act of rebellion that causes the Noldor who follow him to be exiled, and leads to the terrible suffering and hardship, and also the heinous crimes, of these Elves. But the rebellion also leads to great heroism and, if it had not been for the presence of the Noldor fighting Morgoth, Middle-earth would almost certainly have been utterly dominated by him, dooming all the other races to lives of slavery.

Fingolfin is Fëanor's brother, the second son of Finwë and the mightiest of all the Noldor. Fingolfin follows his brother into exile, becoming High King of all the Noldor of Middle-earth after Fëanor's death. Fingolfin himself dies in single combat with Morgoth, although he manages to strike the god seven times, causing wounds that never heal. Finarfin is the third son of Finwë, the most beautiful and the wisest of the Noldor. He refuses to follow Fëanor and becomes High King of the few Noldor who remain in the Undying Lands.

The powerful Lords of the Noldor who dominate the First Age are too numerous to list here, as are all their noble, and ignoble, deeds. But one is certainly worthy of further mention. Galadriel went with the Noldor into exile from the Undying Lands, despite her father Finarfin staying behind. But she does not follow Fëanor; instead she goes to Middle-earth because she wishes to rule a realm of her own. By the time of the Third Age, Galadriel has her wish and is the Queen of Lothlórien, as well as the most powerful and most beautiful Elf in all of Middle-earth. However, Galadriel has learned the lessons of the First Age, which saw all of her brothers and cousins killed, and directs her power wisely. Probably the most powerful opponent of Sauron in Middle-earth, with the possible exception of Gandalf, Galadriel's powers and strength are in passive resistance rather than active opposition. Galadriel also possesses Nenya, the Ring of Water, one of the three great Elven Rings. She uses its power to hide Lothlórien from Sauron, rather than confronting him openly.

'I perceive the Dark Lord and know his mind, or all of his
mind that concerns the Elves. And he gropes ever to see me
and my thought.' [183]

Even Gandalf is pushed to the limit to hide Frodo and the Ring from the
searching eye of Sauron, as he does when Frodo places it on his finger to
escape Boromir on top of Amon Hen. For Galadriel to have such an
advantage over Sauron means that her powers must be vast. But her powers, to see hidden events and the minds of others, are used to offer advice
and aid rather than to make war. An example is Galadriel's testing of the
Company of the Ring when they enter Lothlórien. In this, she follows the
wisdom of her mentor of the First Age, Melian the Maia.[184] It is Galadriel
who originally wishes Gandalf to be the head of the White Council, the
Council of the Wise, a role he turns down. Saruman takes the position
instead, but he never forgives Galadriel for favouring Gandalf.

One of the clearest signs of Galadriel's wisdom is her refusal to take
the One Ring from Frodo, even when freely offered. Galadriel's pride
and lust for power caused her to join the exile of the Noldor from the
Undying Lands. The same pride, as well as a love for the lands of
Middle-earth, leads her to refuse the Pardon of the Valar after the defeat
of Morgoth at the end of the First Age. But when Frodo freely offers her
the Ring – the power she has always wanted – she chooses to refuse it.
She is then able to return to the West after the defeat of Sauron and the
destruction of the Ring, with Gandalf and the Ring-bearers.

Most of the Noldor return to the Undying Lands after the defeat of
Morgoth at the end of the First Age, but some remain. Leaving
Galadriel aside, two other Noldor dominate the Second Age, which sees
the first rise and fall of Sauron.

Celebrimbor was the grandson of Fëanor himself, and the greatest jewel
smith since his grandfather. In the Second Age, he ruled the Elves of
Eregion. It is Celebrimbor who is deceived by Sauron in his fair disguise of
Annatar, the Lord of Gifts, into aiding the Dark Lord in forging the Rings
of Power,[185] which they make together. When Sauron makes the One Ring
to rule all the others, and puts it on, his true nature is revealed and war
between Mordor and the Elves of Eregion follows. Eregion is destroyed

and Celebrimbor killed. Sauron gains power over the nine mortal Ring-bearers, eventually creating his greatest servants, the Nazgûl or Ringwraiths. He also gains a far lesser influence over the Seven Dwarven Rings. But Celebrimbor forges Nenya, Vilya and Narya, the three Elven Rings, alone and Sauron never has any part in their creation. Although they are still subject to the control of the Ruling Ring, the Elves use their Rings secretly and keep them hidden, and Sauron is unable to use them against their wielders. Once Sauron is defeated at the end of the Second Age and the One Ring lost, the Three can be used more safely, being wield-ed in secret during the War of the Ring by Elrond, Galadriel and Gandalf.

The architect of Sauron's defeat at the end of the Second Age is Gil-galad, the High King of the Elves in Middle-earth. Also a Noldor, he is the son of Fingon, who was in turn the son of Fingolfin, both High Kings before him. Gil-galad, along with Elendil, the Dúnedain King and founder of Gondor and Arnor, the Dúnedain realms in exile, leads the Last Alliance of Elves and Men which destroys Sauron's armies. Sauron kills Gil-galad and Elendil in that great battle, before himself falling to Elendil's son Isildur.

By the Third Age the Noldor are very few in number, outnumbered by the Sindar and the far more numerous Silvan Elves. Apart from Galadriel, the two most worthy of mention are Glorfindel and Gildor. All three have Vanyar blood.

The Teleri are the Sea Elves. They love the water and are unmatched sailors. They learned all they could from Ulmo, the god of the Sea, and his Maiar servants, including the art of making the beautiful Swan Ships. The first crime of the Noldor, when they defy the Valar in the First Age, is the Kinslaying of the Teleri. Fëanor and his followers demanded that the Sea Elves sail them to Middle-earth. When the Teleri refuse, they demand the beloved Swan Ships. When the Teleri refuse again, saying the ships are their greatest treasures, the Noldor steal them by force, slaughtering their cousins. This is the greatest crime of the Noldor, although only a minori-ty are actually with Fëanor at the time. The majority of the Noldor follow behind with his brother Fingolfin and are blameless.

The Sindar, or Grey Elves, are the Teleri who began, but never finished, the journey to the Undying Lands. Many stay behind in Middle-earth with

King Thingol Greycloak in his realm of Doriath. The Sindar are not as powerful as the Noldor, as they have never seen the Light of Aman, and have not learned from the Valar themselves and their Maiar servants. But they are still wise and very powerful in the eyes of Men. They maintain some contact with, and learn from, the Vala Ulmo, who never abandons the Elves of Middle-earth. The sea longing that afflicts those Elves who have been to the West remains strong in the Sindar: it merely sleeps, to be awoken when Ulmo wishes. Like the Teleri, the Sindar are great sailors and mariners, and it is the Sindar Elves who pilot all the ships sailing West to the Undying Lands from Middle-earth. Doriath, the Sindar realm of Thingol and Melian in the First Age, is one of the most powerful Elven kingdoms in Middle-earth. The power and wisdom of those two rulers elevates the Sindar almost to the level of their Noldor cousins.

But relations between the Sindar and Noldor are frosty at best, murderous at worst. When Thingol discovers the reason for the exile of the Noldor, and especially the Kinslaying of the Teleri – the cousins of the Sindar – he bans all Noldor of the Houses of the sons of Fëanor from Doriath. Relations between the two groups are not helped when those same sons of Fëanor destroy Doriath some years later. After the death of Thingol at the hands of the Dwarves, which leads Melian to abandon Middle-earth and return to the West, their grandson Dior rules Doriath. When Dior comes into possession of a Silmaril, it awakes the great Oath sworn by all the children of Fëanor, to never rest until they have recovered the jewels their father had made. They destroy the Sindar kingdom and kill Dior, although the Silmaril escapes with Dior's daughter Elwing, who later becomes the mother of Elrond.

One result of the hostility between the Noldor and Sindar is a change in their language. The Sindar refuse to speak Quenya, and so Sindarin becomes the common language which all the Elves use to communicate. Sindarin is similar to Quenya, as they have the same roots, but the two languages had grown apart when the Noldor travelled to the Undying Lands.

By the Third Age, the Sindar left in Middle-earth are relatively few, although more common than the Noldor. They make up the majority of the ruling nobles of the Elven kingdoms, with the Silvan Elves making up the vast majority of their populations. Celeborn, the husband of Galadriel and King of Lothlórien, was originally a great Sindar Prince of Doriath. Thranduil, the King of the Elves in Mirkwood, is also a Sindar. Círdan, the master of the Grey Havens, is not only a Sindar but also the only Elf ever known to have a beard. It is Círdan who was originally the bearer of Narya, the Elven Ring of Fire. When the Istari travel from the Undying Lands to Middle-earth to join the struggle against Sauron, after around a thousand years of the Third Age, Círdan gives the Ring to Gandalf. The Sindar Lord, understanding in his wisdom the role Gandalf will play in Sauron's downfall, realises that its power to kindle the fires in the hearts of Men and Elves will be more useful to the Grey Wanderer.

Most famously Legolas, the Elf who joins the Company of the Ring in Rivendell, is a Sindar. He is the son of Thranduil, the King of Mirkwood, and fights alongside Aragorn and Gimli against the armies of both Saruman and Sauron. Remarkably, he befriends Gimli and escorts the Dwarf to the Undying Lands at the end of the Third Age.[186] However in his clothing, manner and many of his skills, Legolas more resembles the Silvan Elves who make up the majority of his father's kingdom than the Sindar lords of earlier times.

The Silvan Elves, also known as Wood Elves or Green Elves, are those who never even began the journey to the West and the Undying Lands. This earned them the title Avari, or the Unwilling. While some hid from the Vala Oromë who brought the summons, others refused because they had already fallen in love with the lands of Middle-earth and had no wish to leave them. By the Third Age and the time of *The Lord of the Rings,* Silvan Elves make up the vast majority of the populations of all the Elven Havens, especially Lothlórien and Mirkwood. As Sam the Hobbit says after seeing them in the Golden Wood:

> '...I reckon there's Elves and Elves... Now these folk aren't wanderers or homeless, and seem a bit nearer to the likes of us: they seem to belong here...' [187]

While it may be a stretch of the imagination to see any Elves as like Hobbits, the essence of Sam's observation is true. While the Noldor

Elves are exiles, and even the Sindar are creatures of power and wisdom whose time has passed, the Silvan Elves are firmly of Middle-earth. They are not as great, or as wise, or as powerful as the Noldor, or even the Sindar, but they are far more at peace in the world. The Silvan Elves forge no great items of power, rule no great kingdoms and commit no great evils. However, in some respects they are more skilled than their cousins. Although all Elves are light-footed and stealthy, the Silvan Elves are unmatched at woodcraft. They wear little armour and use bows as their main weapons. They favour hit-and-run tactics and ambushes, at which they are masters, over conventional battles. Most of all, they love and understand everything about the lands in which they live, from the animals and plants to the trees and rivers.

Legolas, although a Sindar Elf, is obviously influenced by the Silvan Elves of his father's domain. He dresses in green and brown and uses a bow and knife rather than a sword. Few Silvan Elves are actually named in the history of Middle-earth, as they are rarely part of the councils of the great and wise. Haldir, the Elf who escorts the Company of the Ring into Lothlórien, is a Silvan Elf. Many of his Silvan companions do not even speak the common language of Westron.

The Dúnedain Prince of Dol Amroth, one of the great nobles of Gondor, is believed to have Elven blood from a marriage between a Silvan Elf and a distant ancestor. Dol Amroth itself was once an Elf-haven and gained its name from the tragic story of two Elf lovers. Amroth was the Sindar King of Lothlórien, before Galadriel and Celeborn.[188] He loved Nimrodel, a Silvan Elf. They wanted to sail to the Undying Lands together but Nimrodel became lost in the mountains. A great storm came and swept the ship, which Amroth had already boarded, out to sea. He leapt overboard to swim to shore and find his love but was drowned. The Gondorian city of Dol Amroth is built by the site of the small Elf-haven from which the ship sailed.

Finally, there are the Peredhil, the Half-elven. In the First Age there were two marriages between Men and Elves. The first was Beren and Lúthien Tinúviel; the second was between Tuor and Idril Celebrindal.[189] The granddaughter of Lúthien and Beren was Elwing, who married the son of Tuor and Idril, Eärendil the Mariner. It was Eärendil, representing both Elves and Men, who managed to sail to the West and beseeched the Valar to intervene against Morgoth in the final battle of the First Age. Elrond and Elros were the sons of Eärendil and Elwing. As the Elves are immortal and Men are doomed to die, any union of Man and Elf results in an exceptional circumstance, one that requires those involved to choose between membership of the two peoples. Beren and Lúthien choose to be mortal and die. Tuor and Idril are granted leave to enter the Undying Lands as Elves. Eärendil and Elwing also choose immortality and Eärendil sails the heavens in the flying ship Vingilot, with the Silmaril on his brow as the Evening Star. Elros chooses to be mortal and found the Dúnedain of Númenor. Aragorn is his distant descendant, and his marriage to Elrond's daughter Arwen at the end of the Third Age is the closing of the circle between the two races of Men and Elves. [190]

Elrond, brother of Elros, chooses to live as an Elf. He carries not only the blood of the Sindar elves, from his mother's side, and the Noldor Elves, from his father's side, along with that of the race of Men, but also that of a Maia, from Melian, his great, great grandmother. He is even descended from the Vanyar Elves via his great, great, great grandmother Indis, the second wife of Finwë, the first High King of the Noldor. With a bloodline like that, it is unsurprising that Elrond is one of the most important figures of the Third Age.

Although Galadriel is the most powerful Elf in Middle-earth by the Third Age, Elrond can certainly rival her for the title of wisest. All the peoples of Middle-earth know him as a great lore master. Boromir, the Lord of Gondor who joins the Company of the Ring, travels to Rivendell to gain the answer to a riddle, having heard that there was no-one wiser than Elrond in all of Middle-earth. The fact that it is the Council of Elrond, in Rivendell, that decides the fate of the One Ring, and that all present defer to Elrond's knowledge and wisdom, says much. It is also Elrond, along with Círdan of the Grey Havens, who had been present at the defeat of Sauron at the end of the Second Age and advised Isildur, unsuccessfully, to destroy the One Ring.

Elrond's realm of Rivendell (or Imladris, to give its Elven name), is the foremost haven in Middle-earth. It provides rest, healing and aid for the Rangers of the North, who protect all the lands that were once the kingdom of Arnor, as well as all Elves and Elf-friends. Elrond is the greatest healer of the Age. No one else could have saved Frodo from the wound inflicted by the knife of the Black Rider.

Elrond also possesses the greatest of the three Elven Rings of Power, Vilya, the Ring of Air. While its powers are never detailed, we do know that all the Elven Rings stave off the weariness of the world that afflicts the immortal Elves, as well as aiding their powers of concealment. Both of these powers can be seen at work in Rivendell. Rivendell is a hidden haven, and its greatest protection from Sauron is his inability to discover precisely where it lies. The location of Galadriel's realm Lothlórien is known by almost no one outside of the Elves of her kingdom, and the woodlands are a natural protection and disguise for the Elves. The location of Rivendell, although by no means public knowledge, is not nearly as secret as Lothlórien. As well as being a haven and refuge for the Elves and Rangers of the North, Rivendell can also be found at need by Dwarves and even Lords of Gondor such as Boromir:

> 'long have I wandered by roads forgotten, seeking the house of
> Elrond, of which many have heard, but few knew where it lay.' [191]

The fact that some know the actual location of the Valley of Imladris, and that more know the general location, puts Rivendell in grave danger. The possibility of treachery and the efforts of the spies of Sauron mean that only great magic could have hidden the refuge for so long.

The other indication of the power of Vilya at work is Rivendell's reputation for healing. Elrond himself is a master healer, but a stay in his house heals not just the body but also the mind, and refreshes those tired in both body and spirit. All who stay there are rejuvenated by their experience.

Elrond is not only important for his wisdom, power and healing. He was married to Celebrían, the daughter of Galadriel, and was the father of one daughter, Arwen, and two sons, Elladan and Elrohir. His sons are great warriors and trackers, and journey often with the Rangers of the North. His daughter becomes the beloved of Aragorn himself, the heir to the thrones of Gondor and Arnor and rightful wielder of Narsil, the sword broken by Sauron when he killed Aragorn's ancestor Elendil.

Narsil is reforged in Rivendell, and renamed Andúril, Flame of the West.

Aragorn has been brought up in Rivendell, and is loved as an adopted son by Elrond. But when Elrond learns that Arwen and Aragorn have fallen in love, he forbids their marriage. Elrond knows the hard choice that comes with the union of a Man and an Elf, and he has no wish to lose his daughter to mortality. Eventually he relents, but only partly, saying that he will allow his daughter to marry no less a man than the King of Gondor and Arnor. Elrond may have set Aragorn this virtually impossible task to ensure the marriage would never happen. But it is more likely that this is the wisdom of Elrond at work, and that his words spur Aragorn on to achieve the seemingly unachievable: the destruction of Sauron and the restoration of Isildur's line in Gondor and Arnor.

After the defeat of Sauron and the end of the Third Age, the Elves' time is truly over. They must

> 'depart into the West, or dwindle to a rustic folk of dell and cave, slowly to forget and be forgotten.' [192]

From the glorious, awe-inspiring, almost god-like figures of the First Age, through the secretive and subtle, though still wise and powerful, figures of the Third Age, the Elves are always central to the fate of Middle-earth. But the defeat of Sauron and the destruction of the One Ring is also their end. As Galadriel foresees, those Elves who do not sail for the West will diminish and be forgotten. The Fourth Age is the Age of Men, and from that time on the Elves play no part in its history, for better or for worse.

The Ents

The Ents are the 'Shepherds of the Trees'. Back in the time of darkness, before the awakening of the Elves or the creation of the Stars, Sun or Moon, the goddess of the Earth, Yavanna,[193] was afraid for the growing things of her domain. While animals could run and hide, the trees had no protection against the Dark Lord's evil, and the axes of his Orcs. But Ilúvatar, the Creator, spoke to Yavanna and said that he had heard her prayers. Powerful spirits answered her call and took the forms of living trees to protect the forests. While originally Maiar, once the spirits had taken shape they were bound to their new forms and became the race of Ents.

Ents vary in appearance as much as the trees they love, resembling huge oaks or birches or firs. All are tall, at least twelve feet high, and are covered in a rough skin that resembles bark. The oldest have beards of moss and their fingers and toes, which can number anything between three and nine, resemble branches and roots. Those fingers are as strong as the roots of an ancient oak, cracking and splintering stone or steel, and doing a century's worth of damage in seconds. Due to their tree form, Ents sleep standing up, and can barely bend in the middle. The Ents are so long-lived as to be practically immortal, although they are prone to becoming more tree-like over time, growing sleepier and eventually becoming indistinguishable from the forests they protect. Mysteriously, the same process works in reverse, with some trees 'waking up' and becoming more Ent-like. Due to their immense lifespan, all Ents are slow, but not slow-witted like Trolls. Rather they think in terms of seasons rather than minutes. The Entish language reflects this, being a low, rumbling tongue that takes hours to say anything:

'It is a lovely language, but it takes a very long time to say anything in it, because we do not say anything in it, unless it is worth taking a long time to say...' [194]

For convenience, however, the Ents use Westron, the common tongue of Men, or else one of the Elvish tongues, to speak with the other races. No non-Ent, not even Gandalf, has ever mastered theirs.

Fangorn is the oldest of the Ents, living in the forest originally named after him. Better known as Treebeard, he takes in the Hobbits, Merry and Pippin, after they escape from the Uruk-hai. Interestingly, some of the power of the Ents comes from the water they drink, the Entwash. Merry and Pippin drink some of the cool, refreshing liquid while with Treebeard and begin to grow – becoming the tallest Hobbits ever recorded. Ancient and awesome, Treebeard himself is one of the very first Ents, remembering a time when almost all of Middle-earth was forested. By the time of the War of the Ring, only a few patches of the old woods remain. It is Treebeard who calls the council of Ents to discuss the threat posed by Saruman, and it is he who leads the assault on Isengard.

The Trees shepherded by the Ents are known as Huorns. The Huorns are also active, able to move and attack their enemies. Although intelligent, they are wilder and more primitive than the Ents, and far more vicious and cruel. The dark, malevolent atmosphere of Fangorn felt by Merry and Pippin is caused by the Huorns watching them. Huorns also have the power to wrap themselves in shadow, moving so swiftly and silently that, before their victims even realise something is wrong, they are surrounded by the branches of the Huorns. Old Man Willow, the tree that tries to eat Pippin in the Old Forest, is a Huorn, although it is Tom Bombadil rather than an Ent that tends that particular wood. When the Ents march to war they herd whole forests of Huorns, which can swallow even the most powerful army without trace.

Although when roused to anger the fury of the Ents is terrifying and almost unstoppable, they are never rash, taking an age to make any decision. This reluctance to be hasty is illustrated by the fact that there are only two recorded instances of the Ents going to war. The Dwarves were never popular with the Tree-herds, as their axes were used to cut wood. In the First Age the Dwarven Army of Nogrod sacked the Elven kingdom of Doriath, following their murder of King Thingol Greycloak. The King's wife was Melian the Maia,[195] one of the most powerful figures of the First Age. When he dies, she, in grief, withdraws her protection, known as the Girdle of Melian, from Doriath and returns to the Undying Lands. This, in turn, allows the Dwarves to attack the woodland kingdom. When the Dwarves march home, Beren, the son-in-law of Thingol and Melian, ambushes them. Part of the army escapes the ambush, only to meet a forest of Ents and Huorns. The Ents slaughter every last Dwarf in revenge.

In the Third Age it is Saruman who feels the wrath of the forests. When Treebeard learns of the treachery of the wizard from the Hobbits, he calls an Entish council. After a remarkably swift three days of debate, they march to war, a very hasty decision for the Ents. This is because the Tree-herds are individually already angry and concerned at the activities of Saruman's Orcs, who have chopped down large sections of the forest and already wounded several Ents. But the Ents have their revenge. When Saruman's army is routed by the Rohirrim at Helm's Deep, the Uruks and Wild Men of Dunlending flee into a dark forest that has sprung up overnight. None are heard of again. Then, when Gandalf and King Théoden arrive at Isengard itself, they find it already under the control of Treebeard. The Ents have torn the stones of the stronghold apart like paper, with only the magical walls of the Tower of Orthanc resisting them, a vivid illustration of their terrifying fury:

> '...striding and storming like a howling gale, breaking pillars,
> hurling avalanches of boulders... tossing up huge slabs of
> stone into the air like leaves...' [196]

Although vulnerable to fire and axe, the Ents' immense strength and power makes them utterly devastating when working in concert. But despite all their strength, by the time of *The Lord of the Rings* the Ents are actually a dying race. Their partners, the Entwives, have been lost and no new children, or Entings, are being made, meaning eventually that all the Ents will fall asleep or 'go treeish'. While the male Ents cared for, and resembled, the great trees of the Forest like the oak and the fir, the Entwives cultivated the crops of the field or orchard, like corn or apples. Many years before the War of the Ring, the Entwives left Fangorn and crossed the Anduin, teaching the local men many secrets and sharing their knowledge. Unfortunately, Sauron discovered their presence and without the protection of the Ents he destroyed them. When Treebeard went to look for them, and Fimbrethil his own beloved in particular, he found their garden paradise a wasteland and the Entwives gone.

This means, despite the defeat of Sauron and Saruman and the Entish victory, that it is only a matter of time before these great guardians of the forest are lost forever amid the woods they once cared for.

HOBBITS

Nothing is known about the exact origins of this peculiar race. The Hobbits themselves have no records, or even legends, other than a time spent just to the east of the Misty Mountains, followed by their moving west and settling in Eriador, in the lands around the Shire, in the Third Age. The great histories of the Elves or Men, that record the important events of earlier times, pay no attention to this insignificant race. But it is precisely this insignificance that makes the Hobbits so important in the defeat of Sauron and the destruction of the One Ring.

All Hobbits consider themselves as being descended from three distinct groups, the Harfoots, the Stoors and the Fallohides. Hobbits of Harfoot stock are shorter than others, and prefer hillsides and hobbit holes. They are the most common type of Hobbit. The Stoors are heavier, with larger feet and the ability to grow a beard, and prefer rivers and flatlands. They followed the Harfoots west, staying longer by the banks of the River Anduin. The Fallohides are the least common of the three breeds, but also the most adventurous. They prefer trees and woodlands, and are less skilled with handicrafts than the others, although better at hunting and more skilled with language and songs.

However, all Hobbits have much in common. Between two and four feet tall, they are all very stealthy, and disdainful of the clumsiness and noise of the 'big folk'. They wear no shoes, having hairy feet with tough soles. They are as skilled at hiding and sneaking as the Silvan Elves, although there is no magic involved. They are all close to the land, and dislike any technology more advanced than a loom or waterwheel. Although they had originally all lived in holes in the ground, by the time of the War of the Ring most Hobbits live in houses, the art of building having been learnt from Men. They all have good eyesight and hearing, and are good archers or stone throwers. However, they are anything but warlike, and any weapons they possess in the Shire are kept in the local museum. All Hobbits love their food, and apparently like at least six meals a day. And of vital importance to wizards and Dwarves is their discovery of pipe-weed, and the invention of the habit of pipe smoking.

Far less obvious, in these seemingly innocuous creatures, is their inner strength. This is both mental and physical, and proves to be vital to the events of the end of the Third Age. No one but the Hobbits could have destroyed the One Ring of Sauron, and saved Middle-earth. This may seem to be a bold statement, but it is undeniably true. The Hobbits' combination of humility and insignificance, together with their quite remarkable toughness, makes them a unique combination which manages to surprise everyone involved in the quest to unmake the Ring, even the non-Hobbit who knows them best and has the most faith in them, Gandalf.[197]

The first reason for the Hobbits' success is their complete unimportance, combined with their plain 'good sense'. The One Ring was a dreadful creation, which augmented the power of anyone who used it, but corrupted with evil as it did so. Any of the great – whether Man, Elf or even Dwarf – would have found their own power and strength of will boosted enormously by the Ring's power. But the temptation to use this power, even for nothing but the best motives, would have given the Ring a hold over them which would have had only one outcome: disaster and a new Dark Lord. Goodness or pure motives alone are not enough to resist such corruption. The warriors and sorcerers who used the Nine Rings all fell under Sauron's influence, and the only difference that their original 'goodness' made was the amount of time it took for them to succumb. Although such figures as Galadriel and Gandalf prove their own virtue by refusing to take the Ring, they would still have succumbed to its influence if they had actually been forced to carry it for any length of time. Gandalf fears even to touch it, so great is his awareness of the risks:

'sooner or later – later, if he is strong or well meaning to
begin with, but neither strength nor good purpose will last
... the dark power will devour him.' [198]

Yet Bilbo carries the Ring for 60 years. In that time he uses its power infrequently, having no need to do so, and then only for minor tricks such as avoiding unwelcome guests. It is precisely because of Bilbo's lack of ambition, power and significance that the Ring has so little power over him. Likewise Gollum, although quickly turned into a pitiful and evil creature by the influence of the Ring, makes no real use of it at all. While he lives in his secret hideaway underneath the Misty Mountains, where he is first discovered by Bilbo in *The Hobbit*, Gollum uses the most powerful and dangerous item in all of Middle-earth for nothing more than easy fishing and the occasional murder of a lone Orc. When Sam carries the Ring, albeit briefly, it tempts him with a vision chosen directly from his subconscious. The greatest temptation that can be mustered is the sight of all the dead lands of Mordor turned into a beautiful garden. But even this simple and personal, though beautiful, vision is resisted by the Hobbit through his love of Frodo and his own 'good sense':

> deep down in him lived still unconquered his plain hobbit-sense... The one small garden of a free gardener was all his need and due... [199]

This lack of power, ambition and 'greatness', which gives the Ring so little to work on, means its malign influence is far, far less on Bilbo, Frodo and Sam, or even Gollum, than it would have been on even the weakest Man or Elf. Another weakening influence on the Ring was the remoteness of both Gollum and Bilbo. Gollum lurks deep underneath a mountain, Bilbo in an insignificant village in an unimportant corner of the world. This means that Sauron's searching eye is unaware of the Ring's reappearance for many, many years, a delay that would in the end prove fatal.

But even more vital to the quest to destroy the Ring is the Hobbits' incredible toughness, both their mental strength and their physical endurance. After the Black Riders injure Frodo on Weathertop they immediately retreat, believing the power of the morgul-knife will subvert Frodo within mere hours. A shard from the magical blade has entered the Hobbit's shoulder and is working towards his heart. Under its malign influence, Frodo becomes much more vulnerable to the power of the Ringwraiths, Sauron and the Ring. But Frodo resists such powerful sorcery for a total of 17 days, something that amazes even Gandalf:

> 'it seems that Hobbits fade very reluctantly. I have known strong warriors of the Big People who would quickly have been overcome by that splinter...' [200]

Despite the rather comic and ineffectual appearance of Hobbits, under-neath they are stronger than anyone imagines. Merry and Pippin are driven by the Orcs across half of Rohan, maltreated and wounded, and yet still retain the strength of will to give a signal to the pursuing Aragorn, Legolas and Gimli and to escape when the opportunity aris-es. Pippin here also displays a quick wit and the famed Hobbit 'good sense'. He is able to free himself but keep this hidden from the Orcs. Pippin then discards his Elven brooch as a sign to his comrades, and finally tricks the Orc Grishnákh with hints of the Ring, enabling he and Merry to escape when things look at their most desperate.

This physical stamina is aided by wills of iron. The power of the Ring, which grants immortality to its wearer, comes at a price. The wearer slow-ly fades and turns into a wraith, becoming part of the shadow world inhab-ited by Sauron and his Nazgûl. Yet Gollum, after almost 500 years, is still whole, although pale and thin and mentally tormented. Bilbo, after bear-ing the Ring for more than 60 years, still seems remarkably untouched:

> 'I feel all thin, sort of *stretched*, if you know what I mean:
> like butter that has been scraped over too much bread.' [201]

The Ring's influence can be seen in Bilbo's 'accidentally' forgetting to leave it for Frodo and his violent suspicion and reaction to Gandalf's urg-ing at the last. But Bilbo's strength of will is so great that he does, in the end, give the Ring up voluntarily – the only creature ever to have actu-ally done so. Frodo carries the burden for a far shorter time, but under far greater pressure and malign influence. It is amazing that such an ordi-nary Hobbit should prove so extraordinary. Frodo is not a great warrior, or a sorcerer, and yet he resists the temptation of the Ring under the direct will of Sauron, on Amon Hen after the treachery of Boromir. Although Gandalf himself aids Frodo, shielding him until Sauron's eye passes, it would have been for nothing if Frodo had yielded. Frodo car-ries the gnawing weight of the Ring for days, through fatigue and pain, in Mordor itself, where Sauron's power is strongest. Again the interven-tion of Gandalf and Aragorn, who keep Sauron's attention firmly direct-ed westwards, helps him – but it is highly unlikely that anyone else could have carried the burden so far without succumbing.

This strength of will and endurance is not just restricted to Frodo. Pippin's foolish decision to look into the Palantír leads him into a direct confrontation with Sauron, and this time there is no Gandalf to intervene. Although saved by Sauron's own impatience and greed, who assumes that Pippin has been captured by Saruman and is in Isengard, Pippin still manages to avoid revealing his mind and all the plans and hopes of the West, when confronted by the most powerful will in all of Middle-earth.

The bravery of the Hobbits may also be surprising to some. As any avid viewer of old war movies will know, courage is not a matter of not being scared when faced with danger. That is stupidity. Courage is when you are afraid of doing something, but overcome that fear and do it anyway. On that score the Hobbits of *The Lord of the Rings* can be said to be the most courageous creatures in Middle-earth. They are small and weak, taken out of familiar territory and placed in some of the most dangerous places in the world. They have no great skills or powers to help them, and yet they acquit themselves admirably. Between them, the four Hobbits in the Company of the Ring are either responsible for, or major players in, the destruction of the One Ring, the death of the Witch-king of Angmar, the rousing of the Ents to destroy Isengard, and the saving of the life of Faramir, the son of the Steward of Gondor. Then, without any outside help, they defeat a fallen Saruman who has taken his revenge on the Shire. All in all, a remarkable list of achievements for so humble a race.

Individually, all the Hobbits are worthy of mention. Although by the time of *The Lord of the Rings* Bilbo Baggins is too old for adventuring, it was his youthful wanderlust that began the whole saga. The discovery of the Ring seemed, at the time, to be incidental to Bilbo's quest with Thorin Oakenshield and the Dwarves to rid the Lonely Mountain of the dragon Smaug.[202] Bilbo found the Ring when lost and helpless in the Goblin caverns underneath the Misty Mountains, as is detailed in *The Hobbit*. After defeating Gollum in a riddle game he discovered, by accident, the Ring's power to grant the wearer invisibility. He uses this power to escape both Gollum and the Orcs and brings the Ring out into the open. At work here is the will of the Ring itself. Gollum's small-mindedness had seen it hidden under a mountain with no hope of returning to its true master, and so it finds another to carry it. Fortunately for the West, it finds Bilbo.

Bilbo proves his courage and his wits beyond doubt during the course of his quest. It is he who rescues the Dwarves from the Elves of Mirkwood, tricks Smaug into revealing his one weak spot and steals the Arkenstone to give to the mortal Lord Bard and the Elven-king Thranduil, in an attempt to avert a battle between the Dwarves, Elves and Men. In the end, it is the arrival of the Goblin army that unites these forces, but Bilbo cannot be faulted for trying.

Most admirable, and surprising, is Bilbo's ability voluntarily to give up the Ring to Frodo when he chooses to 'retire' to Rivendell on his eleventy-first, or 111th, birthday. Bilbo is the only Ring-bearer to do such a thing (although Frodo offers the Ring to both Gandalf and Galadriel, but is refused). Bilbo is too old, and too long influenced, for such a dangerous quest as the destruction of the Ring, but it is his example – his friendship with the Elves, his wanderlust, his innate good nature and his strength of character – that inspire the other Hobbits to journey into the unknown.

It is Frodo, Bilbo's nephew, who carries the Ring into Mordor, through quite unimaginable danger and hardship. Frodo's mental and physical strength is astonishing. Despite being wounded by the Black Riders, poisoned by Shelob, manhandled by Orcs and journeying under the most inhospitable conditions, and in the teeth of Sauron's terrible will, Frodo succeeds in reaching Mount Doom. By the end of that journey, every step is torture. As well as the physical hardship of thirst, starvation and exhaustion, Frodo carries the Ring:

> a burden on the body and a torment to his mind. [203]

Such is the power of the Ring that, even without its presence being known, it almost destroys the hobbit – and certainly destroys any pleasure in life, as the lesser Rings have done to the mortal lords who have become the Ringwraiths. [204]

> 'No taste of food, no feel of water, no sound of wind, no memory of tree, grass or flower, no image of moon or star are left to me.' [205]

At the final hurdle, standing before the Crack of Doom where the Ring was made, Frodo finally balks at his task, and is unable to destroy the Ring he has carried for so long. But it is extremely doubtful whether any other creature in all of Middle-earth could have gone so far, or done so well, with such an evil and powerful burden.

Despite his courage and endurance, Frodo would have failed it if it had not been for his faithful companion Sam Gamgee. A simple Hobbit, enchanted from an early age by Bilbo's tales of Elves, Sam endures all that Frodo does out of a love of his friend. Sam's contribution to the quest to destroy the Ring goes far beyond simple moral support and practical good sense. It is Sam who deals with questions of rope, cooking utensils and other routine, though vital, matters. But it is Sam who defeats the evil spider demon Shelob, with help from the Phial of Galadriel,[206] and rescues Frodo from the Orcs of Cirith Ungol. Sam also carries the Ring, if only for a short time, and so comes to understand something of his master's suffering. For all his seeming simplicity, Sam is actually very shrewd. He is the only one to work out Frodo's intentions when he tries to evade the rest of the company and continue the quest to Mordor alone after the treachery of Boromir. Without Sam's practical assistance and unflinching support of Frodo through the Dead Marshes, Ithilien and Mordor itself, the quest to destroy the Ring would surely have failed.

The other two Hobbits, Merry and Pippin, although they are separated from Frodo and the Ring after being captured by Orcs at Amon Hen, also manage to achieve more than would have been thought possible. It is Pippin's quick thinking while in the hands of the Orcs that first alerts the pursuing Aragorn, Gimli and Legolas that they are still alive. Pippin then engineers the escape of both Hobbits into the Forest of Fangorn. While in Fangorn they meet the Ent Treebeard and convince him to call the Entish council that declares war on Isengard. Without the intervention of the Ents, and their destruction of Isengard, Rohan could still have fallen and Saruman could have been victorious, as Théoden's army is in no shape to assail Saruman's stronghold after their costly victory at Helm's Deep. It is while in Fangorn that Pippin and Merry both drink Ent-draughts, the drink of the Ents. This magical liquid, vital to an Enting growing strong and tall, has much the same effect on the Hobbits, turning them quickly into the two tallest Hobbits in the history of the Shire.

Peregrin Took, better known as Pippin, is an impetuous mixture of bravery, quick wits and foolishness. Although he proves both bravery and intelligence in his tricking of the Orcs, he may also be responsible for rousing the Balrog in Moria. It is Pippin who, from curiosity, drops a stone down a well as the Company travels through the Mines. This is swiftly answered by the sound of hammers, apparently Orcs signalling to each other. Later, the lesson unlearnt, Pippin gazes into the Palantír of Orthanc, and is interrogated by Sauron himself. However, both these seeming acts of folly instead prove to work entirely in the favour of the West, and against Sauron.

The meeting with the Balrog of Moria leads to the death of both it and Gandalf. But Gandalf's spirit returns from the dead, as Gandalf the White, more powerful than ever, while the threat of the Balrog is destroyed forever. And Sauron's haste to physically retrieve the hobbit means that he neglects to question him at length, leading to his mistaken assumption that Pippin is a captive of Saruman in the Tower of Orthanc. But equally important is the timely discovery that the stone is actually a Palantír, as Gandalf himself had been thinking of testing it. If he had, and had been caught in a direct battle of wills with Sauron, not only would his presence have been revealed but quite possibly the entire plan to destroy the Ring would have been given away, dooming it to failure.

It is also Pippin who alerts Gandalf to the madness of Denethor, the Steward of Gondor, and prevents the death of Faramir, Denethor's son. He also, despite his small stature, manages to kill one of the mighty Olog-hai in the battle between the armies of the West and Sauron at the gates of Mordor, although he is knocked unconscious by the weight and smell of the Troll when it lands on top of him.

Meriadoc Brandybuck, better known as Merry, also proves the worth of Hobbits. As well as his part in the events leading to the destruction of Isengard, Meriadoc swears allegiance to King Théoden and becomes a squire of Rohan, as Pippin is similarly made a knight of Gondor by Denethor. Journeying with the army of Rohan,

Merry resists the terror of the Nazgûl and helps the shieldmaiden Éowyn, in her disguise as the warrior Dernhelm, to kill the greatest of the Ringwraiths, the Witch-king of Angmar.

But quite possibly the most remarkable Hobbit of all, and certainly the most notorious, is Gollum himself. Originally a Stoor known as Sméagol, he was fishing with his friend Déagol on his birthday when Déagol found the Ring. Sméagol demands the Ring as a birthday present and strangles his friend when he refuses to hand it over. As his possession of the Ring begins, so it continues, as Sméagol uses its power to steal and spy until his own family throw him out. Under the influence of the Ring, Sméagol becomes Gollum, named after the gurgling noise he makes in his throat. He becomes a pitiful and wretched thing, thin and bony, with huge eyes. Hiding from the Sun under the Misty Mountains, he is consumed with hate, loathing the light and all living things, as well as the dark and even the Ring itself.

If any more proof of the toughness of Hobbits is needed, Gollum is it. He possesses the Ring for more than 500 years, its power extending his life far beyond its natural span, and yet he resists being turned into a wraith or creature of shadow. Instead, the Ring torments his mind, always trying to find its way back to its true master. The mere fact that Gollum proves intractable for century after century, hiding always in the dark under the mountains, is astonishing. But even more astonishing are Gollum's actions after the Ring abandons him for Bilbo. Driven by his all-consuming lust for the Ring, he braves the Sun and the outside world to hunt for the Hobbit.

It is that search which leads him to Mordor, where he is captured by Sauron and interrogated. This is how Sauron learns of the Ring's rediscovery and the existence of 'Baggins' and the Shire. Gollum is released by Sauron, but his will is so strong that even after meeting Sauron in person, the most powerful creature in all of Middle-earth, Gollum still retains a selfish desire to take the Ring for himself and cheat the Dark Lord. It is hard to imagine any other figure in Middle-earth who could have been subject to the direct will of Sauron, and yet not be enslaved, especially after 500 years of being tormented by the will of the Ring.

Gollum is captured by Aragorn, after eight years of searching, and imprisoned by the Elves of Mirkwood. But his determination from then on is worthy of admiration, although his motives deserve condemnation. Gollum escapes from the Elves of Mirkwood and continues to hunt the Ring. He is so skilled at stealth and sneaking, after centuries of practice, that while following Frodo and the Ring he evades capture by Aragorn, the greatest tracker in all of Middle-earth, the Elves of Lórien, the Rangers of Ithilien and the Orcs of Mordor. His remarkable talent for survival, as well as his desperation, can be seen in his pact with a creature as evil, selfish and powerful as Shelob – to provide better food for her larder.

If the journey of Frodo and Sam to Mount Doom is an incredible story of endurance and survival, no less so is that of Gollum's pursuit. And in the end, despite Gollum's crimes, it is only due to him that the Ring is finally destroyed at all. The hobbit, or former hobbit, that found the Ring more than 500 years before, is the same one who finally carries it to both their destructions.

After the defeat of Sauron, the Hobbits have one last battle to fight. Upon returning to the Shire, they discover the depths to which Saruman has fallen. Under the name Sharkey, the wizard is ruling as a petty tyrant over Hobbiton and the neighbouring areas, destroying the land the Hobbits hold so dear. Without any help from Gandalf or any of the Kings or Lords they have met on their journeys, the Hobbits defeat Sharkey and his ruffians, proving they are, in Gandalf's words:

> 'Grown indeed very high; among the great you are, and I have no longer any fear at all for any of you.' [207]

All that remains, once the Shire is free, is for the Ring-bearers, Frodo and Bilbo, to travel to the West in the company of some of the most powerful figures of the Third Age. Along with Gandalf, Galadriel and Elrond, the two hobbits, rewarded with this special grace for their vital role in the destruction of the Ring and Sauron, sail to the paradise of the Undying Lands. They leave the Shire behind them to revert once more to a sleepy country, full of contented Hobbits, in a forgotten corner of the world.

Men

Men are the second born race, called the Atani or Edain by the Elves who came first. While the Elves awoke in a world lit by the stars, by the time of the birth of Men, the Sun and the Moon were in existence. Originating in the dark lands of the East, the first Elves met by Men were the Wild or Dark Elves, the Silvan Elves. [208] Hearing of the lands to the West, and the gods who dwelt there, three kindreds of Men travelled to Beleriand where the Elves were battling Morgoth, the original Dark Lord.

Although there was initially some mistrust between the Sindar and Silvan Elves and the Edain, many of the great Noldor kings quickly accepted Men as extra warriors in the war against Morgoth. The three peoples who came west, the Houses of Bëor the Old, Marach and the Haladin, become known as Elf-friends. Almost all the races of Men who were later to fight against Sauron, from the Dúnedain to the Rohirrim, are descended from these three Houses.

The Men of the House of Bëor are dark haired, with grey eyes and the closest in temperament to the Noldor. They are always eager and quick to learn, skilled craftsmen and lovers of lore.

Those of the House of Marach are the most warlike. They are brave, strong and tall as well as quick to anger or laugh. They are mostly blonde and blue eyed.

The third House of Elf-friends is the woodland people called the Haladin, known later as the House of Haleth. They are more solitary in nature, shorter and less eager to learn all the skills the Elves wish to teach. They are also dark haired and dark eyed.

All three of these Houses, having been taught directly by the Elves, are greater than the Men who follow, collectively known as Easterlings, in order to differentiate them from the Edain. Although Tolkien uses the word Edain generically to mean second born, or Men, it is often used to refer only to the Houses of the Elf-friends. The Easterlings, who came into Beleriand later, are short and broad with dark hair and dark eyes. Two Houses of these Eastern Men are mentioned in the histories of the First Age. One, that of Bór, faithfully fights Morgoth. The other, the House of Ulfang the Black, betrays the Elves to the Dark

Lord. The Fifth Battle, or the Battle of Unnumbered Tears, when Morgoth finally breaks the Elven resistance to his rule in Beleriand, is only won because of the treachery of the Easterlings of Ulfang.

What is more surprising is that such treachery is so rare. Men awoke in the East of Middle-earth, a region almost entirely dominated by Morgoth. Unlike the Elves, the Valar did not send an emissary to summon them to the West, or go to war to protect them. Fortunately for Mankind, the dark god's attention is focussed on the West and the crushing of his enemies in Beleriand, and he does not give the corruption of Men the attention it requires. But he does cast a great shadow over the whole race, a shadow that means they are always easier to corrupt, enslave and turn to treachery than the Elves.

Morgoth's malign influence has two main results. The first is to sow dissension between Men and Elves, to divide his foes. As we saw in the Lessening of the Ages chapter, this is always one of the prime tactics of evil, and one of its most successful. Although the three Houses of the Elf-friends all fight Morgoth, and are instrumental in his downfall, they also bring misery and disaster to many of the Elven kingdoms.

The second, and even more despicable, effect of Morgoth's lies is to turn death from a blessing into a curse, casting a great shadow over Men's lives. While the Elves are immortal, Ilúvatar gives Men a different fate, to die and go onto something else. This is intended as a blessing. Men will strive to achieve things in a short lifetime, without the centuries the Elves have at their disposal to wander or to waste. The afterlife should also have been a thing of joy and anticipation. Men were intended to go into Ilúvatar's great design, presumably some sort of Heaven, without fear or trepidation. But Morgoth uses lies, deceit and malice to turn the thought of death into a terrible fear, of darkness and the unknown. This is the greatest of his crimes against Men. For the rest of time the fear of death will be a constant friend of evil, leading Men to follow the Shadow with the promise of eternal life and an escape from mortality.

Although all are mortal, the 'greatness' of any particular race of Men can almost always be seen by measuring their lifespan. Those peoples who serve the Shadow always live shorter lives, despite the promises of the Dark Lord which they serve. On the other hand, those races closest to the Elves in both blood and temperament and 'goodness' almost always live longer. The people of the Three Houses of the Elf friends all have a lifespan of centuries. The Dúnedain of Númenor, their Second Age descendants, are all blessed with a long life. The wisdom of those Dúnedain is also shown in the fact that their kings abdicate in favour of their children while still whole in mind and body, not waiting for infirmity and senility to take them. When they later turn away from the Valar, becoming cruel and proud, their lifespan shortens and they abandon this practice, holding greedily onto power until death takes them. Likewise, in the Third Age, the slow decline in the power and wisdom of the Dúnedain is marked by a decline in their lifespan.

Although the Elves dominate the events of the First Age of the Sun, Men do play an important part in the struggle against Morgoth. Certain heroes undertake great deeds, and are as powerful as the highest Elven Lords. However, such heroes are also the carriers of great Dooms, and suffering often follows in their wake.

Beren is the first man to marry an Elf. His destiny, or Doom, is so great that not even the Girdle of Melian around Doriath can keep him out of the kingdom. There he meets, and falls in love with, Lúthien Tinúviel, the most beautiful Elf ever to live in Middle-earth. Her father, Thingol, demands a Silmaril from Morgoth's Iron Crown as her dowry. Against all the odds, after a long and dangerous journey and at first the cost of his hand, then his life, Beren succeeds. By Lúthien's intervention with Mandos, Beren is permitted to escape death and to live again, but when he dies a second time, of old age, Lúthien dies with him, as a mortal. For this loss alone the Elves would call the story a tragedy, but the gift of the Silmaril itself leads eventually to the destruction of Doriath and the second Kinslaying of Elf by Elf.

Túrin Turambar is another great hero, the slayer of the first dragon, Glaurung.[209] Unfortunately, he also kills his best friend, the Sindar Elf Lord Beleg Strongbow, abandons his Elven beloved to her death, and marries his sister under a spell of forgetfulness. In the end, after killing Glaurung – the cause of much of his misery – he kills himself.

Túrin's father Húrin was the mightiest mortal warrior to have ever lived, and a friend of the Elven King Turgon of the hidden realm of

Gondolin. But his story is actually the most tragic of all. He is captured by Morgoth at the Battle of Unnumbered Tears and chained in a high tower to watch all the events of Middle-earth, interpreted through Morgoth's lies and malice. After 28 years of torture, incredibly still unbroken but embittered, Húrin is released. Morgoth claims Húrin's freedom is granted out of pity, but of course it is merely another act of cunning cruelty.

Seeing him released with pomp and ceremony by Morgoth's own forces, Húrin's own people believe him a traitor and shun him. The hero travels to the vicinity of Gondolin and calls out to Turgon and the Eagles of Manwë to let him in. They also think him a traitor and ignore him, but the damage is already done. Morgoth's spies are following Húrin and now know the general area where the hidden stronghold of Gondolin is located. They concentrate their efforts on the area until they catch the Elf Maeglin, and convince him to turn traitor, spelling the end of Gondolin.

But Húrin's Doom is not yet finished. He then travels to Doriath, having found the graves of his son and daughter and watched his wife die of a broken heart. Although the power of Melian the Maia breaks Morgoth's hold on his mind, allowing Húrin to find peace, the mortal hero gives King Thingol the Nauglamír. This necklace is a great Dwarven treasure, found in the ruined city of Nargothrond, where Húrin's son Túrin had killed Glaurung. This final act brings doom to a second Elven kingdom, as Thingol's decision to employ Dwarves to attach the Silmaril, brought by Beren, onto the Nauglamír leads to the Elven King's murder. [210]

But Men do not only bring disaster. The hero Tuor, aided by none other than the Vala Ulmo himself, becomes a great lord in Turgon's hidden Elven kingdom of Gondolin before its fall. So high does Tuor rise in the Elven King's eyes that he is even allowed to marry Turgon's daughter Idril. Although this match enrages the jealous Elf Maeglin, who betrays the kingdom to Morgoth, Tuor and Idril escape its destruction. It is their son Eärendil, the result of the second marriage of Elves and Men, who sails to the West and convinces the Valar to take pity on both Men and Elves and to intervene against Morgoth.

Thus although the First Age is dominated by the actions of the Elves, with Men as supporting players, it is a figure representing both peoples that saves Middle-earth. From then on, the role and importance of the Elves will decline, and that of Men increase.

After the overthrow of Morgoth, the gods rewarded the three faithful Houses of Elf-friends. The Maiar, the servants of the Valar, went among them and taught them many skills and great knowledge and wisdom. They were given the Island of Númenor as their home, specially raised in sight of the Undying Lands. The three peoples mingled, becoming known as the Dúnedain, or Men of the West, and became the greatest of their race that has ever been. They became taller, stronger and longer-lived than any other men, with great wisdom and learning that rivalled the Elves. The disadvantage of this longevity was that they had few children and bred slowly.

Elros, the son of Eärendil and Elwing, was their first king, ruling for 410 years. The Half-elven, or Peredhil, were forced to choose between the races of their parents, to live as either Men or Elves. The first son of Eärendil and Elwing, Elrond, chose immortality, and played a crucial role in *The Lord of the Rings*. [211] The second son and brother of Elrond, Elros, chose mortality and became the greatest of the new race of Dúnedain.

The decline of the Dúnedain of Númenor into pride and folly is detailed in the Lessening of the Ages chapter, but it is appropriate to say here that at the height of their power they were the greatest force in Middle-earth in the Second Age. This was the beginning of the decline of the Elves and the dominance of Men. While the Elven havens were still great, their numbers and their great Lords were far fewer than in the previous age. They also had little to do with the other peoples of Middle-earth, and kept themselves mainly to their own affairs. This allowed the Númenoreans to found a series of trading coastal kingdoms, which later became colonies and dominated the lesser men of the mainland. Although the Dúnedain individually could not match the greatest of the Elves, as a whole they were their equals, and in their direct influence on Middle-earth, they surpassed them.

But this independence and strength, unmatched militarily, did not protect them from the Shadow. Their final descent into evil comes about under the influence of Sauron but their initial decline, shown clearly by their growing obsession with death and how to avoid it, is nobody's fault but their own. The shadow cast upon the hearts and minds of Men by Morgoth, back in the First Age, continues even after the Black Enemy is thrust outside the world into the Void. While Sauron became the focus and ruler of the old minions of Morgoth, the seeds of evil planted by Morgoth can never be entirely rooted out, and bear fruit without any outside influence.

Pride leads to the Dúnedain turning away from the Valar, resenting the ban placed on their sailing west to the Undying Lands. They change from the wise and benevolent teachers and trading partners of the other men of Middle-earth to tyrannical empire-builders. Ar-Pharazôn, the last ruler of Númenor, takes the title King of the World, and sails with a huge army to destroy Sauron. But his reason is not an altruistic desire to defeat a Lord of evil, but rather a selfish pride that brooks no rivals. Sauron surrenders without a fight, seeing the might of the Númenorean army, but swiftly becomes the chief adviser of the King, persuading him to rebellion against the Valar. That rebellion, as detailed in the Lessening of the Ages chapter, leads to the total destruction of Númenor and the survival of only a few faithful Dúnedain led by Elendil, as well as some Black Númenoreans, who are fortunate enough to be based in their cruel colonies at the time.

Elendil, with his sons Anárion and Isildur, founds the Dúnedain realms in exile of Gondor and Arnor, the two greatest realms of Men in Middle-earth in the Third Age. But Sauron also survives the destruction of Númenor, although he loses the power to take on a beautiful shape. He marshals his forces in Mordor to finally crush his enemies. Standing against him is the Last Alliance of Elves and Men. Led by Gil-galad, the Elven High King, and Elendil, the King of the Dúnedain Faithful in exile, their armies manage to defeat Sauron, but at great cost. Anárion dies in the war, while Sauron kills both Gil-galad and Elendil. Isildur avenges his father and cuts the One Ring from Sauron's finger, vanquishing him.

The fact that it is a man who defeats Sauron, rather than one of the great Elven Lords, is a sign that the balance of power between the two peoples has shifted. Unfortunately, the Elves have learned wisdom while Men, it appears, have not. Isildur refuses to destroy the Ruling Ring, against the advice of Gil-galad's herald Elrond, and takes it as reparation for his father's death. It is this act of folly that allows Sauron to reform in the Third Age and threaten Middle-earth once again.

The Ring brings its master's killer nothing but evil, as he is soon ambushed by Orcs and attempts to flee by swimming across a river while invisible. The Ring, known henceforth as Isildur's Bane, slips from his finger and is lost in the waters. Until, of course, its discovery nearly 2500 years later by the Hobbit Sméagol – who becomes Gollum under the Ring's foul influence.

But the rise and fall of the Dúnedain of Númenor is not the whole story of Mankind in the Second Age. There are many men in the South and East of Middle-earth who serve neither the Valar nor Morgoth, but live wild and free. Unfortunately, with the defeat of Morgoth, his mortal servants flee Beleriand and swiftly dominate their cousins, becoming kings among them. This means that almost all the men of mainland Middle-earth, with the exception of those areas around the Elven havens and the Númenorean coastal kingdoms, are dominated by Sauron and evil. When the Númenoreans turn to darkness, and even their lands become cruel colonies, it means that there are few men except for the Dúnedain Faithful free from the Shadow.

And it is from these men, touched by the Shadow, that Sauron chooses nine of the greatest to bear his Rings of Power. None are named but all are said to have been great sorcerers, kings or warriors, even before they received the Rings. Three were Dúnedain of Númenor, but six were of the Easterlings, Haradrim or other races of Men from the mainland. The Power of the Nine Rings grants their bearers great wealth, power, glory and exceptionally long life. But the Rings also slowly make that life seem tasteless and miserable. The Rings grant their wearers the power to become invisible, and to see into the shadow world, but they also give Sauron the power to control what they see there. Eventually, all nine become wholly of the shadow world, wraiths under the control of Sauron: the Úlairi or Nazgûl, the Dark Lord's greatest Servants.

Interestingly, not all were evil or corrupt to begin with, although none could resist Sauron's power forever:

> one by one, sooner or later, according to their native strength
> and to the good or evil of their wills in the beginning, they
> fell...under the domination of the One... [212]

In the end all become phantoms, wholly subservient to Sauron and wholly dependent on his power. When Sauron slowly builds up his power in the Third Age, not declaring himself openly until he is sure of victory, it is the Úlairi that he uses to pave the way for his return. The Nazgûl secretly gather armies in Mordor, and capture Minas Ithil from Gondor – later renamed Minas Morgul, or the Tower of Black Sorcery – the stronghold originally set to keep watch on the Land of Shadow. It is the greatest of the Nine, the Witch-king, who commands the evil armies of Angmar and successfully divides and destroys the Northern Dúnedain realms of Rhudaur, Cardolan and Arthedain. And it is the Black Riders that Sauron sends to the Shire to find the One Ring, and who chase Frodo and the others to Rivendell.

The Nazgûl have no true physical form, but exist solely as spirits in the shadow world. When Frodo puts on the One Ring on Weathertop, he sees their forms as they appeared when still living. The Ring's power to turn its wearer invisible makes them a part of the spirit world of Sauron and the Black Riders, thus making Frodo even more vulnerable to their power.

Those powers are formidable. Although the Nazgûl's eyesight is poor, being restricted to the shadow world, the hearing and smell of the Ringwraiths is far better than a normal man's. Their evil presence alone causes fear and panic among their enemies, and their breath is poison. They carry special weapons, the Morgul-knives, which break off inside their enemies, quickly finding their hearts and turning their victim into another wraith, a weaker version of themselves. Weapons that strike the Nazgûl melt upon touching them. On top of these supernatural powers, they also possess their own skills as warriors or sorcerers from life. Although the Nazgûl could be individually faced down by the greatest of heroes, together they were nigh unstoppable.

The Nazgûl do have some weaknesses, however. Weapons forged by the Elves or the Dúnedain of Númenor can harm them, although the weapon is still destroyed in the process. The Nazgûl are also, oddly, afraid of fire, although they can face it if they have to. But one of the most powerful weapons against them is the name of the holiest of the Valar, the Queen of the Heavens who created the Stars, Elbereth Gilthoniel. Even when the Ringwraiths are seemingly defeated, they are very hard to kill. Their bodies could be destroyed, as they are by the flood of the river outside Rivendell, but their spirits would then fly back to Mordor to be reclothed in another body by Sauron. Although the Witch-king is destroyed by the Rohirrim shieldmaiden Éowyn, in her disguise of the warrior Dernhelm – aided by Merry, one of the Hobbits – his death would have been temporary if Sauron had been victorious. But the destruction of the One Ring finally vanquishes both the Dark Lord and all his nine servants.

In the Third Age, the learning of the Dúnedain split Men into three general groups, as Faramir tells Frodo and Sam in Ithilien:

> 'the High, or Men of the West, which were Númenoreans;
> and the Middle Peoples, Men of the Twilight....and the Wild,
> the Men of Darkness.' [213]

The High Men are the Dúnedain of Gondor and Arnor, the Black Númenoreans and the Corsairs of Umbar. Although they still counted themselves as greater than the other men of Middle-earth, by the end of the Third Age the difference was lessening. A low birth rate had led to interbreeding with the common men of their areas, resulting in a shorter lifespan, while time and constant wars had led to a decline in their learning and lore.

All the Dúnedain are tall, dark haired and grey eyed. They were descended from the great lords of old, and even those who had turned to evil were still mighty among Men. By the time of the War of the Ring, Gondor was the foremost realm of the Dúnedain. The Northern realm of Arnor had long since been destroyed by the greatest of the Ringwraiths, the Witch-king of Angmar. The rise and decline of these two Dúnedain realms in exile is dealt with in detail in the Lessening of the Ages chapter, but here we can mention some of the foremost figures in the story.

The ruler of Gondor during the War of the Ring is the Steward Denethor, father of Boromir and Faramir. Denethor had been a great and powerful noble but he was also proud and had used the Palantír to match his strength against that of Sauron, which eventually drove him to madness and death. His son Boromir was a great warrior and joined the Company of the Ring, but he succumbs to temptation and attempts

to wrest the One Ring from Frodo. It is this act that leads to the break-
ing of the Fellowship, and to Frodo and Sam choosing to journey to
Mordor alone. Boromir soon repents and dies unsuccessfully defending
Merry and Pippin from a great band of Orcs. More on Boromir and, in
particular, Denethor's struggle with Sauron, is detailed in the
Lessening of the Ages chapter.

Arnor had long been destroyed by the time of *The Lord of the Rings*,
the only remnants of its strength being the Rangers of the North. These
Dúnedain, who travel the wilds of the North fighting the creatures of
Sauron, are the descendants of the last Kings and Nobles of Arthedain.
Their chief is none other than Aragorn, the direct descendant of Isildur.

Aragorn is not only a great warrior and Ranger, the rightful heir to
the thrones of both Gondor and Arnor, but also the greatest mortal in
Middle-earth. He had been fostered as an adopted son by Elrond himself
in Rivendell and had fallen in love with Elrond's daughter Arwen. But
Elrond forbade their marriage, not wanting to lose his daughter, until
Aragorn was King of both Gondor and Arnor. By the time of the War of
the Ring, there was little Aragorn had not done. In his youth he had
served as a captain in the armies of both Gondor and Rohan, as well as
travelling deep into the wild lands to the South and East. He had journeyed with, and learned much from, the wizard Gandalf and was a welcome guest in both Rivendell and Lothlórien. Galadriel's daughter
Celebrían had been the wife of Elrond, before her death in an Orc
ambush many years before, and Arwen was Galadriel's granddaughter.
The Elven Queen supported the match and gave much advice and wisdom to Aragorn. By the time of *The Lord of the Rings* Aragorn was

> the most hardy of living Men, skilled in their crafts and lore,
> and was yet more than they; for he was elven-wise [214]

It is Aragorn, under the name of Strider, who escorts the four Hobbits
from Bree to Rivendell, battling the Black Riders along the way.
Aragorn is second in command of the Company of the Ring, taking over
its leadership when the Balrog kills Gandalf. When a distraction is desperately needed to turn Sauron's attention away from Frodo and his

perilous journey through Mordor, it is Aragorn who gazes into the Palantír. This action directly challenges the Dark Lord, something not even Gandalf or Galadriel have ever risked, and plays on Sauron's fear that one of the great among his enemies will take the Ring and use it against him. As the heir of Isildur, the Dúnedain King who defeated Sauron at the end of the Second Age, Aragorn is the obvious choice for such a gamble. The time of Men is coming, with the waning of the Elves, and Aragorn is the greatest of them. Fortunately, Aragorn is wiser than his ancestor and sees the need to destroy the Ring rather than use it, in stark contrast to the greatest Men of Gondor, Denethor and Boromir. Confirmation of Aragorn's status as rightful heir to the thrones of the Dúnedain nations, if any is needed, comes when Aragorn enters the Paths of the Dead and commands the Army of the Dead to follow him against Sauron. Bound by an oath made to Isildur, they obey.

After the defeat of Sauron, Aragorn is crowned King Elessar, the monarch of both Gondor and the old realm of Arnor. He marries Arwen Evenstar at last, with Elrond's blessing, and rules for the first 120 years of the Fourth Age. His marriage to Arwen, the last union of Men and Elves, harks back to the great unions of the First Age and closes the joint histories of the two peoples. After the death of King Elessar, the Elves will wane and the history of Middle-earth will be a history of Men.

But the High Men of the Third Age are not all enemies of Sauron. The Black Númenoreans, who survived the destruction of their homeland, continue to fight against Gondor from their home of Umbar. As well as being the most strategic port of the South, Umbar is where the Dúnedain Army that had humbled Sauron and carried him back to Númenor in chains had landed in the Second Age. Gondor eventually defeats the Black Númenoreans after a thousand years of the Third Age, making Umbar a Gondorian stronghold and allowing Gondor to dominate the lands of the Haradwaith. Unfortunately, after the Kin-strife five centuries later, the exiled supporters of Castamir the Usurper occupy the port and use it as their base to harry and war with Gondor until the end of the Third Age. They become known as the Corsairs of Umbar, and are only finally defeated by Aragorn and the Army of the Dead in the War of the Ring.

The Middle Men, or Men of Twilight, are those lesser peoples of the

North West of Middle-earth who are not Dúnedain but who fight against Sauron. These people are sometimes known collectively as the Northmen, but include such disparate peoples as the Men of Dale, the Beornings and the Rohirrim. These are all descended from the Elf-friends from the First Age, the Houses of Bëor, Malach and Haladin, but from those who refused to go to Númenor and stayed instead in Middle-earth. Although they are not blessed with the same gifts of learning and long life as the Dúnedain, they are still enemies of Sauron. Several important figures from Bilbo's adventures in *The Hobbit* are Men of Twilight. Bard the Bowman, who kills the dragon Smaug, is a Lord of the Men of Dale, and his line become the kings of that region after him. The Beornings are few in number, but as well as being vegetarians who are famous for their honey cakes, they are fearless warriors with special powers. Some among them can transform themselves into bears. Beorn, the Beorning shape-changer who aids the Dwarves on their journey to the Lonely Mountain, is one of these. His intervention in the Battle of the Five Armies is decisive. In the shape of a huge bear he rescues the dying Dwarf Thorin Oakenshield from the battlefield, before singlehandedly smashing his way through the Goblin bodyguard to crush their leader, Bolg.

But the most important of the Middle Men, at least militarily, are the Rohirrim. Originally a group of Northmen known as the Éothéd, they are unmatched horsemen who come to the aid of Gondor against an army of Orcs and Easterlings in the early 26th century of the Third Age. They are rewarded with the gift of the land of Rohan. From this time they take their new name of Rohirrim, or Horse Lords, and remain staunch allies of Gondor. They are the greatest heavy cavalry in Middle-earth, and, in the War of the Ring, defeat the armies of Saruman before, once again, riding to the rescue of Gondor.

The Rohirrim are tall and blonde, speaking their own language of Rohirric as well as the common tongue of Westron. Their King at the time of the War of the Ring is Théoden. Théoden falls under the malicious influence of Saruman, through the traitor Gríma Wormtongue. This dark influence not only enfeebles him, but also turns him against his nephew Éomer. Gandalf, with the aid of Narya, the Elven Ring of Fire, rekindles the fires of his heart and convinces him to ride to battle against Saruman. After victory at Helm's Deep and the Entish destruction of Isengard, Théoden leads his army into battle at Pelennor Fields where he personally, at the age of 71, kills both the chieftain and the standard bearer of the Haradrim, scattering the enemy cavalry.

> Fey he seemed... borne up on Snowmane like a god of old, even as Oromë the Great in the battle of the Valar when the world was young. [215]

Théoden is only stopped by the greatest of the Ringwraiths, the Witch-king of Angmar, and even resists the terror of the Nazgûl to try to rally his troops. Unfortunately, he is trapped under the body of his dying horse and crushed. The Witch-king himself is stopped by the remarkable shieldmaiden, Éowyn. The niece of Théoden, she disguises herself as a man, the warrior Dernhelm, to ride to war with her people. With the aid of the Hobbit Merry, she kills the Witch-king, fulfilling the prophecy that the Nazgûl would not die by the hand of man. Although Éowyn loves Aragorn forlornly, she is wooed by Faramir, the brother of Boromir, and marries him after the defeat of Sauron. Éomer, Éowyn's brother, succeeds his uncle Théoden as King of Rohan.

The Wild Men, or Men of Darkness, include the Easterlings and Haradrim of Sauron's armies, as well as the Dunlendings, who fight for Saruman. The Easterlings of the Third Age are descended from the original mortal servants of darkness, the Easterlings of Ulfang in the First Age. They war constantly with Gondor and the Northmen throughout the Third Age, invading on a number of occasions before the War of the Ring. A disparate group of tribes from around the Sea of Rhûn, the Easterlings are bitter enemies of both the Dúnedain and the Rohirrim. Dark and wild, many of them are expert horsemen. The chiefs of at least one tribe, the Wainriders, who invade Gondor early in the Third Age, fight in great war chariots.

The Haradrim of the South are also a constant thorn in the side of Gondor. The term Harad is used to refer to all the lands south of Gondor. This includes Near Harad, or Harandor, and Far Harad, which includes the land of Mûmakan where the great war elephants and their mobile archery platforms come from. Near Harad was actually under the control of Gondor at the height of its power, and became the southernmost border of the Dúnedain kingdom. But this was always a land disputed with Gondor's enemies further south in Harad. The stronghold of Gondor's enemies is Umbar, and the area between changed hands on many occasions throughout the Third Age. The Haradrim are known as a cruel people, but are also proud, brave and valiant warriors. After the destruction of the One Ring and the collapse of Sauron's armies, many Haradrim, and Easterlings too, fight to the death against their enemies, even after the battle is clearly hopeless for them.

The Dunlendings who serve in the armies of Saruman have a slightly different origin. They originally lived in and around the White Mountains that mark the borders of Northern Gondor. With the foundation of the Dúnedain realm in exile, they were slowly forced to migrate northward. The granting of Rohan to the Éothéd forced many even further north and west to the other side of the Misty Mountains. Many settled in Eriador, in the lands that were once the realm of Arnor, and became the common stock, settling down and turning to peaceful agriculture and industry. The men of the town of Bree next to the Shire, for example, are originally of Dunlending stock. But the wildest and most aggressive of these men occupy the rugged area of Dunland, hating both the Dúnedain and the Rohirrim, whom they call strawheads, with a passion. Saruman finds many willing recruits from among these Dunlendings, who welcome the chance to fight against their old enemies, even if it means consorting with Orcs. It is Dunlendings that Saruman uses to breed his half-orc spies. The slanty-eyed southerner seen consorting with Bill Ferny in Bree is just such a half–orc.

The people of the Paths of the Dead were also once of the same people as the Dunlendings. These were a tribe that lived in the White Mountains at the end of the Second Age. They and their King swore a great oath to come to the aid of Isildur in War but when Isildur called on them, at the time of the Last Alliance of Elves and Men, they broke their oath and stayed in their homes in the mountains. Isildur cursed them. They haunt the mountains until the chance comes to redeem themselves and fulfil their promise. Aragorn, as the Heir of Isildur, calls upon that ancient tie and they follow him, a whole Age later. The chief weapon of the Army of the Dead is fear, which they use to defeat the Corsairs of Umbar and capture their fleet.

The most notable exception to Faramir's categories of Men must be the Woses, the Wild Men of Druadan forest, who show the Rohirrim a secret way through the White Mountains to come to the aid of Minas Tirith. First heard of in the First Age living among, but not part of, the woodland House of Haleth, they are short, squat and ugly, with what little facial hair they grow forming straggly beards. The Woses are short-lived, but as skilled as the Silvan Elves at woodcraft and in plant lore, with a keen sense of smell that can find an Orc long before the Orc sees them. As well as their natural talent for ambushes, for which they use poisoned darts, the Woses can actually enchant their carved stone statues, or Púkel-men. These strange carvings act as watchers or even animate to attack their enemies. The Woses are hated enemies of the Orcs, although the Rohirrim also hunt the Wild Men like animals, thinking them nothing but dumb beasts. Ghân-buri-Ghân is their chief in the War of the Ring. In return for the Woses' help against Sauron, they are granted Druadan forest as their own domain. Wild the Woses certainly are, but they are the epitome of the 'noble savage', and never turn to evil.

After the defeat of Sauron comes the Fourth Age, the Age of Men. With the departure of the most powerful Elven Lords into the West, and the waning of those remaining, Men are clearly the dominant race. The Maiar who dominated their destinies, such as Sauron, Saruman and Gandalf, have also become part of history, leaving Men to lead the wars and struggles between their nations.

But the Men themselves are destined to wane too. The rule of King Elessar, as Aragorn is known after his coronation, is a short-lived renaissance harking back to the ancient days of Númenorean splendour. After 120 years, Aragorn chooses to abdicate his throne and give up his life in peace, before senility takes him, as his ancestors had done thousands of years before:

> 'I am the last of the Númenoreans and the latest King of the Elder Days; and to me has been given … the grace to go at my will, and give back the gift.' [216]

With the death of Aragorn, the last remnants of that ancient knowledge, splendour and power is also lost. Over the following centuries the differences between the Dúnedain and the Middle and Wild Men will inevitably diminish, then disappear. While the future fate of Middle-earth is firmly in the hands of Men, those same Men are set to become pale shadows of their former glory.

Orcs

The Orcs are the ancient enemies of Elves, Men and Dwarves and have made up the foot soldiers of the armies of evil since the First Age. Bred by Morgoth, through twisted experiments on captured Elves, the Orcs are mockeries of that noble race. The life of an Orc is nasty, brutish and short. Created in darkness and through cruelty

> deep in their dark hearts the Orcs loathed the Master whom
> they served in fear, the maker only of their misery. [217]

Although the pawns and slaves of Morgoth, the Orcs are not mere robots, obeying only the commands of their creator. As they were originally creatures with independent life, they still have their own wills, although they can be easily cowed by anyone more powerful than themselves. The Orcs serve whatever evil is nearest and greatest, controlled through fear and violence. Left to their own devices they would raid the weakest enemy, torturing and eating whoever they found, purely for fun.

Created in darkness, in the depths of Angband before the coming of the Sun and Moon, Orcs fear the day, and will not fight, or even travel, during daylight unless some great terror forces them to. On the other hand, they can see in the dark and can track by scent alone, as well as any trained bloodhound. If forced, they can actually show great stamina, and are able to run tirelessly for days. Although individually cowardly, Orcs can be devastating in battle, if they have overwhelming superiority in numbers and strong commanders.

The Orcs are made up of many different tribes, some of which even make pacts with Wargs, huge wolves from the North, and use them as mounts like horses. One particular tribe, the Orcs of the Misty Mountains, are known as Goblins, with their leader being called the Great Goblin. These different tribes all speak different guttural variations of Westron, the common language of Middle-earth, and communication between different tribes is therefore difficult. To overcome this, and to make the Orcs more useful soldiers, in the Second Age Sauron created a common language of evil known as the Black Speech, which he taught to all the Orcs and servants of Mordor.

In the Third Age there appeared a new type of Orc, known as the Uruk-hai. Where Morgoth had bred the Orcs in mockery of the Elves, Sauron crossed them with Men in another series of twisted experiments. Commonly known as Uruks, or soldier Orcs, these creatures contemptuously refer to their lesser cousins as Snaga, the Black Speech word for slave. The Uruk-hai are taller and stronger than their predecessors, as well as much braver, and are found in the armies of both Sauron and Saruman. But the most terrifying difference between the Uruks and the lesser Orcs is that the Uruks have no fear of sunlight and can fight as well during the day as the night.

Saruman also makes use of half-orcs, who are human enough to pass for ugly men, as his spies. The mysterious friend of Bill Ferny at Bree, the squinty-eyed Southerner, is later revealed as a half-orc.

Orcs of all kinds possess a malicious cunning and intelligence, which is always centred around hurt or pain. They can forge their own weapons and armour, which are always functional but never beautiful. They are at their most creative when devising new tortures or punishments. Instead of the Elven Lembas, or waybread, the Orcs have a fiery drink that rejuvenates tired limbs but is foul in taste. They even make their own healing salve, although it leaves ugly scars. Generally, the Orcs prefer to live in the mountains or underground, and are passable cavers, although again, unlike Dwarves, their halls are never beautiful or more than functional.

The common bond that keeps Orcs together is simple: hatred and fear. They hate everyone else slightly more than they hate each other.

When there are no Elves, Men or Dwarves to fight, they fight amongst themselves. Only a figure stronger than they are, who can inspire terror, can unite the Orcs, and even then the effect is temporary and less effective the further from the source of their fear that the Orcs travel. This can be clearly seen in the relations between the Orcs in *The Lord of the Rings.*

When the Hobbits Merry and Pippin are captured by Orcs after the death of Boromir, they soon discover that there are three competing bands arguing over them. The first, made up of Uruks, is led by Uglúk and wear the White Hand of Saruman as their token. The second, comprising lesser Orcs led by Grishnákh, serve Mordor and Sauron. A third group, from the Misty Mountains, are seemingly just there for torture and booty. The main conflict is between Uglúk and Grishnákh. Both have orders that the prisoners are to be taken, unmolested, back for questioning. But for Uglúk that means Isengard, and for Grishnákh, Mordor. Within minutes of waking, Merry and Pippin see how the Orcs settle debates – Uglúk kills two of the lesser Orcs. The Uruks then dominate the group and lead it towards Isengard. There are constant disagreements, always accompanied with at least the threat of violence and, when the Riders of Rohan cut them off, it is only the Uruks that show any stomach for the fighting. All are killed, most of the lesser Orcs as they run away. Even as the Rohirrim slaughter the Orcs, they are still squabbling and betraying each other.

This violence and hatred, controlled only by fear, is not only seen when bands of Orcs serving different masters come into conflict. When Frodo and Sam are crossing Mordor they overhear a squabble between an Uruk and a lesser Orc tracker. Despite both serving Sauron, their frustration with not having found their prey leads swiftly to threats of retribution. The Uruk threatens the tracker with the wrath of the Nazgûl, whose power would normally be enough to cow any sign of rebellion. But for Orcs, out of sight is out of mind:

> 'Go to your filthy Shriekers, and may they freeze the flesh off
> you! If the enemy doesn't get them first. They've done in
> Number One, I've heard, and I hope it's true!' [218]

Not only does the lesser Orc defy the threat of the Nazgûl, he applauds the death of their leader. Orcs respect only power and strength, and as soon as the Ringwraiths, and by extension Sauron, look vulnerable, dissension is sure to follow. Unsurprisingly, upon hearing such rebellious talk, the Uruk tries to spear the tracker, only to be shot through the eye.

Even when there seems to be some common cause between the Orcs, they are only ever one step away from bloody violence. Shagrat and Gorbag are both Uruk leaders. Shagrat is garrison commander for Cirith Ungol, Gorbag the commander of a contingent of Uruks from Minas Morgul. They obviously know each other and plan together what they will do after Sauron's victory in the war:

> 'you and me'll slip off and set up somewhere on our own
> with a few trusty lads, somewhere where there's good loot
> nice and handy, and no big bosses.' [219]

Although fear is the only way to control such creatures, they still dream of a life without it – or at least a time when they are the only ones dealing it out. But even two Uruk-hai, supposedly responsible senior commanders and even friends, are not to be trusted. Within hours of their meeting, the two groups slaughter each other over loot, with Gorbag strangling Shagrat while being himself knifed. Frodo's mithril coat proves too tempting, even though all the Orcs are well aware of the direct orders from the Nazgûl and Sauron that all such booty is to be sent on. If booty, albeit almost priceless booty, can drive such creatures to murder so quickly, and against the threat of punishment from the Ringwraiths themselves, then we can see why Orcs must be considered unreliable servants at best. They may be effective in battle but their discipline, even among the considerably better-trained Uruk-hai, is never strong.

This is well known by Sauron, and Morgoth before him. Cirith Ungol was originally a fortress designed to keep watch on Sauron and the forces of Mordor. After its capture by the Dark Lord, he uses it for the same thing:

> for he [Sauron] had few servants but many slaves of fear,
> and still its chief purpose as of old was to prevent escape
> from Mordor. [220]

Even as dreadful and powerful a master as Sauron is forced to spend much of his time and effort keeping his own troops loyal, and preventing them from deserting.

The Orcs are foot soldiers, swiftly bred and excellent cannon fodder, but of the poorest quality as soon as they are out of direct control. This is a weakness neither Morgoth nor even Sauron ever overcomes. Although their overwhelming numbers, ferocity and cruelty make the Orcs devastating pawns of evil, they are never a true match for the Elves they were bred from, or the Men and Dwarves they fight for millennia. This is something that is extremely fortunate for the free peoples of the West.

Trolls

The Trolls were another creation of Morgoth, as he bred his armies in Angband back in the First Age. As the Orcs were bred in mockery of the Elves, Trolls were the result of twisted experiments on the Ents. And as with the Orcs, they were poor imitations of the original. As Treebeard says to the Hobbits Merry and Pippin, before tearing apart the walls of Isengard like paper:

> 'Trolls are only counterfeits, made by the Enemy in the Great
> Darkness, in mockery of Ents... We are stronger than Trolls.
> We are made of the bones of the earth.' [221]

They may not be the equals of the Ents, but Trolls are still very powerful opponents. Like the stone used in their creation, they are incredibly strong and tremendously hard to hurt. They are also very, very stupid. Most are barely capable of speech, and have no more intelligence than a trained animal. Although powerful shock troops, they are only of use as part of a larger force, as they always need someone to direct their malice. Bred in the darkness of Angband before the creation of the Sun, the Trolls – like the Orcs – are vulnerable to daylight. But while the Orcs hate and fear the Sun, the sorcery used in the Trolls' creation is actually undone by the Sun's power and turns them back into the stone from which they came.

The three Trolls encountered by Bilbo Baggins, the Dwarves and Gandalf in *The Hobbit* are undoubtedly the Einsteins of their kind. Although easily outwitted by Gandalf, Bill, Tom and Bert speak in sentences, make fire, and can plan an ambush. If all Trolls had been so intelligent they would have been far more dangerous servants of the enemy. In the later ages, Sauron attempts to make better use of these stupid monsters and manages to teach them some rudimentary language, so it may be that these three had had the benefit of a tutor. However, Sauron is still discontented with the Trolls and chooses to improve them dramatically.

Just as Sauron's breeding of Orcs and Men produced the Uruk-hai, his twisted experiments with Trolls produce the Olog-hai. These Black Trolls are faster, stronger and far more intelligent. They can all use weapons, carry shields, and speak the Black Speech of Mordor. Most dangerous of all, they are unaffected by the sunlight. However, these effects are the direct result of Sauron's will, and with his destruction, the Olog-hai lose any power of independent thought. Whether they have the power to recover after Sauron's downfall, or are unmade by his destruction, never to threaten the West again, is unknown.

CHAPTER FIVE

GANDALF: THE FIRE IN MEN'S HEARTS

he Hobbit occupies an uneasy place within Tolkien's works. Written for children, it describes events in a way that often seems incongruous with the heroic seriousness of *The Silmarillion* and *The Lord of the Rings*. The frivolous song of welcome sung by the Elves of Rivendell to the company of Thorin, for example, is a striking contrast in tone to the dignified proceedings in Elrond's house in *The Lord of the Rings*. For our purposes here, however, the fact that *The Hobbit* is a children's story is of secondary interest to the events that it describes: events which are deadly serious, and moreover deeply significant within Middle-earth's history. For example, when Tolkien published *The Hobbit* in 1937, he had only a limited idea of the full significance of the Ring. Here, however, we will look at the events described in *The Hobbit* in the way Gandalf does in *The Lord of the Rings*: as part of the history of Middle-earth. And it is clear that Gandalf placed great significance on Bilbo's finding of the Ring.

We learn in the Appendices to *The Lord of the Rings* (Appendix B) that the Istari, the five wizards, arrive in Middle-earth around the year 1100 of the Third Age. Of the five, the two Blue wizards, Allatar and Pallando, are described elsewhere as leaving for the East. They play no significant part in the known history of Middle-earth. Radagast the Brown's historical role is also minor. Interested more in plants and animals than in the affairs of Men, he is easily duped by Saruman into luring Gandalf to Orthanc, although Saruman's description of Radagast as 'Radagast the Bird-tamer! Radagast the Simple! Radagast the Fool!' [222] is arguably a little harsh. It is the two eldest wizards,

White and Grey, Saruman and Gandalf, who are the true wizardly powers in Middle-earth. In the *Unfinished Tales,* we learn that Círdan of the Grey Havens, meeting Gandalf on his arrival in Middle-earth, perceives him as the wisest and greatest spirit of the Istari. Círdan gives Gandalf Narya, one of the three Elven Rings, the Ring of Fire.

The White Council, the alliance of the Wise of Middle-earth (comprising Elrond, Galadriel, Círdan, various other senior Elves, Saruman and Gandalf) is formed in the year 2463 of the Third Age, in response to the fear that Sauron may have returned to Dol Guldur, his fortress in Mirkwood. The doings of the White Council are described in *The Silmarillion* in some detail.[223] It is around this time that Saruman becomes seduced by thoughts of the One Ring and begins actively searching for it. To this end, in 2851, Saruman counsels against a direct assault on Dol Guldur, even though Gandalf has found incontrovertible evidence that the power there is Sauron himself. Saruman does this in the hope that the Ring, in seeking its maker, will appear, and in the fear that if Sauron is driven from the area the Ring may remain hidden. This is a dangerous tactic for Saruman to employ, as there is no guarantee that he will be the first to seize the Ring, should it indeed appear. In 2941, Saruman changes his tactics. Deciding that the risk of Sauron finding the One Ring outweighs his own chances of procuring it should it come to light, and desiring also to search the Anduin River area unhindered, Saruman agrees to the White Council's assault on Dol Guldur.

Before we proceed to the events of *The Hobbit*, we need to consider briefly an earlier event in the history of Middle-earth: the fall of Erebor, the Lonely Mountain, to Smaug the dragon. In 2770, drawn by rumours of the fabulous wealth of the Lonely Mountain, the great Dwarven fortress of Thror, Smaug, the greatest dragon of the age, attacks the region, driving out the Dwarves and laying waste to the surrounding area. Thror and his son Thrain II escape from a secret side entrance in the mountain, later meeting Thrain II's son Thorin Oakenshield, who had been away from the mountain during the assault. Their doings prior to *The Hobbit* are described in the section on 'The Dwarves' in chapter four.

It is against this background that we approach the events of *The Hobbit*, and Gandalf's role therein. The year is 2941, and Gandalf has yet to attend the meeting of the White Council that will finally vote to attack Dol Guldur. Gandalf fears greatly that Sauron plans to attack Rivendell, and then to regain the deserted lands of Angmar in the north-west of Middle-earth. It appears that Sauron has Easterling forces that he can deploy to this end. [224]

We begin to get a glimpse of Gandalf's strategic acumen. The description of the background to the Quest of Erebor (in essence a summary of *The Hobbit*) in *Unfinished Tales* provides a fuller and slightly more informative analysis of the situation as Gandalf sees it. Gandalf realises that while Sauron is based in Dol Guldur, he is in a powerful position to attack the two great hidden strongholds of the West: first Lorien, then Rivendell:

> 'I thought then, and I am sure now, that to attack Lórien and Rivendell, as soon as he was strong enough, was his original plan. It would have been a much better plan for him, and much worse for us.' [225]

Gandalf is speaking here after the downfall of Sauron. Gandalf also realises that the Dwarves of the Iron Hills, whilst a strong bulwark against the East and a great strategic asset in the area, are compromised by the presence of Smaug in the Lonely Mountain:

> 'To resist any force Sauron might send to regain the northern passes in the mountains and the old lands of Angmar there were only the Dwarves of the Iron Hills, and behind them lay a desolation and a Dragon. The Dragon Sauron might use with terrible effect.' [226]

Gandalf realises that the Dwarves of the Iron Hills are located in a potentially disastrous position. To their west lies Smaug and 'scorched earth', and to the east, as noted before, lie Sauron's Easterling resources that, if deployed, would be marching west. The Iron Hills are located between hammer and anvil. Interestingly, Gandalf uses the verb 'to use' in reference to Smaug as opposed to the verb 'to send' in reference to Sauron's Eastern resources. Smaug, like the Balrog and Shelob, is a powerful figure of evil not directly under Sauron's control. Such creatures are useful to Sauron, however, and can be exploited.

But Gandalf has other even more pressing concerns. He believes it is imperative that Sauron be dislodged from Dol Guldur, and thus far Saruman, senior to him at the White Council, has resisted this idea (for reasons we have already described). Gandalf describes his own priorities in the following passage:

> 'Often I said to myself: "I must find some means of deal-
> ing with Smaug. But a direct stroke against Dol Guldur is
> needed still more. …I must make the Council see that."' [227]

It is at this point that Gandalf meets Thorin Oakenshield while travelling towards the Shire to rest and think. Thorin's mind is full of thoughts of vengeance upon Smaug and he asks Gandalf for help towards this end, but Gandalf is too much of a military realist to entertain Thorin's plans for all-out war against Smaug. And then something strange happens. Gandalf hears news of a Hobbit he has always been fond of but has not seen for some twenty years. These years have blunted the Hobbit's insatiable curiosity about the world beyond the Shire, and have made him into, well, it is probably best to let Gandalf describe him:

> '… he was getting rather greedy and fat, and his old
> desires had dwindled down to a sort of private dream.' [228]

Gandalf realises that there is still something within this Hobbit that might make him a useful companion to Thorin. The Hobbit's name is Bilbo Baggins. This is a moment of profound intuition on Gandalf's part. Gandalf realises that he has found a potential solution to the problem of Smaug.

The strange thing about this chapter of *Unfinished Tales* is that

Gandalf never describes exactly why he selects Bilbo for the quest. Gandalf does suggest in *The Hobbit* that a burglar will have a better chance of success in the quest than a warrior will: especially when Gandalf remembers finding a lone raving Dwarf imprisoned in Dol Guldur during his perilous visit there. This Dwarf gave him a key and a map 'for his son', and Gandalf suddenly realises that the Dwarf is none other than Thrain II, Thorin Oakenshield's father. The map is of the Lonely Mountain, and the key opens the very side door in the mountain from which Thror and Thrain II escaped during Smaug's attack. From the description of Hobbits with their stealth and 'long clever brown fingers' [229] it is clear that a Hobbit would make a consummate burglar, but it is Gandalf's intuitive recognition of the sleeping dream of adventure within Bilbo that underlies his decision.

It is also in keeping with Gandalf's preferred way of doing things to send a thief rather than a warrior on such a quest. Throughout the events leading up to and during the War of the Ring, Gandalf always prefers to avoid overt displays of power. The reason for this is that such acts of power attract unwelcome attention from forces whose attention it is better not to attract. Gandalf is realistic enough to realise that, powerful though he is, he is not a match for some of these forces face to face. An example is the moment in the Caradhras pass when Gandalf is forced reluctantly to light a fire magically in order to keep the Company of the Ring alive:

> 'If there are any to see, then at least I am revealed to them,' he said. 'I have written *Gandalf is here* in signs that all can read from Rivendell to the Mouths of Anduin.' [230]

It is this kind of self-knowledge and humility that differentiates Gandalf from the arrogance that characterises the forces of evil in Middle-earth. Stealth plays an integral part in the strategy Gandalf devises for the West during the War of the Ring, though Gandalf is not frightened to stand face-to-face against the forces of evil when he has no other option. And Gandalf realises that his piece of intuitive improvisation to deal with the threat of Smaug can be made to work with his primary strategic priority: the ousting of Sauron from Dol Guldur:

> Time was getting short. I had to be with the White Council
> in August at the latest, or Saruman would have his way
> and nothing would be done. And quite apart from other
> matters, that might prove fatal to the quest: the power in
> Dol Guldur would not leave any attempt on Erebor unhin-
> dered, unless he had something else to deal with. [231]

Gandalf realises that for the quest against Smaug to succeed, his primary goal of an assault on Dol Guldur must also be achieved. If Gandalf can succeed in both of his strategic goals, Sauron will lose a great strategic asset in Smaug; the bulwark of the Dwarves in the Iron Hills will be greatly enhanced by a repopulated Lonely Mountain; Rivendell and Lorien will be protected; and Sauron will lose his foothold in an area perilously deep within the West.

The one thing that Gandalf does not have a great deal of, is time. Still (and this is one of the most admirable things about Gandalf), he does not regard Bilbo and the Dwarves as a means to an end. Despite the fact that his primary goal is to sway the White Council in the matter of Dol Guldur, he dedicates as much time to the Lonely Mountain quest as he can possibly afford.

The Hobbit starts out humorously, but the action becomes progressively darker as the story develops. The encounter with the Trolls at the start of the book, when a hidden Gandalf keeps them arguing until sunrise turns them to stone, is very funny. It is also in keeping with Gandalf's preferred method of doing things: to select the subtle, elegant solution in preference to brute force. And lest we think that this is a particularly childish, incongruous exploit for Gandalf the Grey, let us not forget that Gandalf often displays a keen sense of humour. The flight from the Goblins and Wargs and the subsequent rescue of the party from the burning trees by the Eagles is a much more serious affair.

In terms of the developing story of *The Hobbit*, Gandalf's departure from Bilbo's quest under the shadow of Mirkwood is an important structural moment: it is time for Bilbo to develop his leadership qualities without Gandalf's aid. Bilbo's battle to save his companions from the giant spiders of Mirkwood is frankly terrifying. Mirroring the darkening of the story is Bilbo's developing resourcefulness and courage. At the start of the story he is ineffectual, and Gandalf has to convince his companions that he is capable of fulfilling the tasks required of him. At the end of the story, Bilbo is the undoubted leader of the party, and it is not really his fault that his plans to prevent the final Battle of the Five Armies fail.

Aside from its dramatic contribution to the development of Bilbo as a hero, Gandalf's departure from Thorin's company is made for pressing strategic reasons of his own. Gandalf has given the party as much time as he can possibly afford – he absolutely must get to the meeting of the White Council for the quest against Smaug to have any chance of succeeding. However, Gandalf also realises that it is time for Bilbo to carry on without his help. And yet, despite the fact that Gandalf realises that his presence at the White Council is vital to the security of a free Middle-earth, he does not shirk from risking his life to help Bilbo and the Dwarves when he has to. After their escape from the Goblins in the Misty Mountains, Gandalf, Bilbo and the Dwarves are trapped again by the Goblins and Wargs in the burning fir trees. Gandalf could certainly save himself at this point, but he does not for a moment consider deserting his companions. Instead, he prepares to sell his life dearly:

> ... he got ready to spring down from on high right among
> the spears of the goblins. That would have been the end of
> him, though he would probably have killed many of them
> as he came hurtling down like a thunderbolt. [232]

It is this very human quality of loyalty that differentiates Gandalf from the likes of Saruman. Saruman regards conscious beings as objects, as chess pieces to be moved around to his advantage. Gandalf seldom does this, and only when he has absolutely no other alternative. This quality is illustrated during the horrifying moment before the gates of Mordor, when the Mouth of Sauron rides out to present terms for the surrender of the West. He is carrying Frodo's mithril armour, his Elven cloak and his sword and offers to trade Frodo's life for terms that would spell absolute disaster for the West. In a moment of great courage, even though it causes him agony, Gandalf finds the strength to reject the terms:

> 'These we will take in memory of our friend [Frodo's effects],' he cried. 'But as for your terms, we reject them utterly. Get you gone, for your embassy is over and death is near to you. We did not come here to waste words in treating with Sauron, faithless and accursed; still less with one of his slaves. Begone!' [233]

Sauron is indeed 'faithless'. There is no question that he will honour any terms made with the West. Gandalf does the only thing possible: he rejects the terms and prepares the forces of the West for battle, even though all hope seems to be gone. And yet it must be clear to Gandalf that Sauron has not yet gained the One Ring. If he had, he would not be attempting to treat with the West. Gandalf must be thinking that there is still a chance that Frodo is alive and that the quest to destroy the Ring might still be completed. It is a mark of Gandalf's brilliant mind and great courage, that he can still reason whilst in an agony of doubt and fear for someone he loves.

Gandalf shows similar qualities during the Battle of the Five Armies at the climax of *The Hobbit*. Gandalf has returned from meeting with the White Council. He has been successful in his aim, and Sauron has been driven from Dol Guldur. Yet we read in various sources (*Unfinished Tales* and Appendix A III of *The Lord of the Rings*) that this victory for Gandalf is a false one. Sauron had been preparing his return to the fastness of Mordor, and fled there during the White Council's assault on Dol Guldur. Later on, Gandalf would see this move as a critical error by Sauron.

The Battle of the Five Armies is of profound strategic significance to the West. The dragon may be dead, but that will count for little if the Goblins and the Wargs can destroy the armies of the Elven King and the Dwarves. This outcome would place the Iron Hills and the Lonely Mountain directly into Sauron's hands and give him dominance of the whole north east of Middle-earth. It would also destroy the stronghold of the Wood Elves in Mirkwood, giving the whole area over to the Shadow. An assault on Lorien and Rivendell would almost certainly follow this eventuality. As the day wears on and the battle appears to be lost, Gandalf once more prepares to go down fighting:

> Gandalf too, I may say, was there, sitting on the ground as if in deep thought, preparing, I suppose, one last blast of magic before the end.[234]

It is the arrival of the eagles that saves the day for the West, and much later Gandalf describes the immense strategic significance of this battle. When the War of the Ring is over, Gandalf talks to Frodo and Gimli in Minas Tirith:

> 'When you think of the great Battle of the Pelennor, do not forget the battles in Dale and the valour of Durin's folk. Think of what might have been. Dragon-fire and savage swords in Eriador, night in Rivendell. There might be no Queen in Gondor.[235] We might now hope to return from the victory here only to ruin and ash. But that has been averted – because I met Thorin Oakenshield one evening on the edge of spring in Bree. A chance-meeting, as we say in Middle-earth.[236]

Throughout *The Lord of the Rings* Gandalf is the most mobile of all the significant characters of the story. He is constantly moving, structuring the defence of the West. When the narrative of the story switches from any of the other main characters, it is always picked up again directly where it left off. Gandalf often acts 'off-screen', and often describes his own actions in retrospect. During the Council of Elrond, Gandalf describes his actions just prior to and during Frodo's journey from Hobbiton to Rivendell. Gandalf, at Radagast's behest, visited Saruman at Orthanc. There Saruman tried to sway Gandalf to his own cause, revealing to Gandalf that he had abdicated as Sauman the White, and had become Saruman 'of Many Colours'. Gandalf replies to Saruman's claim that white is a mere beginning that can always be overwritten:

> 'In which case it is no longer white... And he that breaks a thing to find out what it is has left the path of wisdom.' [237]

Here Gandalf demonstrates a clear understanding of the genetic fallacy. A complex thing such as virtue is far more than the mere sum of its parts. Deconstructing it, in the way a prism splits white light into its constituent colours, is an act of degeneration. Having failed to persuade Gandalf to his cause, Saruman imprisons him on the pinnacle of Orthanc. Gandalf remains there, exposed to the elements, and beset by fears and doubts, until he is rescued by Gwaihir of the Eagles.

Gwaihir bears Gandalf to Rohan, where he attempts to warn King Théoden of the various threats that face his realm. Théoden, however, has already been swayed by Saruman's lies and will not listen, insisting that Gandalf take a horse and leave his kingdom. Gandalf, to Théoden's displeasure, takes Shadowfax, the greatest of the horses of Rohan, and rides to the Shire, arriving a mere six days after Frodo has left. He then follows Frodo to Bree, and hears that he has left in the company of Strider. Comforted by this news, and realising he has little chance of finding Frodo in the wilderness, Gandalf then rides to Weathertop to draw the Ringwraiths away from Frodo, and to buy him more time. This is a particularly courageous thing for Gandalf to do: he has no trouble dealing with the Ringwraiths during daylight, but he fights a strenuous battle with them at night on the summit of Weathertop. The Ringwraiths are at the height of their powers during the hours of darkness, and even Gandalf is hard pressed to hold them at bay. He escapes at sunrise, and deliberately draws four of the Nine Ringwraiths after him through the dangerous Troll fells north of Rivendell. This entire episode portrays perfectly the nature of Gandalf: his courage and resolution when things appear hopeless; his speed and mobility; his ability to assess situations and to make hard decisions; and his willingness to fight and to risk his life when his preferred tactics of speed and stealth have failed.

The reason that Gandalf's original plan has failed at this point, incidentally, is that Barliman Butterbur, innkeeper of Bree, forgets to send the letter Gandalf which writes to Frodo before setting out for Orthanc. The letter advises Frodo to leave for Rivendell no later than the end of July. Frodo does not in fact depart until 23 September. Nearly two months have been wasted and the Ringwraiths are hot on Frodo's trail. Typically though, Gandalf forgives Butterbur this lapse, recognising that:

'... fat men who sell ale have many calls to answer...' [238]

As we mentioned before, Gandalf knows that neither he nor the greatest figures of the West have the strength to face Sauron directly. While Aragorn decides the Company of the Nine should attempt to cross the Misty Mountains by the Redhorn pass after leaving Rivendell, Gandalf believes this to be too exposed. He has another plan, and it is clear he has already discussed it with Aragorn:

'But there is another way, and not by the pass of Caradhras [the Redhorn pass]: the dark and secret way that we have spoken of.' [239]

For Gandalf, this way – the route through the mines of Moria – has the virtue of secrecy. Driven back by harsh weather in the Redhorn Pass, it is the route they finally have to take. Aragorn, who has made the journey once before, is unhappy about this course of action. In a moment of prophecy he warns Gandalf:

'It is not of the Ring, nor of us others that I am thinking now, but of you, Gandalf. And I say to you: if you pass the doors of Moria, beware!' [240]

This prophecy is a true one. Before entering Moria, however, Gandalf must solve the riddle carved on the doors: 'Speak, friend, and enter'. Here we get a glimpse of the wizard that Gandalf truly is: 'subtle, and quick to anger'. Pippin has the temerity to question Gandalf about the riddle. Gandalf responds:

> 'Knock on the doors with your head,Peregrin Took,' said Gandalf. 'But if that does not shatter them, and I am allowed a little peace from foolish questions, I will seek for the opening words.' [241]

This waspish irritability is also a hallmark of Gandalf. However, if he is quick to anger, he is also quick to forgive, where forgiveness is due. [242]

Gandalf's attempt at a stealthy passage through the mines is unsuccessful. The stone Pippin drops into a deep well wakes things best left undisturbed, and after a fierce battle with Orcs, the Balrog attacks the Company near the eastern exit to Moria, on Durin's bridge. Once again, Gandalf shows his willingness to risk his life for his friends, facing down the Balrog on the bridge, even though he knows he is desperately tired. And this time it appears that he really has sacrificed himself, falling with the Balrog into the depths below the bridge, yet buying his friends time to escape from the mines.

Gandalf does not appear again for many chapters, but there is a moment later on in *The Fellowship of the Ring* when we hear his voice. This happens when Frodo is on top of Amon Hen, the Hill of Sight. Boromir has tried to wrest the Ring from Frodo, and in a panic Frodo puts it on, and flees to the summit of the hill. There he looks out over Middle-earth, and his eyes are slowly drawn eastwards to Mordor. Frodo suffers a terrible internal struggle at this point. He feels Sauron seeking him and is agonisingly balanced between two choices: to deny Sauron or to submit to him:

> He heard himself crying out: *Never! Never!* Or was it: *Verily I come, I come to you?* He could not tell. [243]

And at this point Frodo hears another voice in his head. It is easy to miss the tone and significance of this second voice:

> Then as a flash from some other point of power there
> came to his mind another thought: *Take it off! Take it off!*
> *Fool, take it off! Take off the Ring!* [244]

The voice comes from 'another point of power', and enables Frodo to take control of himself, and to take off the Ring. Whose voice, whose tone is this but Gandalf's? This is confirmed later on in *The Two Towers* when Aragorn, Legolas and Gimli meet Gandalf again – Gandalf reborn as Gandalf the White. He talks of the very moment of struggle above:

> 'Very nearly it [the Ring] was revealed to the Enemy, but it
> escaped. I had some part in that: for I sat in a high place, and
> I strove with the Dark Tower, and the Shadow passed.' [245]

Gandalf describes his fall into the depths with the Balrog, and how he pursued him to the peak of the highest mountain in Middle-earth, where he cast him down. What Gandalf describes next is very strange indeed. He talks of 'straying out of thought and time' and states that

> 'Naked was I sent back – for a brief time, until my task
> is done.' [246]

It seems clear that Gandalf left the physical realm of Middle-earth for a while, and was in some way actually reborn. When Gwaihir the Eagle bears him from the mountaintop to Lorien, Galadriel recognises the significance of this and clothes him in white. Gandalf has now taken up the role of Saruman. As he himself says:

> 'Yes, I am white now,' said Gandalf. 'Indeed I *am*
> Saruman, one might almost say, Saruman as he should
> have been.' [247]

In his new role, Gandalf is already thinking strategically again. He analyses the dangers posed by both Sauron and Sauruman in detail. Saruman, by covertly waging war on Rohan, is preventing Rohan from aiding Gondor. Sauron knows that two Hobbits were taken to Isengard and is in fear lest Saruman has found the Ring. Saruman, meanwhile, knows he has not found the Ring. Unaware of whether his Orcs were bringing Hobbit prisoners to him or not, he believes it is possible that the Ring was lost during the recent battle where his forces were utterly destroyed by the Rohirrim. He is therefore in an agony of fear in case it is found by the forces of Théoden, and is preparing to deploy all his forces against Rohan.

Meanwhile, Gandalf knows that the Ring is nowhere in the vicinity, but is in fact on its way into Mordor. Saruman's forces did not capture Frodo the Ringbearer, but Merry and Pippin. Gandalf's next goal, therefore, is to enable the forces of Rohan to fight back against Saruman, finally allowing them to come to the aid of Minas Tirith. To do this he must first free Théoden from the malign influence of the lies of Saruman. Gandalf succeeds in this task by revealing to Théoden the plan to destroy the Ring, and by exposing the lies of Wormtongue, Théoden's advisor, and lackey of Saruman.[248] The forces of Rohan are deployed at the fortress of Helm's Deep, where they fight a terrible battle with Saruman's army of Orcs and Wild Men. Once more the forces of evil are too strong to overcome in a pitched battle, and Théoden, unwilling to die cornered, rides out with his forces to fight and die.

But once more Gandalf makes good use of the powers at his disposal. He rounds up the scattered troops of Rohan's Westfold, under the command of Erkenbrand. Gandalf also brings an army of Huorns, the semiconscious trees shepherded by the Ents, to the mouth of the pass. Saruman's Orcs are caught between the charging forces of Théoden, Erkenbrand's men, and the Orc-hating army of Huorns, and are utterly destroyed. This is a piece of brilliant generalship by Gandalf, and once more demonstrates his ability to find intuitive solutions to apparently hopeless situations. After breaking the power and the staff of Saruman at Isengard, and organising the Ents' custodianship of the area, Gandalf rides with Pippin to Minas

Tirith to organise its last defence.

The importance of the Battle of Helm's Deep, and Gandalf's role in it, cannot be overestimated. Without this victory over Saruman the forces of Rohan would not have been able to come to the aid of Minas Tirith, which they do at the eleventh hour. Not even Minas Tirith, the greatest fortress and city of the West, can withstand a direct assault by Sauron. The dividends of the Battle of Helm's Deep are seen here, in one of the most magnificent passages of *The Lord of the Rings*, where Gandalf is once more facing down an enemy he cannot hope to defeat in single combat. The Witch-king, the Lord of the Nazgûl, is about to ride in through the broken gates of Minas Tirith, at the head of Sauron's besieging army. Gandalf, sitting alone on Shadowfax, bars his way, and speaks defiant words. The Witch-king laughs:

> 'Old fool!' he said. 'Old fool! This is my hour. Do you not know Death when you see it? Die now and curse in vain!' And with that he lifted high his sword and flames ran down the blade.
>
> Gandalf did not move. And in that very moment, away behind in some courtyard of the City, a cock crowed. Shrill and clear he crowed, recking nothing of wizardry or war, welcoming only the morning that in the sky far above the shadows of death was coming with the dawn.
>
> And as if in answer there came from far away another note. Horns, horns, horns. In dark Mindolluin's sides they dimly echoed. Great horns of the North wildly blowing. Rohan had come at last. [249]

The Witch-king withdraws from his position facing Gandalf at the shattered gates of the City, and moves to engage King Théoden on the field. This is a fight Théoden has no chance of winning, as the Witch-king cannot be harmed by a mortal man. Théoden is killed, but the Witch-king is wounded in the knee by Merry. This gives Eowyn, Théoden's daughter who has stowed away with the army in disguise, her opportunity to strike a deadly blow against the Witch-king. With the arrival of Aragorn and the army he has mustered from southern Gondor, the Battle of the Pelennor Fields becomes a temporary, yet ultimately significant, victory. The breathing space allows Gandalf to argue for his final throw of the dice, to distract Sauron from his true peril – the journey of Frodo and Sam towards Mount Doom.

The journey of the Ringbearer is the crucial element in Gandalf's strategy to defeat Sauron. Everything else is ultimately a side-show. The Ring cannot be used by any of the great figures of the West, as its very nature is to corrupt those who bear it. It cannot be safely kept unused, as there is no stronghold in Middle-earth that Sauron could not finally conquer. It cannot be hidden or thrown away, as it is the Ring's nature to seek its master. The Ring presents a deadly danger to the West in more than one way. Its very existence is a temptation. Gandalf, Galadriel, even Sam all resist this temptation when it is offered to them. Boromir and Saruman are corrupted by it. It is this last danger that Gandalf decides to exploit. Sauron, in his arrogance, cannot believe that one of the great figures of the West will not try to use the Ring against him. The course of action that Gandalf recommends, and that the Council finally selects, is a desperate one: they decide to attempt the destruction of the Ring. For this to be accomplished the Ring must be carried into Mordor and cast into the furnace, fiery Sammath Naur in Mount Doom, where it was made. This apparently suicidal course of action has one great strategic benefit: it is the last thing Sauron expects the West to attempt. Gandalf makes this clear:

> 'Well, let folly be our cloak, a veil before the eyes of the Enemy! For he is very wise, and weighs all things to a nicety in the scales of his malice. But the only measure that he knows is desire, desire for power; and so he judges all hearts. Into his heart the thought will not enter that any will refuse it, that having the Ring we may seek to destroy it. If we seek this, we shall put him out of reckoning.' [250]

Gandalf is right. It is in Sauron's nature to fear that a champion of the West will confront him with the Ring, as power and domination are the only modes of thinking he understands. In an extended meditation, Gandalf reveals more of his thinking to Legolas, Gimli and Aragorn after rejoining them in Fangorn forest:

'Indeed he [Sauron] is in great fear, not knowing what mighty one may suddenly appear, wielding the Ring, and assailing him with war, seeking to cast him down and take his place. That we should wish to cast him down and have *no* one in his place is not a thought that occurs to his mind. That we should try to destroy the ring itself has not yet entered his darkest dream.' [251]

Gandalf realises that in constantly looking towards the West for the Ring, Sauron is making a serious error. He is ignoring the one place the ring is slowly going: his own realm. After his apparent defeat and explulsion from Dol Guldur, Sauron appeared to have outwitted the White Council, fleeing to his prepared stronghold in Mordor. But, as Gandalf ultimately realises, this was a fundamental error on Sauron's behalf:

'He [Sauron] returned at once to Mordor, and in ten years he declared himself. Then everything grew dark. And yet that was not his original plan; and it was in the end a mistake. Resistance still had somewhere where it could take counsel free from the Shadow. How could the Ringbearer have escaped, if there had been no Lórien, or Rivendell? And those places would have fallen, I think, if Sauron had thrown all his power against them first, and not spent more than half of it in the assault on Gondor.' [252]

The best strategy for Sauron would have been a direct and immediate assault on the hidden places of power in Middle-earth. Having failed to exploit this opportunity, Gandalf realises that Sauron, ensconced in Mordor, made another strategic blunder. Instead of capitalising on the natural strength of Mordor as a defensive position, and using all his powers to look for the Ring, Sauron launched the attack that started the War of the Ring:

> 'For if he had used all his power to guard Mordor, so that
> none could enter, and bent all his guile to the hunting of
> the Ring, then indeed hope would have faded: neither
> Ring nor bearer could long have eluded him. But now his
> eye gazes abroad rather than near at home; and mostly he
> looks towards Minas Tirith.' [253]

Sauron chooses the worst of the options available to him. Instead of striking at the West immediately, he returned to Mordor. And then instead of fortifying Mordor, he strikes outwards. It is upon this error – Sauron's belief that the West will seek to use the Ring – and his own natural arrogance, that Gandlaf's desperate strategy is based. And it is this strategy that dictates Gandalf's last tactical move, argued for in the Last Debate:

> '...we cannot by force defeat his [Sauron's] force. But we
> must at all costs keep his Eye from his true peril. We can-
> not achieve victory by arms, but by arms we can give the
> Ring-bearer his only chance, frail though it be.' [254]

This is Gandalf's last move then: to muster the remaining forces of the West, and to march out to confront Sauron before the gates of Mordor. This he believes will convince Sauron that Aragorn is displaying 'the pride of the new Ringlord', [255] and will cause him to bend all his attention to capturing him. The aim is to buy Frodo any extra time possible to complete his quest. It is, indeed, a desperate gambit. That it succeeds is down to the great wisdom Gandalf displays in his first conversation with Frodo about the Ring. When Gandalf talks to Frodo of Gollum and his game of riddles with Bilbo, Frodo evinces disgust and says that it was a pity Bilbo had not killed him. Gandalf's responds with some of his wisest words:

'Pity? It was Pity that stayed his hand. Pity, and Mercy: not to strike without need… Many that live deserve death. And some that die deserve life. Can you give it to them? Then do not be too eager to deal out death in judgement. For even the very wise cannot see all ends.' [256]

While the implications of Bilbo's merciful impulse are never properly explored in *The Hobbit*, Gandalf's commentary above says everything necessary about the virtues of pity and mercy. These words come back to Frodo when he first meets Gollum in the Emyn Muil and cause him to spare Gollum's life. And it is finally Gollum who achieves what Frodo at the end cannot bring himself to do, falling into the Cracks of Doom with Frodo's Ring-adorned severed finger, at the very moment of his triumph.

Gandalf, then, is the most significant historical figure in the history of the Third Age. Wise and courageous, intuitive and resourceful, terse yet kindly, he is a model of integrity and a source of inspiration for those who read of his exploits. In the last chapter of *The Lord of the Rings*, Gandalf departs from the Grey Havens to the Undying Lands, from where he first came to Middle-earth. With him also depart the Ring-bearers Bilbo and Frodo, as well as Elrond, Galadriel and other High Elves. Of the five Istari or wizards who came to Middle Earth, Gandalf is the only one who returns to the Uttermost West at the end of the Third Age – his mission accomplished. Waiting to set sail from Middle-earth, Gandalf wears openly for the first time Narya, the Elven ring of fire, which he has used to kindle fire in the hearts of those who have opposed Sauron.

CHAPTER SIX

TALES BY THE FIRE: FURTHER READING

s was said in the first chapter, there is no way we can do more than scratch at the surface of Tolkien's legacy. What began as a hobby, the creation of a new language, has become a massive international publishing and merchandising property, spawning four films, a number of radio serialisations, television documentaries, games and toys and, of course, many, many books.

And then there's the Internet. Quite what Tolkien would have made of that is anybody's guess...

FURTHER READING

The greatest benefit Tolkien readers will reap from the release of the New Line Cinema version of *The Fellowship of the Ring* is the re-release of pretty much every book or collection even remotely relating to the Professor, his life and his mythology. Volumes previously rather tricky to track down have been dragged from obscurity, their old covers replaced with flashy new ones showing images from the latest films, and have been stacked, floor to ceiling, in your local bookshop.

There are so many quality publications that it would take a book the size of this one just to detail them. With this in mind, here is a list of the best volumes for new Middle-earth explorers to seek out, once they've finished *The Silmarillion*, *The Hobbit* and *The Lord of the Rings*.

UNFINISHED TALES

After the publication of *The Silmarillion*, this was the next volume of Tolkien's Middle-earth work to be published. It is a curious book because, as the title suggests, there are no complete stories contained therein. Instead, there are glimpses and explanations.

The glimpses are of moments in Middle-earth's history of deep beauty and significance, from all of the Ages. Incidents merely touched on even in *The Silmarillion* are told in as much detail as exists. At times, this is deeply satisfying, such as the unused conversation between Gandalf, Frodo, Merry, Pippin and Gimli, told by Frodo, telling the background to the story we know of as *The Hobbit* and setting the story nicely within the events of *The Lord of the Rings*. Gandalf's telling of the Hunt for the Ring is equally compelling.

At other times, the abrupt or fragmentary nature of the stories will frustrate the Tolkien fan, leaving them with ragged dreams of what might have been (and possibly with nightmares of what they have yet to get through, namely all twelve volumes of *The History of Middle-earth*). The most wonderful, magical and frustrating example is the first tale in the collection, *Of Tuor and his Coming to Gondolin*, which simply stops. In the end, Christopher Tolkien can only paraphrase the jottings that show the direction the rest of the story was to take.

The explanations, notes and occasional alternative sections of text offered by Christopher Tolkien set each story in context both within the mythology and within the development of the mythology. The individual reader's reaction to these should give said reader some idea as to whether or not they are of a mind to explore yet further.

At times enough to make one weep, for all sorts of reasons, *Unfinished Tales* (George Allen & Unwin, 1981) is still an absolute must-have for Tolkien fans who want to extend their Middle-earth tour.

THE HISTORY OF MIDDLE-EARTH, VOLS 1-12

In his foreword to the first volume of *The Book of Lost Tales*,

Christopher Tolkien points out that

> ... many who read *The Lord of the Rings* with enjoyment
> would never wish to regard Middle-earth as more than
> the *mise-en-scene* of the story, and would delight in
> the sensation of 'depth' without wishing to explore
> the deep places. [257]

The same could be said of *The Silmarillion*. However, the simple knowledge that a vast amount of Tolkien's text was left unpublished, even after the *Unfinished Tales* were released in 1981, was just too much for many fans of Tolkien's work. Equally, Christopher Tolkien had always admitted that *The Silmarillion* was always going to be his interpretation of his father's work. Without the addition of comments from critics and commentators, Christopher Tolkien knew of the need for a commentary on the creative process that led his father to the creation of *The Silmarillion*, and a commentary that mere biography could not provide.

With no original plan, nor idea as to how long it would take in the writing, the result by 1996 was *The History of Middle-earth*, a detailed twelve-volume examination of the creation of and, as the title of the collection hints, the history of Middle-earth. Even by the end, not all of Tolkien's work in Middle-earth had been put on show.

Christopher Tolkien deserves applause for his exhaustive work, but be aware that these are books for only the most dedicated explorers of Middle-earth. Stories, chapters, brief jottings are presented (and sometime re-presented in a later, altered form), then dissected with lengthy commentaries placing the text in its correct historical place, both within the mythology and the development of that mythology. At times, it can be confusing and overwhelming.

The result for the reader is a greater understanding of Tolkien's seemingly haphazard creative process, and a deepening respect for Tolkien as a writer (despite lacking a hard and fast plan for where his writing was heading). Finally, the reader gains a respect for

Christopher Tolkien himself, for embarking on what at times must have seemed like an impossible task!

The volumes in *The History of Middle-earth* are:

J R R Tolkien: A Biography

Written by Humphrey Carpenter, a contemporary of Tolkien, this is the official, authorised biography of the Professor, first published back in 1977 by George Allen & Unwin. This is not a biography of Tolkien's writings, but of the man himself. Those looking for a history of the writing will not be dissatisfied by reading Carpenter's work, but will learn nothing here on the compiling for publication of, for example, *The Silmarillion*.

Although Tolkien himself did not believe that biography could always tell the reader about an author's work, Carpenter's very readable book does give clues here and there as to where Tolkien may have taken his inspiration. His life was not without incident and adventure, and Tolkien's readers will enjoy the journey.

It should be noted that Humphrey Carpenter also wrote *The Inklings: C.S. Lewis, J.R.R. Tolkien, Charles Williams and their friends*, and compiled *Letters of J.R.R. Tolkien*, both published by George Allen & Unwin in 1978 and 1981 respectively. Together with the biography, they give a comprehensive study of the life and character of Professor Tolkien.

THE ROAD TO MIDDLE-EARTH

Published by George Allen & Unwin in 1982 and revised ten years later, Tom Shippey here set out to explore in one volume what Christopher Tolkien was, at the time Shippey put pen to paper, to do in twelve. Shippey taught the same syllabus that Tolkien had taught at Oxford, lecturing in Old English (Anglo-Saxon). He is also a renowned science fiction author in his own right. Shippey even communicated with Tolkien on the subject of *The Road To Middle-earth*.

This is a fascinating book, truly, but it is not an accessible book. Its very subject, perhaps, prevents it from being an easy read, though it is well worth persevering with. While Carpenter deals with Tolkien's life as a whole, and how external forces worked upon the Professor and his writings, Shippey is almost entirely concerned with Tolkien's professional life.

The Road To Middle-earth deals with Tolkien's fascination with language; the history of languages, how they were constructed and how they developed. Shippey then shows how all of this impacted on the creation of *The Lord of the Rings* and the rest of the mythology. Extensive examples, fascinating quotes and comparisons, compelling and complex discussion, all serve to fill gaps left in Humphrey Carpenter's biography. At the end, the reader can only conclude that both simple life history and detailed professional study had equal parts in the creation of Tolkien's mythologies.

Bored Of The Rings

It was with no small delight, and a faint twinge of conscience, that the authors of this book welcomed the news that the Harvard Lampoon's parody *Bored of the Rings* was to be reprinted in time for the release of the new film. First printed in 1969, much has since been said of this work of... well, this work, and much of it by people who really should have been more polite.

Although it does sag a little towards the end, this is a mostly funny, occasionally truly inspired, always affectionate spoof of *The Lord of the Rings*. If you grow tired of endless reams of deadly serious text concerning the eminent Professor and his works, this clever little book is the perfect antidote. It will, no doubt, attract as large and as dedicated following amongst the student fraternity, in whose direction the humour is firmly aimed, as it did last time around.

The BBC Radio Series

Not strictly further reading, it must be said, but well worth a mention here, are the BBC Radio adaptations of *The Hobbit* and *The Lord of the Rings*. Available both from bookshops and on-line, both on CD and audiocassette, these are exceptional. Potential listeners may be put off by the thought that a radio production cannot possibly do justice to such intricate works. Put such thoughts aside immediately. The high production values, effects, music and voice talents do the stories justice.

Groundbreaking and award-winning, *The Lord of the Rings* is especially worth a mention, as Ian Holm, who plays Bilbo Baggins in the upcoming New Line Cinema version of *The Fellowship of the Ring*, puts in an astonishing performance as Frodo Baggins. The series borrows from *Unfinished Tales* to provide extra dialogue and scenes to fill gaps and explain some things that newcomers might miss. Thoroughly recommended!

THE ANIMATED MOVIE

In the 1970s, an ambitious director by the name of Ralph Bakshi attempted to create an animated version of *The Lord of the Rings*. The project ran into money troubles. Short cuts were taken and, in the end, the film (released in 1978) covered events only as far as Gandalf's arrival at Helm's Deep. A second film never materialised.

Fondly remembered by some, vilified by the majority, the movie is available on DVD in the UK (released in November, 2001), and will surely be seen many times on television in the run-up to the cinematic release of *The Fellowship of the Ring*. It is worth noting that Peter Woodthorpe gave voice to Gollum and played the same role in the BBC Radio adaptation, and that Anthony Daniels (*Star Wars*'s C-3PO) provided the voice for Legolas.

TOYS, GAMES AND MERCHANDISE

Way back in 1982, *The Hobbit* became a text *and* graphics adventure on a number of home computer formats. Although there had been a few Tolkien-related computer games released before this date, this game, produced by Beam Software and distributed by Melbourne House, is the one most fans remember as the first.

Since then, there have been many more computer games set in Tolkien's mythology. The efforts of technologically-minded fans have kept many of these ancient titles alive and, with the appropriate software on your modern PC, you can relive the heady days of the ZX Spectrum or the Commodore 64.

Tolkien Games (http://www.lysater.liu.se/tolkien-games/) have a comprehensive listing and a detailed, illustrated history of these games, and have links to the best download sites for the emulators and the games themselves.

Sierra will be releasing a new game, *The Fellowship of the Ring*, across a number of formats, a little before the eponymous film is released in late 2001. At the time of writing, little information is available from Sierra themselves (http://www.sierra.com/), but that will no doubt have changed by the time you read this.

The Lord of the Rings is full of battles, sieges and skirmishes, making it a perfect setting for a table-top wargame. Games Workshop have a reputation for producing quality fantasy and sci-fi wargames aimed at the teenage buyer, but which are popular also with many adult gamers. Although the UK company, the biggest of its kind in the world, has previously stuck religiously to settings of their own devising, the lure of *The Lord of the Rings* has proved too tempting to resist.

Tolkien collectors and gamers alike can discover more about Games Workshops contribution to the latest merchandise frenzy by visiting the company stores, the company website (http://www.games-work-shop.com), or by writing to the company directly.

In the UK, write to:
Games Workshop Ltd.
Willow Road
Lenton
Nottingham
NG7 2WS

In the US, write to:
Games Workshop Inc.
6721 Baymeadow Drive
Glen Burnie
Maryland
21060 6401

With a background as detailed as Tolkien's mythology, and with many of Tolkien's admirers being, or having been, higher education students, it should come as no surprise that role players have always sought adventure in Middle-earth. For many years, the US company Iron Crown Enterprises (ICE for short) met the huge demand with the much admired *Middle-earth Role Playing* system, or *MERP* as it is more popularly known.

An adapted version of ICE's own *Rolemaster* system, the supplements to this game allowed imaginative and creative players to adventure in any Age of Tolkien's mythology, and in any part of Middle-earth. There were, before the licence was dropped, over 40 supplemental books published, giving exhaustive detail on geography and population, flora and fauna, politics and intrigue, for every square inch of Middle-earth. It is still possible to pick up new and second-hand copies of these excellent books at the likes of Legend Games (http://www.legendgames.co.uk) who, incidentally, have available a number of free *MERP*-related downloads. They can also be found at your local games store or at conventions.

Picking up where ICE left off, Decipher Inc. (http://www.decipher.com) will be releasing a role playing system and a card game (fully illustrated with images from the new film) in time for the release of *The Fellowship of the Ring*. Decipher have a well-deserved reputation for providing excellent customer support, and their products are generally of a high standard. Collectors and gamers will not, one imagines, be disappointed.

Collectable miniatures such as those produced by Games Workshop are not a new thing. Mithril Miniatures, founded back in 1987, produce beautiful, very finely detailed 25mm scale miniatures of Middle-earth personalities, including everyone and everything from the likes of Gandalf and Galadriel to merry drinkers from the inn at Bree. The company website (http://www.mithril.ie) has all the details, but interested parties can also write to the company at

Mithril Miniatures
Kilnamartyra
Macroon
Co. Cork
Ireland
Or call them on **00-353-26-40222**.

The central plank of any movie merchandising campaign these days seems to be the action figure. Currently, there are two companies producing Middle-earth plastic people. Toy Vault (http://www.toyvault.com) have a licence which expires in 2002. Their range of figures are, in truth, not that inspiring, although the Galadriel figure is pretty good. Repackaged several times, they have an appeal for completist collectors.

In time for the release of the New Line Cinema version of *The Fellowship of the Ring*, Toy Biz are producing the usual six-inch figures, as well as nine- to twelve-inch collector's figures. There will be double packs, deluxe editions and, no doubt, collector's exclusives.

Add to the merchandise lists the posters, statues and busts, tie-in books and re-covers, magazines, mugs, stickers, calendars, T-shirts, and lunchboxes, and the next three years or so are likely to be an intense time for Tolkien collectors everywhere. If you are wondering how to keep track of all of the excitement, the Internet is the place to turn.

TOLKIEN ON THE INTERNET

The Tolkien Society
http://www.tolkiensociety.org/
This section could both begin and end with this one link. From the simple but resoundingly useful site of the Tolkien Society, a traveller on the Internet can journey far and wide and with such satisfaction that any site not listed on the society's links page seems scarcely worth mentioning.

Without even being a member of the Society, an international group of fans of all ages and from all walks of life, the browser can find much to satisfy their thirst for information. Biographies, whole essays, thought provoking discussions, extensive lists, informative reviews; everything you could need and more. The Tolkien Society even has a bookshop where you can pick up the texts needed to fill the gaps in your collection.

Those of you who do not have Internet access can contact the Tolkien Society in the UK at the following address:

> **Membership Enquiries**
> **Trevor Reynolds**
> **65 Wentworth Crescent**
> **Ash Vale**
> **Surrey**
> **United Kingdom**
> **GU12 5LF**

Remember to include the appropriate type of stamped, self-addressed envelope (particularly if you are writing from overseas). By far the best and easiest way to join the Society is on-line at their website.

The Official Lord of the Rings Movie Site
http://www.lordoftherings.net/index.html

Between Christmas 2001 and Christmas 2003, New Line Cinema will release the most complete cinematic representation of *The Lord of the Rings* yet to be attempted. Inevitably, the very notion of a live-action film has caused controversy amongst Tolkien fans. We all know, in our heads, what Gandalf looks like, how Gollum sounds, and how dark Moria actually is.

This new interpretation of Tolkien's works, drawing as it does from (amongst other volumes) the Appendices of *The Lord of the Rings* to flesh out the likes of Arwen, and creating new characters such as Saruman's orc creature Lurtz, will no doubt be loved and hated in equal measures by the critics, much as Tolkien's original novels will always be.

The official site for the new films contains details of the cast, the filming, the merchandise and, needless to say, the source material. It is a little slow to download for those of us with more ancient Internet connections, but it is a genuine challenge to even the most purist of Tolkien fans not to be just a little excited by director Peter Jackson's interpretation of Middle-earth.

TheOneRing.net
http://www.theonering.net/

As the official site slowly took form, there was one site on the Internet where Tolkien fans could head for information and images, rumours and debate about the Peter Jackson films. Once the official site became established, TheOneRing.net was still the best place to go for up-to-the-minute news, images, rumours and debate.

With information gathered by individuals on the ground in New Zealand, augmented by reports of *Lord of the Rings* coverage from around the globe, TheOneRing.net remains one of the finest, most positive on-line fan communities today. Its input has been appreciated by those involved in the making of the new films, to the extent that the site is now the home of the Official Peter Jackson Fan Club.

Extensive links pages, not to mention the usual reviews, polls, discussion and so on, make it easy to see why this well organised, well designed site has attracted the following it has.

The Tolkien Sarcasm Page
http://www.speakeasy.org/ ~ ohh/tolksarc.htm

Every now and then, a work of true genius is thrust upon the world. One such work is *The Tolkien Sarcasm Page*. It is very easy to get caught up in the seriousness of Tolkien's works; to get lost in the language, the structure, and the stories. This site is an instant cure for the tendency to take Tolkien overly seriously. Purists need not apply.

A visit to this site allows the browser access to the extremely rare *Lord of the Rings* board game (*not* the Hasbro version), the complication cards from which will raise many a chuckle. You will be able to read the lost texts of Shakespeare's *The Tragedie of Frodo Baggins*, and Sir Arthur Conan Doyle's *Sherlock Holmes in Middle-earth*. Finally, you may wish to peruse *The Tolkien Crackpot Theories Page*, to learn the truth about the likes of the Balrog's slippers, why Elves and Dwarves don't get along, and the Witch-king's secret identity of Tom Bombadil.

This is by no means a comprehensive list of even the very best Tolkien related websites. Entering the name 'Tolkien' in the Yahoo! search engine brings up a listing of more than 187,000 web page matches. Enter *The Lord of the Rings* and the list is for 222,000 pages. With the release of the movies, this is certain to increase.

The sites listed here have links pages that will take the browser on a very long journey indeed. You will travel the world as you search for Middle-earth on the Internet, encountering Tolkien aficionados from Australia, Britain, Russia, Japan, the USA, South America, Africa and every point in between.

Despite the fact that Tolkien was uneasy about the attention which his mythology brought upon him personally, it cannot be doubted that his books have struck a chord with readers throughout the world. We said at the beginning of this book that, once encountered, the stories, people and places of Middle-earth stay with you all your life. Tolkien created a mythology of such depth and complexity, yet with such simple and profound roots, that it can take a lifetime to explore without ever the journey becoming dull.

Good luck in your travels!

Bibliography

Carpenter, Humphrey, *J.R.R. Tolkien: A Biography*, George Allen & Unwin, 1977

Carpenter, Humphrey, *The Inklings: C.S. Lewis, J.R.R. Tolkien, Charles Williams and their friends*, George Allen & Unwin, 1978

Carpenter, Humphrey (editor), *Letters of J.R.R. Tolkien*, George Allen & Unwin, 1981

Day, David, *A Tolkien Bestiary*, Harbour Publishing, 1984

Harvard Lampoon, *Bored of the Rings*, Signet, 1969

Kocher, Paul H, *Master of Middle-earth: The Achievement of J.R.R. Tolkien*, Thames and Hudson, 1973

Kocher, Paul H, *A Reader's Guide To The Silmarillion*, Thames and Hudson, 1980

Noel, Ruth S, *Mythology of Tolkien's Middle-earth*, Panther, 1979

Shippey, Tom, *The Road To Middle-earth*, George Allen & Unwin, 1982 (revised edition, Grafton, 1992)

Tolkien, Christopher (editor), *The History of Middle-earth* comprising:

I: *The Book of Lost Tales, Part One*, George Allen & Unwin, 1983
II: *The Book of Lost Tales, Part Two*, George Allen & Unwin, 1984
III: *The Lays of Beleriand*, George Allen & Unwin, 1985
IV: *The Shaping of Middle-earth*, Unwin Hyman, 1986
V: *The Lost Road and Other Writings: Language and Legend before The Lord of the Rings*, Unwin Hyman, 1987
VI: *The Return of the Shadow: The History of The Lord of the Rings, Part One*, Unwin Hyman, 1988
VII: *The Treason of Isengard: The History of the Lord of the Rings, Part Two*, Unwin Hyman, 1989
VIII: *The War of the Ring: The History of the Lord of the Rings, Part Three*, Unwin Hyman, 1990
IX: *Sauron Defeated: The End of the Third Age (The History of the Lord of the Rings, Part Four)*, Harper Collins, 1992
X: *Morgoth's Ring*, Harper Collins, 1993
XI: *The War of the Jewels*, Harper Collins, 1995
XII: *The Peoples of Middle-earth*, Harper Collins, 1997

Tolkien, J R R, *The Hobbit: or There and Back Again*, George Allen & Unwin, third edition,1966

Tolkien, J R R, *The Lord of the Rings*, George Allen & Unwin, second edition, 1966

Tolkien, J R R, *The Silmarillion*, George Allen & Unwin, 1977

Tolkien, J R R, *Unfinished Tales of Numenor and Middle-earth*, George Allen & Unwin, 1981

NOTES

Page references given below for Tolkien's major works are to the latest editions published during the author's lifetime:

The Hobbit, third edition, George Allen & Unwin Ltd, 1966

The Fellowship of the Ring, second edition, George Allen & Unwin, 1966

The Two Towers, second edition, George Allen & Unwin, 1966

The Return of the King, second edition, George Allen & Unwin, 1966

The Silmarillion, first edition, George Allen & Unwin, 1977

Unfinished Tales, first edition, George Allen & Unwin, 1980

Chapter One

We could not hope to equal, for example, Tom Shippey's scholarly *The Road to Middle-earth* (George Allen & Unwin,1982)

2 In his very readable authorised biography (*J. R. R. Tolkien a biography*, George Allen & Unwin, 1977) Humphrey Carpenter points out that Tolkien himself did not believe that the true meaning and motives of the author could be successfully gleaned from study of the author's life. Indeed Carpenter himself concludes that more can be learned about the Professor from his work, as '...the work was his biography...'

Chapter Two

3 *The Silmarillion,* 'Ainulindalë' p.15

4 The parallel with Satan in Judeo-Christian mythology is so obvious as to be almost not worth remarking on.

5 Ibid. p.15

6 Ibid. p.16-17

7 It is vital to realise that whilst the universe now exists, the complex world the Ainur see within it exists only *in potentia.*

8 The Ainur see part of the developing history of Eä, but it is suggested that their vision fades before they see it all.

9 *The Silmarillion,* 'Ainulindalë' p.19

10 Ibid. p.19

11 The idea that the greatest perfection is achieved using flawed materials is a fascinating one. The most perfect (three-dimensional) geometric form that can be imagined is the sphere. Indeed, of the pre-Socratic philosophers, Parmenides insisted that the world was a perfect, eternal, changeless sphere, and so much the worse for our flawed senses. Most of us who live and think in this flawed world, however, would agree that 'flaws' mean difference, difference diversity, and diversity life.

12 Rose A Zimbardo 'Moral Vision in Lord of the Rings', *Tolkien and the Critics,* Isaacs and Zimbardo, Notre Dame, 1968

13 *Silmarillion,* 'Ainulindalë' p.16

14 *Silmarillion,* Chapter 1, Of the Beginning of Days, p.37

15 Ibid. p.39

16 Ibid. p.38

17 Ibid. p.40

18 Ibid. p.40

19 Ibid. p.40

20 *Silmarillion,* Chapter 2, Of Aulë and Yavanna, p.43

21 Ibid. p.43

22 Ibid. p.46

23 It is interesting to note that the polar

natures of Aulë and Yavanna are expressed perfectly in a very few lines at the end of Chapter 2. Yavanna warns Aulë that his children had better beware when they walk in the forests. Aulë's marvellously laconic reply is worth quoting in full: '"Nonetheless they will have need of wood", said Aulë, and he went on with his smith-work.'

24 Christopher Tolkien identifies most of the stars and constellations created in the index of *The Silmarillion*: Wilwarin = Cassiopeia; Menelmacar = Orion; Valacirca = Ursa Major (the Great Bear, The Plough, the Big Dipper). He does not identify Carnil (Red Star) but I would imagine this is Mars. Neither does he identify Telumendil which Ruth S Noel translates in *The Languages of Tolkien's Middle-earth* as 'Devoted to the Dome of Heaven' or 'Point of the Dome'. From this I would guess that the word describes either the star Polaris, or the constellation that contains it, Ursa Minor.

25 *The Lord of the Rings,* The Fellowship of the Ring, Book 1, Chapter 12, p.210
26 *The Lord of the Rings,* The Two Towers, Book 4, Chapter 9, p.330
27 *The Lord of the Rings,* The Return of the King, Book 6, Chapter 1, p.179
28 *Silmarillion*, Chapter 7, Of the Silmarils and the Unrest of the Noldor, p.67
29 The parallel between Fëanor and Prometheus here is remarkable.
30 *Silmarillion*, Chapter 7, Of the Silmarils and the Unrest of the Noldor, p.69
31 The name Fëanor itself means 'Spirit of fire'

32 Ruth S Noel notes (*Mythologies of Tolkien's Middle Earth* p.149) that in Anglo-Saxon and Norse mythology the name 'ring-giver' is synonymous with 'good ruler'. Much here might be said about the irony of the name Sauron chooses for himself.
33 These Elves were the people of Celebrimbor, grandson of Fëanor, the greatest smith in the history of Middle Earth whom we have already mentioned.
34 The One Ring was completed around the year 1600 of the Second Age, over 4500 years before Bilbo finds the One Ring in the Goblin warrens, in the year 2941 of the Third Age, as detailed in *The Hobbit*.
35 *Master of Middle Earth*, p.59 (Thames and Hudson,1973)
36 *The Lord of the Rings*, The Fellowship of the Ring, Book 2, Chapter 2, p.266
37 These events are described in detail in *The Hobbit,* Chapter 5, Riddles in the Dark.
38 Sauron took up residence in Dol Guldur in Mirkwood upon returning to Middle Earth in the year 2060 of the Third Age, although there were hints of a dark power growing there long before this. In Third Age 2063, Gandalf investigated Dol Guldur, and Sauron retreated to the East. He returned in 2460 and remained there until 2941, the year in which Bilbo found the Ring. In this year the White Council united to drive Sauron from Mirkwood. Sauron, having laid his plans well, returned in secret to Mordor. In 2953, Sauron declared himself openly in Mordor.
39 *The Lord of the Rings*, The Fellowship of the Ring, Book 1, Chapter 2, p.65

40 *The Hobbit* Chapter 5, p.97

41 *The Lord of the Rings*, The Fellowship of the Ring, Book 1, Chapter 2, p.69

42 *The Lord of the Rings*, The Return of the King, Book 6, Chapter 1, p.177

43 We should also note the case of Saruman. The desire for the Ring was also part of his downfall. However for him this was also encompassed by his deep study of the works of Sauron, and the fact that he finally gave in to temptation and used one of the *Palantíri* (seeing stones), whence he was snared by Sauron. The case of Saruman is a classic example of Nietzsche's caveat 'He who studies monsters should take care lest he become a monster; and when you look into the abyss, beware - for the abyss also looks back into you.'

44 *The Lord of the Rings*, The Return of the King, Book 6, Chapter1, p.188

45 *The Lord of the Rings*, The Fellowship of the Ring, Book 1, Chapter 1, pp 70-71

46 *The Lord of the Rings*, The Fellowship of the Ring, Book 2, Chapter 8, p. 381

47 ibid. p.381

48 ibid. p.381

49 ibid. p.381

50 ibid. p.381

51 *The Lord of the Rings*, The Fellowship of the Ring, Book 2, Chapter 2, p.281

52 The Council in fact considered another option: that of giving the Ring to Tom Bombadil to guard. Tom is described as virtually omnipotent within in his small realm of the Old Forest and the Barrow Downs, and the One Ring has no power over him: a fact clearly seen when he dons the Ring, and does not disappear from the sight of the startled hobbits. But Tom's strength is limited to his own tiny realm, and linked to the earth itself, which Sauron has the power to torture and disrupt. Even it, according to Gandalf, could not withstand a concentrated assault by Sauron indefinitely. See this volume: Chapter 4: Foul and Fair: The Cast of *The Lord of the Rings*: section on Maiar.

53 *The Lord of the Rings*, The Fellowship of the Ring, Book 2, Chapter 10, p.417

54 It should be noted however that Hobbits are remarkably resilient. Bilbo bore the Ring for a long time without much ill-effect, and Sméagol possessed the Ring for 478 years. It had a dramatic effect on him, certainly, but he never became a Ringwraith, as a man surely would have done.

55 *The Silmarillion* 'Of the Rings of Power and the Third Age', p.304

56 *The Lord of the Rings*, The Fellowship of the Ring, Book 2, Chapter 7, p.380

57 *The Silmarillion* 'Of the Rings of Power and the Third Age', p.304

Chapter Three

58 *The Silmarillion*, Ainulindalë, The Music of the Ainur, p.22

59 *The Silmarillion*, Chapter 3, Of the Coming of the Elves, p.52

60 *The Silmarillion*, Chapter 9, Of the Flight of the Noldor, p.88

61 *The Silmarillion*, Chapter 9, Of the Flight of the Noldor, p.81

62 *The Silmarillion*, Chapter 8, Of the Darkening of Valinor, p.73

63 As detailed in Chapter 2: Creation. Morgoth produces these monsters as twisted mockeries of the Elves and Ents. This is said to be his greatest evil.

64 *The Silmarillion*, Chapter 18, Of the Ruin of Beleriand and the Fall of Fingolfin, p.150

65 Fëanor's words to the Valar upon his defying of their ban and urging the Noldor to follow him to take vengeance upon Morgoth. *The Silmarillion*, Chapter 9, Of the Flight of the Noldor, p.85

66 During the Fall of Gondolin, Ecthelion of the Fountain kills Gothmog, the Lord of the Balrogs. And Glorfindel, the namesake of the Elf in *The Lord of The Rings*, also kills one of the Valaraukar as the Elves flee the ruined city.

67 *The Silmarillion*, Chapter 18, Of the Ruin of Beleriand and the Fall of Fingolfin, p.153

68 *The Silmarillion*, Chapter 20, Of the Fifth Battle: Nirnaeth Arnoediad, p.195

69 Eärendil is the son of Tuor, a human hero, and Idril Celebrindal, the granddaughter of Fingolfin.

70 *The Silmarillion*, Chapter 24, Of the Voyage of Eärendil and the War of Wrath.

71 Beleriand is the land in Middle-earth where the events of *The Silmarillion* take place. Its destruction encompasses Morgoth's hold of Angband, almost all the Elven strongholds and the Dwarven Mansions of Nogrod and Belegost.

72 The parents of Elrond and Elros are Eärendil and Elwing. Eärendil, as we just mentioned, is the son of Tuor, a Man, and his Elven wife Idril Celebrindal. Elwing is the granddaughter of Beren, another mortal, and Lúthien, the result of the union of Thingol Greycloak, the Sindarin King, and Melian the Maiar. This means Elrond and Elros carry the blood of three great races.

73 *The Silmarillion*, Akallabêth, p.260

74 The Valar forbid the Dúnedain from sailing west, as that way lies the Undying Lands, reserved for the Elves alone.

75 Ilúvatar has made Men mortal. It is a gift. But through the lies and evil of Morgoth, death comes to be seen as a curse, something to be feared and strived against. It is said to be one of his greatest evils against Men.

76 Of Sauron's nine Ringwraiths, or *Nazgûl*, three are said to have originally been great princes of Númenor corrupted into Sauron's service even before he became adviser to Ar-Pharazôn.

77 *The Silmarillion*, Akallabêth, p.273

78 *The Silmarillion*, Akallabêth p.281

79 *The Silmarillion*, Akallabêth, p.280-81

80 Of these Umbar is the greatest. This sea fortress in the Southern lands of Harad proved to be a constant enemy and rival of Gondor, until its final defeat by Aragorn in the early years of the Fourth Age.

81 *The Silmarillion*, Of the Rings of Power and the Third Age, p.294

82 *The Lord of The Rings*, The Fellowship of the Ring, Book 2, Chapter 2, p.266

83 The Elven army is led by Glorfindel, the powerful Noldor who comes to the aid of Frodo, Aragorn and the other Hobbits as they approach Rivendell, pursued by the Nazgûl.

84 The Haradrim and Easterlings, respectively.

85 Interestingly, it is with the aid of the Northmen that the victory of King Eldacar comes. Yet another example in miniature of the necessity of alliances and understanding between disparate

peoples in the struggle against Sauron and Morgoth.

86 Minas Ithil and Minas Anor were originally twin fortresses, meaning Tower of the Moon and of the Sun, respectively. After its capture, Minas Ithil becomes Minas Morgul, or Tower of Dark Sorcery. Minas Anor is renamed in contest Minas Tirith, or Tower of Guard or Watch.

87 Thus fulfilling the prophecy, spoken by the Elven Lord Glorfindel at the destruction of Angmar, that the Witch-king would not fall by the hand of man. In this great feat, Eowyn had the aid of the Hobbit, Meriadoc Brandybuck, who struck the Nazgûl behind the knee to save her at a vital moment.

88 *The Lord of The Rings*, The Fellowship of the Ring, Book 2, Chapter 2, pp 280-81

89 One of the powers of the Elven Ring of Fire is said to be its ability to kindle the fire in men's hearts. Although not stated explicitly, it is likely that it played a part in Théoden's transformation. For more details see this volume: Chapter 2: Creation and Chapter 5: Gandalf: The Fire in Men's Hearts.

90 *The Lord of The Rings*, The Return of the King, Appendix A, p.377

91 *The Lord of The Rings*, The Return of The King, Book 5, Chapter 1, p.30

92 *The Lord of The Rings*, The Return of The King, Book 5, Chapter 4, p.86

93 Ibid p.87

94 Ibid p.87

95 *The Lord of The Rings*, The Return of The King, Book 5, Chapter 7, p.129

96 *The Lord of The Rings*, The Return of The King, Book 5, Chapter 4, p.87

97 *The Lord of The Rings*, The Return of The King, Book 5, Chapter 4, p.92

98 *The Lord of The Rings*, The Return of The King, Book 5, Chapter 4, pp 98-9

99 *The Lord of The Rings*, The Return of The King, Book 5, Chapter 7, p.129

100 It is also likely that Professor Tolkien's own world view and Catholic upbringing, with its strict prohibition against suicide, colours the condemnation of Denethor's end.

101 *The Lord of The Rings*, The Return of The King, Book 5, Chapter 7, p.129

102 *The Lord of The Rings*, The Return of The King, Book 5, Chapter 4, p.86

103 *The Lord of The Rings*, The Return of The King, Book 5, Chapter 4. P.93

104 *The Lord of The Rings*, The Two Towers, Book 3, Chapter 6, p. 117

105 *The Lord of The Rings*, The Return of The King, Book 5, Chapter 7, p. 129

106 *The Lord of The Rings*, The Return of The King, Book 5, Chapter 4, p.97

107 *The Lord of The Rings*, The Return of The King, Book 5, Chapter 7, p.132

108 *The Lord of The Rings*, The Return of The King, Book 5, Chapter 7, p.130

109 Although Elrond at first opposed the match, reluctant to be parted from his beloved daughter. He refused to allow the marriage until Aragorn became king of both Gondor and Arnor, as befitted the descendant of Elendil. The tale of Aragorn and Arwen, as described in the first Appendix to *The Lord of The Rings*, has many echoes of that of Beren and Lúthien.

110 See *The Silmarillion*, Of the Rings of Power and the Third Age and *The Lord of The Rings*, Appendix B for more details. The Istari are dealt with in greater detail in this volume, Chapter 5: Gandalf: The Fire in Men's Hearts

111 Meaning Hill of Dark Sorcery. For a timeline of events in the Third Age see The Tale of Years, *The Lord of The Rings*, Appendix B

112 See this volume: Chapter 5:Gandalf:The Fire in Men's Hearts

113 *The Lord of The Rings*, The Two Towers, Book 4, Chapter 9, p.332

114 Meaning slave in Mordor's Black Speech: 'snaga' is the contemptuous term the Uruk-hai use to refer to the lesser Orcs.

115 The three specimens encountered by Bilbo and the Dwarves in *The Hobbit* were geniuses of their kind, speaking Westron and understanding basic arithmetic.

116 *The Lord of The Rings*, The Return of The King, Book 6, Chapter 4, p.227

117 The Inscription upon the One Ring is written in Black Speech, rather than Elven or Westron.

118 *The Lord of The Rings*, The Return of The King, Book 5, Chapter 9, p.156

119 *The Lord of The Rings*, The Fellowship of the Ring, Book 2, Chapter 2, p.284

120 *The Lord of The Rings*, The Fellowship of the Ring, Book 1, Chapter 2, pp 68-69

121 *The Lord of the Rings*, The Fellowship of the Ring, Book 2, Chapter 2, p.282

122 Details of Aragorn's rule, and his marriage to Arwen Evenstar, can be found *The Lord of the Rings*, The Return of the King, Appendix A.

123 Along with Gandalf, Bilbo, Frodo, Sam and even Gimli! See the Dwarves section in this volume: Chapter 4: Foul and Fair: The Cast of *The Lord of the Rings*.

124 *The Lord of the Rings*, The Return of the King, Book 5, Chapter 9, p.155

Chapter Four

125 The nature and source of Creation is dealt with in greater detail in this volume: Chapter 2: Creation.

126 The sundering of the Elves into at least four different groups, the Vanyar, the Noldor, the Teleri and the Avari, is dealt with in this volume: Chapter 4: Foul and Fair: The Cast of *The Lord of the Rings*: section on Elves.

127 See this volume: Chapter 2: Creation.

128 For example, Gildor the Elf called her protection upon Frodo as they said farewell in the Shire. *The Lord of the Rings*, The Fellowship of the Ring. Book 1, Chapter 3, p. 94

129 *The Lord of the Rings*, The Two Towers, Book 4, Chapter 10, pp 329-331

130 For more on the greatest servants of the Valar, see this volume: Chapter 4: Foul and Fair: The Cast of *The Lord of the Rings*: section on the Maiar.

131 These events, and others of the First Age, are dealt with in more detail elsewhere in this book. See this volume: Chapter 2: Creation.

132 *Unfinished Tales*, Part 1, Chapter 1, Of Tuor and His Coming to Gondolin, p.29

133 See this volume: Chapter 3: The Lessening of the Ages.

134 For more on Aulë and the origins of the Dwarves, see this volume: Chapter 2: Creation and Chapter 4: the section on Dwarves.

135 For details of this act of creation, see this volume: Chapter 2: Creation.

136 As they are. One Silmaril sits upon

the brow of Earendil the Mariner as he sails the heavens. The others are cast into the sea and a volcano to find their final resting places.

137 As we have seen elsewhere, many of the stories found in the world's myths and legends are also found in other forms in Tolkien's work. The Greek legend of Orpheus and Eurydice, where Orpheus charms Hades with his songs into returning his lost love Eurydice to him, bears some obvious similarities to Tolkien's story of Beren and Lúthien.

138 While the other Valar can easily be equated with pagan gods of the sky, the sea or the dead, Nienna perhaps most resembles the Christian, and especially Catholic, figure of the Virgin Mary.

139 See this volume: Chapter 3: The Lessening of the Ages.

140 *The Lord of the Rings*, The Return of the King, Book 5, Chapter 5, p.113

141 Although there is very little information given on Vaire, we can see there are similarities with the Fates of Greek myth and the Norns of Norse legend. However in both those cases there are three sisters weaving the tapestries of fate, while Vaire does so alone.

142 Lóthlorien, the realm of Galadriel in *The Lord of the Rings*, literally means Dream Flower and is named after the memory of the gardens of Irmo. However Lóthlorien is commonly referred to as the Golden Wood after its full, original title of Laurelindórenan.

143 For an overview of some of the most important events of the First Age, including many of the crimes of Morgoth, see this volume: Chapter 3: The Lessening of the Ages.

144 See this volume: Chapter 2: Creation.

145 For more on the Orcs, Trolls, Dragons and other minions of Morgoth see the appropriate sections of this chapter.

146 See this volume: Chapter 3: The Lessening of the Ages.

147 For more on the forging of the Rings, their powers and purposes, see this volume: Chapter 2: Creation.

148 For details of the Nazgûl, see this volume: Chapter 4: Foul and Fair: The Cast of *The Lord of the Rings*: section on Men.

149 See this volume: Chapter 3: The Lessening of the Ages, and Chapter 5: Gandalf: The Fire in Men's Hearts.

150 For a more detailed examination of the motivations and natures of Morgoth and Sauron, from Tolkien's own notes, see the multi-volume History of Middle-earth, Volume 10, Morgoth's Ring, Part 5.

151 *The Lord of the Rings*, The Fellowship of the Ring, Book 2, Chapter 5, p.344

152 *The Silmarillion*, Chapter 9, Of the Flight of the Noldor, p.80

153 *The Lord of The Rings*, The Two Towers, Book 4, Chapter 9, p.333

154 For more on the different races of Elves, see this volume: Chapter 4: Foul and Fair: The Cast of *The Lord of the Rings*: section on Elves.

155 *The Silmarillion*, Chapter 17, Of the Coming of Men into the West, p.144

156 For more on the Nauglamir, and the troubled history of the Dwarves and Elves, see this volume: Chapter 4: Foul and Fair: The Cast of *The Lord of the Rings*: section on Dwarves.

157 For more on both these crimes against Doriath see this volume: Chapter 4: Foul and Fair: The Cast of *The Lord of the Rings*: sections on Dwarves and Elves.

158 For more on both these crimes against Doriath see this volume: Chapter 4: Foul and Fair: The Cast of *The Lord of the Rings*: section on Ents.

159 *The Lord of the Rings*, The Fellowship of the Ring, Book 1, Chapter 7, p.142

160 *The Lord of the Rings*, The Fellowship of the Ring, Book 2, Chapter 2, p.279

161 For more on all the Dwarves, including those of Belegost, see this volume: Chapter 4: Foul and Fair: The Cast of *The Lord of the Rings*: section on Dwarves

162 *The Silmarillion*, Chapter 21, Of Túrin Turambar, pp 213-214

163 For more on Gandalf, and the chance meeting that saved Middle-earth from Sauron, see the this volume: Chapter 5: Gandalf: The Fire in Men's Hearts.

164 *The Silmarillion* , Chapter 2, Of Aulë and Yavanna, p.44

165 *The Lord of The Rings*, Appendix A, p.360

166 See this volume: Chapter 2: Creation.

167 As detailed in *The Hobbit*

168 See this volume: Chapter 4: Foul and Fair: The Cast of *The Lord of the Rings*: section on Ents.

169 *The Lord of the Rings,* The Fellowship of the Ring, Book 2, Chapter 4, p.318-319

170 As detailed in *The Hobbit*

171 *The Lord of the Rings* The Fellowship of the Ring, Book 2, Chapter 4, p.331

172 See this volume: Chapter 4: Foul and Fair: The Cast of *The Lord of the Rings*: section on Maiar.

173 As detailed in *The Hobbit*

174 *The Lord of the Rings,* The Fellowship of the Ring, Book 2, Chapter 7, p.371

175 *The Lord of the Rings,* Appendix A, p.362

176 See this volume: Chapter 3: The Lessening of the Ages

177 Manwë is the chief of the gods, or Valar. The King of the Sky, he was Lord of all birds and creatures of the air, and the mighty Eagles were his most favoured servants. For more on Manwë and the Valar, see this volume: Chapter 4: Foul and Fair: The Cast of *The Lord of the Rings*: section on the Valar.

178 For more on the dragons, see this volume: Chapter 4: Foul and Fair: The Cast of *The Lord of the Rings*: section on dragons.

179 For details of the fall of these High Men from Grace, and their assault upon Paradise, see this volume: Chapter 3: The Lessening of the Ages

180 As described in *The Hobbit*

181 For more on Elbereth, and the other gods, see this volume: Chapter 4: Foul and Fair: The Cast of *The Lord of the Rings*: section on the Valar.

182 For more on Melian and her protection of the first Sindar Kingdom of Doriath see this volume: Chapter 4: Foul and Fair: The Cast of *The Lord of the Rings*: section on the Maiar.

183 *The Lord of the Rings*, The Fellowship of the Ring, Book 2, Chapter 7, p.380

184 For more on Melian and her relationship with Galadriel, see this volume: Chapter 4: Foul and Fair: The Cast of *The Lord of the Rings*: section on the Maiar.

185 For more on the Rings of Power see this volume: Chapter 2: Creation. To learn more about the Nazgûl, Sauron's Black Riders, see this volume: Chapter 4: Foul and Fair: The Cast of *The Lord of the Rings*: section on Men. And to learn more about the Dwarves, and why they could resist Sauron's influence when Men could not, see this volume: Chapter 4: Foul and Fair: The Cast of *The Lord of the Rings*: section on Dwarves.

186 For more on that remarkable friendship, and why Gimli became the only Dwarf to ever have the privilege of sailing to the West, see this volume: Chapter 4: Foul and Fair: The Cast of *The Lord of the Rings*: section on Dwarves.

187 *The Lord of the Rings*, The Fellowship of the Ring, Book 2, Chapter 7, p.376

188 For more on Amroth, Nimrodel, Galadriel, Celeborn and Lothlórien see *Unfinished Tales*, Part 2, Section 4. Or for the song sung of Amroth and Nimrodel by Legolas in Lothlórien see *The Lord of the Rings*, The Fellowship of the Ring, Book 2, Chapter 6, pp 354-355

189 For more on the unions of Men and Elves see this volume: Chapter 3: The Lessening of the Ages

190 For more on Aragorn, the rightful King of both Arnor and Gondor in The Lord of the Rings, see this volume: Chapter 4: Foul and Fair: The Cast of *The Lord of the Rings*: section on Men.

191 The Lord of the Rings, The Fellowship of the Ring, Book 2, Chapter 2, p.259

192 The Lord of the Rings, The Fellowship of the Ring, Book 2, Chapter 7, p.380

193 For more on Yavanna and the other Valar see this volume: Chapter 4: Foul and Fair: The Cast of *The Lord of the Rings*: section on the Valar.

194 *The Lord of the Rings*, The Two Towers, Book 3, Chapter 4, p.68

195 For more on Melian, and the Maiar in general, see this volume: Chapter 4: Foul and Fair: The Cast of *The Lord of the Rings*: section on the Maiar.

196 *The Lord of the Rings*, The Two Towers, Book 3, Chapter 9, p.173

197 For more on Gandalf and his overwhelming contribution to the fall of Sauron see this volume: Chapter 5: Gandalf: The Fire in Men's Hearts

198 *The Lord of the Rings*, The Fellowship of the Ring, Book 1, Chapter 2, p.56

199 *The Lord of the Rings*, The Return of the King, Book 6, Chapter 1, p.177

200 *The Lord of the Rings*, The Fellowship of the Ring, Book 2, Chapter 1, p.234

201 *The Lord of the Rings*, The Fellowship of the Ring, Book 1, Chapter 1, p.41

202 For more on Smaug and dragons in general see this volume: Chapter 4: Foul and Fair: The Cast of *The Lord of the Rings*: section on dragons.

203 *The Lord of the Rings*, The Return of the King, Book 6, Chapter 3, pp 212-213

204 For more on the Nazgul see this volume: Chapter 4: Foul and Fair: The Cast of *The Lord of the Rings*: section on Men.

205 *The Lord of the Rings*, The Return of the King, Book 6, Chapter 3, p.215

206 See this volume: Chapter 4: Foul and Fair: The Cast of *The Lord of the Rings*: section on Maiar.

207 *The Lord of the Rings*, The Return of the King, Book 6, Chapter 7, p.275

208 For more on the different types of Elves see this volume: Chapter 4: Foul and Fair: The Cast of *The Lord of the Rings*: section on Elves.

209 For more on Glaurung, and his struggles with Túrin Turambar, see this volume: Chapter 4: Foul and Fair: The Cast of *The Lord of the Rings*: section on dragons.

210 For more on Dwarven relations with Doriath and other Elven kingdoms, as well as the Nauglamír itself, see this volume: Chapter 4: Foul and Fair: The Cast of *The Lord of the Rings*: section on Dwarves.

211 For more on Elrond, and the Peredhil, see this volume: Chapter 4: Foul and Fair: The Cast of *The Lord of the Rings*: section on Elves.

212 *The Silmarillion*, Of the Rings of Power and the Third Age, p. 289

213 *The Lord of the Rings*, The Two Towers, Book 4, Chapter 5, p.287

214 *The Lord of the Rings*, Appendix A, p. 341

215 *The Lord of the Rings*, The Return of the King, Book 5, Chapter 5, pp 112-113

216 *The Lord of the Rings*, Appendix A, p.343

217 *The Silmarillion*, Chapter 3, Of the Coming of Elves and the Captivity of Melkor, p.50

218 *The Lord of the Rings*, The Return of the King, Book 6, Chapter 2, p.203

219 *The Lord of the Rings*, The Two Towers, Book 4, Chapter 10, p.347

220 *The Lord of the Rings*, The Return of the King, Book 6, Chapter 1, p.176

221 *The Lord of the Rings*, The Two Towers, Book 3, Chapter 4, p.89

Chapter Five

222 *The Lord of the Rings*, The Fellowship of the Ring, Book 2, Chapter 2, p.272

223 *The Silmarillion* 'Of the Rings of Power and the Third Age',pp 300-304

224 The area of Middle-earth where the action of *The Lord of the Rings* takes place, and which is covered by Tolkien's maps, is about the size of Europe. Gimli says, for example, that it is 300 leagues (900 miles) from the Dark Tower to the Redhorn Pass of the Misty Mountains. (*The Fellowship of the Ring* Book 2 Chapter 3, p.302) Likewise we are informed by Gandalf that it is 200 leagues (600 miles) from the Dark Tower to Orthanc. (*The Two Towers* Book 3 Chapter 11, p. 204) It follows, then, that there is much more to Middle-earth than we can see on the maps. The Easterlings come from far beyond the eastern edge of the easternmost map section of Middle-earth, beyond even the area marked as Rhûn.

225 *Unfinished Tales* III 'The Quest of Erebor', p.322

226 Ibid. p.322

227 Ibid. p.322

228 Ibid. p.325

229 *The Hobbit* Chapter 1, p.10

230 *The Lord of the Rings*, The Fellowship of the Ring, Book 2, Chapter 3, p.304

231 *Unfinished Tales*, 'The Quest of Erebor', p.323

232 *The Hobbit* Chapter 6, p. 117

233 *The Lord of the Rings*, The Return of the King, Book 5, Chapter 10, p.167

234 *The Hobbit* Chapter 17, p.297

235 Arwen Evenstar, daughter of Elrond, who dwelt in Rivendell.

236 *The Lord of the Rings* Appendix A III (A similar passage may be found in *Unfinished Tales* 'The Quest of Erebor'

237 *The Lord of the Rings,* The Fellowship of the Ring, Book 2, Chapter 2, p.272

238 Ibid. p.274

239 *The Lord of the Rings,* The Fellowship of the Ring, Book 2, Chapter 3, p.300

240 *The Lord of the Rings,* The Fellowship of the Ring, Book 2, Chapter 4, p.310

241 Ibid p.320

242 This is not the last time that Pippin will exasperate Gandalf, or the last time that Gandalf will use such a scathing tone. Later on in Moria, Pippin drops a stone down a well, causing Gandalf to suggest that Pippin throw himself down the next well. Later, however, Gandalf speaks kindly to Pippin, recognising his own irritability and his need for a smoke. We also remember Gandalf's fierce reaction after Pippin steals the seeing stone of Orthanc and, looking into it, seeing the face of Sauron himself. Gandalf then comforts Pippin with the words: 'If you meddle in the affairs of wizards you must be prepared to think of such things. But come! I forgive you. Be comforted!' (*The Lord of the*

Rings, The Two Towers, Book 3, Chapter 11, p.199)

243 *The Lord of the Rings,* The Fellowship of the Ring, Book 2, Chapter 10, p.417

244 Ibid. p.417

245 *The Lord of the Rings,* The Two Towers, Book 3, Chapter 5, p.99

246 Ibid. p.106

247 Ibid. p.98

248 The name Wormtongue is not as clumsy as it sounds at first. The derivation is probably from the Anglo-Saxon *wyrm* or 'dragon.' As we remember from *The Hobbit*, dragons are creatures of great subtlety, with very persuasive voices.

249 *The Lord of the Rings,* The Return of the King, Book 5, Chapter 4, p.103

250 *The Lord of the Rings,* The Fellowship of the Ring, Book 2, Chapter 2, pp 282-283

251 *The Lord of the Rings,* The Two Towers, Book 3, Chapter 5, p. 100

252 *Unfinished Tales* 'The Quest of Erebor', p.330

253 *The Lord of the Rings,* The Two Towers, Book 3, Chapter 5, p.100

254 *The Lord of the Rings,* The Return of the King, Book 5, Chapter 9, p.156

255 Ibid. p.156

256 *The Lord of the Rings,* The Fellowship of the Ring, Book 1, Chapter 2, pp 68-69

Chapter Six

257 *The Book of Lost Tales* vol.1, p. 7 (George Allen & Unwin, 1983)

INDEX